A WICKED WAY TO DIE

Tracie whirled around and gasped as she saw a dark figure reaching out for her. The breathing was real! She hadn't imagined it! But before Tracie could open her mouth to scream, strong hands struck her in the small of the back and she was falling into the pool.

Tracie struck out at the hands that were holding her down. It was probably one of the guys and she was going to absolutely kill him when he let her up for air. This was a nasty trick. Tracie hated to be dunked.

Tracie reached up to grab the hands and that was when she realized that the person who'd shoved her was wearing gloves. Why would he wear gloves on a hot summer night?

She had to take a breath of air! Spots began to swirl before her eyes and Tracie hit out with all her strength. But the hands just kept holding her head beneath the water. Tracie struggled frantically, her lungs screaming out for oxygen.

And then her struggles began to cease.

That was when an awful thought crossed Tracie's mind, the last rational thought of her life.

The hands were wearing gloves because they intended to kill her . . .

Books by Joanne Fluke

Hannah Swensen Mysteries

CHOCOLATE CHIP COOKIE MURDER
STRAWBERRY SHORTCAKE MURDER
BLUEBERRY MUFFIN MURDER
LEMON MERINGUE PIE MURDER
FUDGE CUPCAKE MURDER
SUGAR COOKIE MURDER
PEACH COBBLER MURDER
CHERRY CHEESECAKE MURDER
KEY LIME PIE MURDER
CANDY CANE MURDER
CARROT CAKE MURDER
CREAM PUFF MURDER
PLUM PUDDING MURDER
APPLE TURNOVER MURDER
DEVIL'S FOOD CAKE MURDER
GINGERBREAD COOKIE MURDER
CINNAMON ROLL MURDER
RED VELVET CUPCAKE MURDER
BLACKBERRY PIE MURDER
DOUBLE FUDGE BROWNIE MURDER
WEDDING CAKE MURDER
JOANNE FLUKE'S LAKE EDEN COOKBOOK

Suspense Novels

VIDEO KILL
WINTER CHILL
DEAD GIVEAWAY
THE OTHER CHILD
COLD JUDGMENT
FATAL IDENTITY
FINAL APPEAL
VENGEANCE IS MINE
EYES
WICKED

Published by Kensington Publishing Corporation

WICKED

JOANNE FLUKE

KENSINGTON BOOKS
http://www.kensingtonbooks.com

To the extent that the image or images on the cover of this book depict a person or persons, such person or persons are merely models, and are not intended to portray any character or characters featured in the book.

KENSINGTON BOOKS are published by

Kensington Publishing Corp.
119 West 40th Street
New York, NY 10018

Copyright © 2016 by Joanne Fluke

All rights reserved. No part of this book may be reproduced in any form or by any means without the prior written consent of the Publisher, excepting brief quotes used in reviews.

If you purchased this book without a cover, you should be aware that this book is stolen property. It was reported as "unsold and destroyed" to the Publisher and neither the Author nor the Publisher has received any payment for this "stripped book."

All Kensington titles, imprints and distributed lines are available at special quantity discounts for bulk purchases for sales promotion, premiums, fund-raising, educational or institutional use. Special book excerpts or customized printings can also be created to fit specific needs. For details, write or phone the office of the Kensington Special Sales Manager: Kensington Publishing Corp., 119 West 40th Street, New York, NY, 10018. Attn. Special Sales Department. Phone: 1-800-221-2647.

Kensington and the K logo Reg. U.S. Pat. & TM Off.

ISBN-13: 978-1-61773-236-2
ISBN-10: 1-61773-236-2
First Kensington Mass Market Edition: August 2016

eISBN-13: 978-1-61773-237-9
eISBN-10: 1-61773-237-0
First Kensington Electronic Edition: August 2016

10 9 8 7 6 5 4 3 2

Printed in the United States of America

FOR JAMI
One of life's joys

With Special Thanks To:
Ruel, John S., Andrea, John F., & Trudi

With Special Thanks To

PROLOGUE

Summer 1995

It was over a hundred degrees in the shade, and Eve Carrington was too hot even to smile at the handsome truck driver who pulled up beside her at the stoplight. One glance in the rearview mirror told her that he probably wouldn't have reacted anyway. The heat had ruined her expensive new hairstyle, her makeup was streaked by beads of perspiration, and the cream-colored linen blouse she'd bought especially for today was impossibly wrinkled.

The stoplight was a long one, and while she was waiting, Eve did her best to repair the damage. She brushed her midnight-black hair, touched up her makeup, and applied new lip gloss. There wasn't a thing she could do about her wrinkled blouse, but she'd brought four suitcases of clothing with her and she'd change just as soon as she arrived.

The light turned green, and Eve sighed as she

stepped on the gas. Instead of broiling in this horrible heat wave, she could have been enjoying the private beach at Hampton Cove. All her friends had left for the beach last night and this was the first year she hadn't gone with them. At this very moment, she could be sipping an ice-cold drink and reclining on a chaise longue under a striped umbrella while handsome waiters hovered, just waiting for her to beckon for a refill. Why had she ever signed up for this stupid writers' workshop when it was bound to be the hottest, most boring month of her life?

Eve reached out to check the air-conditioning vent. Cool air was pouring out, but the noon sun was so hot, it warmed the frigid air the moment it came out of the vent. The interior of her car felt like a sauna, and it was all Ryan's fault that she was so uncomfortable!

They'd planned to spend the entire month of August at the beach, but Eve's boyfriend, Ryan Young, had signed up for a workshop in creative writing. He'd told Eve that he was sorry he couldn't go to Hampton Cove with her, but he didn't want to pass up the opportunity of a lifetime.

The opportunity of a lifetime? Exactly what was that? she had asked. And Ryan had explained that this particular writing workshop was being led by Professor Hellman, who had connections to several large publishing firms in New York.

Eve had shrugged. So? What good would Professor Hellman's connections do for Ryan?

Ryan had laughed and told her she couldn't

possibly be so dense. She knew he wanted to write historical fiction. He'd told her all about it. This workshop was important because Professor Hellman had promised to take the best three workshop projects and submit them to his publisher friends.

Eve had listened as Ryan had described the workshop. The writers would live in the Sutler Mansion on the edge of campus for four weeks. Professor Hellman would come in every Friday to critique their work and give them advice. Only ten students were being accepted, five guys and five women. That meant there was better than a thirty percent chance that the professor would choose Ryan's manuscript and send it to New York.

Normally, Eve wouldn't have batted an eyelash. There were plenty of handsome guys at Hampton Cove, and she could have had a pleasant vacation without Ryan. But one thing about the workshop worried Eve. Ryan would be spending his vacation with five other women, and he'd be with them day and night. It sounded like a recipe for romance to her, and she wasn't about to let another woman pick up her handsome boyfriend.

Eve had called her father and asked if he could pull some strings. As he was a distinguished alumnus who contributed heavily to various college funds, one word from him had done the trick. Ryan had been delighted when she'd told him that she'd been accepted at the workshop, but he'd also been puzzled. He'd had no idea that Eve was interested in creative writing.

Eve wasn't interested in creative writing, but here

she was, dripping sweat, driving across campus to
the Sutler Mansion. And to make matters even worse,
she didn't have the foggiest notion what her project
would be. It would have to be good. Ryan thought
she was as dedicated as he was, and she certainly
didn't want to make a fool of herself.

She checked her map and drove around the
corner, and there it was, the Sutler Mansion. Eve
gave a groan of dismay as she parked in front. It
looked like something straight out of a horror movie
with its wavy glass windows and dark shutters. Ryan
had told her that they were renovating it for faculty
offices, but it was clear they hadn't started yet. The
Sutler Mansion looked as if it might fall down around
their ears!

Two girls barged out of the front door as she started
to get out of the car. Eve smiled as she recognized
them. Cheryl Frazier and Tracie Simmons, two of
her sorority sisters.

"Hi, Eve!" Cheryl, a pretty redhead with her hair
in a ponytail, rushed up. "You're late."

"I know. I had to stop on the way to pick up some
things."

"We'll help you unload." Tracie brushed her curly
brown hair out of her eyes and grabbed one of Eve's
suitcases. "Everybody's already staked out their
rooms, but Cheryl and I saved the best one for you."

It was no less than what Eve had expected. She
had the best room in the sorority house, too. It was
only right. Since her money paid for most of the
parties, and her father had arranged to have the

whole place redecorated, it wasn't surprising that all Eve's sorority sisters treated her like a queen.

Eve let Cheryl and Tracie carry everything up the front steps. "I can hardly wait to get inside and cool off in front of the air-conditioning."

"Bad news, Eve." Cheryl shook her head. "We don't have air conditioning . . . just fans, and they don't work very well in this kind of heat."

Eve gave a little sigh. This was turning from bad to worse. She followed them into the house and sighed again. It was slightly cooler inside, but not much. "The brochure said there wasn't a pool, but I had no idea we'd be living in a place without air-conditioning!"

"Look on the bright side, Eve," Tracie said. "It's supposed to cool off tonight, and you've got the only room on the girls' floor with a balcony."

"The girls' floor?"

"That's right," Cheryl explained. "The guys are on the second floor, and we're on the third. The fourth floor used to be servant quarters, and those rooms are off-limits."

"Why?" Eve was curious.

"Because they haven't started fixing them up yet. There could be loose boards and weak spots in the floor."

"We've got a surprise for you, Eve." Tracie started to grin. "Your room's right above Ryan's. He's got the second-floor balcony and I thought it might be romantic, like Romeo and Juliet."

Eve sighed. Tracie was always trying to be romantic. "Romance like that I don't need! Did you forget that Romeo and Juliet killed themselves in the end?"

"I never thought about that!"

Eve smiled at her. "I'm glad I have a balcony. I can leave the door open and maybe I'll get a breeze. Who else is on our floor, Tracie?"

"Beth Masters. She's got the room next to you."

"I'm sure you've seen her around campus." Cheryl noticed Eve's totally blank look and she went into detail. "Beth's got light brown hair and she wears glasses. She's had a couple of her poems published in the *College Chronicle*."

Eve shrugged. "I probably know her. It just doesn't ring a bell. Tell me about the guys, Tracie."

"There's Ryan, of course. And Jeremy Lowe's here. I'm sure you remember *him*!"

Eve winced. She remembered Jeremy very well. She still couldn't believe that he'd actually had the nerve to ask her for a date. "Unfortunately, I do. He's the frat guy who put the dead lobster in our pool."

"That's Jeremy." Cheryl sighed. "I just hope he doesn't play any of his dumb practical jokes on us. And then there's Scott Logan. He does those in-depth things for the *Chronicle*."

"I've met Scott. Who else?"

"Marc Costello." Tracie frowned slightly. "His father does the Channel Seven sports and I went out with him once. Marc's cute, but he doesn't have a romantic bone in his body."

Eve knew. Tracie was always looking for romance, but the kind of man she wanted was only found in books.

"Dean Isacs is here," Cheryl went on. "I know

you've seen him around campus. He's a music major, really tall and skinny with long black hair."

"The guy who always carries his guitar?"

"That's him. Dean wants to write a rock musical."

"That's mildly interesting." Eve sighed. With the exception of Ryan, the rest of the guys didn't interest her at all. "I thought there were supposed to be five girls. Who's the other one?"

Tracie looked a little puzzled. "Somebody named Angela Adams. But she's not here yet."

"Angela Adams?" Eve repeated the name. "I don't think I know her."

"We don't know her, either. She's a new freshman and she's enrolling in the fall."

"A new freshman?" Eve was surprised. "I thought this workshop was only for current students."

"So did we. I don't know why they made an exception, but I guess we'll find out when she gets here."

"We have to finish fifty pages a week?" Eve stared at Ryan in shock. "But that's a lot of work!"

"Of course it is. This workshop is intensive. You didn't think we were going to sit around and play games, did you?"

"No. Of course not." Eve shook her head. "But I didn't realize we had to do quite that much. How about this computer keyboard and screen? What's the setup?"

"It's exactly the same as a personal computer. We're all hooked into a network. The main CPU's up in the fourth-floor hallway, along with the high-speed printer. When you want to print out you, just send it up there and the pages print out."

Eve frowned at the small student desk with its secretarial chair. She wasn't looking forward to spending long hours, alone in her room, working on a project that didn't interest her. "How about food? Is it being catered?"

"Catered?" Ryan laughed. "That's a good one, Eve. If I didn't know you better, I'd swear you were serious."

Eve laughed, too, but she hadn't been joking. "Then we have a cook that comes in?"

"No caterer, no cook." Ryan shook his head. "We're roughing it, Eve. We're all going to take turns in the kitchen. The schedule's up on the bulletin board."

This was even worse than she'd thought. "Then I guess we don't have maid service, either."

"No way. It's up to us to keep the place clean. We've got a dishwasher in the kitchen and a laundry room right next to the back door."

"I guess that's . . . handy." There was no way she'd wash her own clothes. Most of her things had to be dry cleaned anyway. She'd just stuff them all in a laundry bag and drive them out to the cleaners.

"You'd better hurry up, Eve." Ryan glanced at his watch. "Get into your grubbies and meet me in the ground floor library. We've got a meeting at four."

"A meeting?"

"With Professor Hellman." Ryan headed for the door. "We're going to discuss our writing projects with him before we start."

"Wonderful. Thanks, Ryan." Eve waited until

Ryan had left, and then she glanced at her reflection the mirror. She thought she looked very fashionable in her red sleeveless dress. She'd put on heels and was wearing her ruby earrings, but perhaps that was too dressy for the crowd here.

Eve thought about it for a moment, and then she went to her closet to see what else she could find. Cheryl and Tracie had been wearing shorts and T-shirts when they'd come out to help her with her luggage, but if that was the way they were supposed to dress for the workshop, she was out of luck.

Why hadn't she stopped at the store to buy some designer shorts and tops? Eve surveyed the contents of her closet. She finally settled for a pair of tan slacks that had been especially tailored for her, and a forest-green silk shell that hugged her figure and almost matched the color of her eyes.

Eve chose a pair of hand-sewn moccasins and slipped them on her feet. She looked casual, but elegant, and that was fine with her. Let the rest of them wear jeans, and shorts, and wrinkled tank tops. She had her standards, and even if Angela Adams was dressed to the teeth, Eve knew she could stand her own.

She was about to leave her room when she heard a creaking sound. Eve stopped, her hand on the doorknob, and shivered slightly. It sounded as if someone were walking softly on the floor above her. But that was impossible. The fourth floor was deserted, and they weren't supposed to be up there.

Old houses creaked. Eve knew that. It was prob-ably nothing but a floorboard expanding in the heat, or a cat or a squirrel running across the roof. Eve glanced up, her heart pounding hard, but there was no way she wanted to go up there and look for the source of the noise. She just pulled open the door and hurried out, into the hallway.

The third floor was deserted and Eve shivered. It gave her a slightly creepy feeling to be up here alone and she felt like glancing around to make sure no one was following her as she rushed to the door that led to the stairs.

Eve arrived at the library, breathless. But no one noticed that she was out of breath. Everyone in the library was gathered around the newcomer. Angela Adams had arrived.

Angela was gorgeous, with long blond hair and a peaches-and-cream complexion. Her lips were full, her teeth were even and white, and her smile was perfectly lovely. Dressed in immaculate white shorts and a lavender-colored stretch top that left absolutely nothing to the imagination, she was holding court in the center of the room. She was tanned to perfection, and her legs and arms were golden from hours in the sun. Angela Adams looked like a model for a designer line of expensive beachwear.

Eve watched intently as Angela spoke. She was too far away to hear what Angela was saying, but everyone else was paying rapt attention. She was telling a story with such graceful gestures, she looked almost as if she were dancing.

As Eve stood there staring, Angela laughed. It was a full-throated laugh, an infectious, happy laugh. Within the space of a second or so, she had everyone else laughing with her.

That was when Eve saw something that made her frown. Angela reached out and put her hand on Ryan's arm. It was a possessive gesture, intimate and warm, and Eve felt her temper flare. Instead of pulling away, as Eve expected Ryan to do, he just smiled at Angela and put his hand over hers.

Eve clamped her lips shut tightly and stood there glaring, unable to tear her eyes away. Ryan was gazing at Angela with an expression that Eve knew well. It was a deeply personal, private look that she'd thought was for her alone. Ryan was gazing at Angela exactly the same way he often gazed at Eve, right before he kissed her good-night.

The lines were drawn.

The battle was on.

Eve glared at her rival with undisguised malice. No one tried to steal Eve Carrington's boyfriend and lived to tell about it. It just wasn't done. Angela Adams was her enemy, and Eve would make her pay. . . .

CHAPTER ONE

"Oh, great! Just what I needed!" Eve spoke the words under her breath, but she needn't have bothered. Everyone was paying attention to Angela, and they wouldn't have heard her if she'd set off a cannon. At least Ryan wasn't holding Angela's hand any longer. He'd stepped slightly to the side, but he was still staring at her like she was the last woman left alive and he was the last man.

So what should she do? Eve wasn't used to being ignored when she entered a room, especially by the guy who was supposed to be her boyfriend. She decided to let it pass, this time, and she walked over to take Ryan's arm. "Hi, Ryan. And you must be Angela Adams."

"Yes, I am." Angela turned to smile at her. "And you're . . ."

"Eve Carrington," Ryan introduced them.

"Of course. You're Ryan's girlfriend." Angela looked perfectly innocent. "Ryan was just telling me about you."

Before Eve could ask what exactly it was that

Ryan had told Angela, an older man in khakis and a dress shirt entered the library. He waved to several students and then walked over to the big library table to take a seat.

"Come on, Eve." Ryan grabbed Eve's hand and led her toward the table. "That's Professor Hellman, and it looks like he's ready to start our first meeting."

When they were all seated, Professor Hellman cleared his throat. "All right. Let's begin. I know some of you, but let's go around the table. Give us your name and tell us what you've chosen to do for your project. Let's start with you, Beth."

Beth looked exactly as Cheryl and Tracie had described her. She was wearing jeans and a tank top, and her long brown hair was pulled back and secured with a leather clasp.

"My name is Beth Masters." Beth smiled at all of them. "And since I write poetry, I'd like to work on a book of poems on a single theme."

Professor Hellman smiled. "Very good, Beth. Next?"

"Jeremy Lowe. I'm going to do something humorous."

Eve squeezed Ryan's hand under the table and leaned close to whisper to him. "That figures. He's the practical joker from the frat house next door."

"I'm Dean Isacs." Dean's voice was soft and Eve could tell he was shy. "I'm a musician, and I'm working on a rock musical."

Professor Hellman nodded. "There's a piano in the living room. You're welcome to use it, Dean."

"Thanks. I brought my keyboard, too. It's got earphones so I won't disturb anybody."

Tracie was next and she smiled at everyone. "I'm Tracie Simmons, and I'd like to write a romance. I just love romances!"

Everyone laughed, including Eve. Tracie had hundreds of romances in her room at the sorority house, and she was always reading a new one. She lived in a dream world where the guys were all handsome and rich. The ordinary guys on the college campus just didn't measure up, and Tracie seldom dated.

"Cheryl Frazier." Cheryl stood up. "I'm doing a cookbook. They're my grandmother's recipes, but I'm going to write little sketches about the family on every other page."

"Good." Professor Hellman made a note in his book.

"Marc Costello." Marc stood up. "I'm working on a sports novel. And it has nothing to do with the fact that my father's a sports reporter for Channel Seven."

Everyone laughed, and then it was Scott Logan's turn. He looked very serious as he faced the group. "I'm Scott Logan and I'm working on an in-depth story about the old brick mansions on the edge of campus. This place is a good example. It's supposed to be haunted by the wife of the man who built it. According to several sources, he killed her and buried her somewhere in the walls."

"Wonderful!" Professor Hellman beamed at Scott. "As far as you're concerned, this workshop couldn't be held in a better place."

Angela was next, and she looked very confident as she stood up. "I'm Angela Adams. I'm a new freshman, and I come from a family of writers."

"Is your father Aaron Adams?" Professor Hellman looked impressed when Angela nodded. "I've read your father's work. He's a brilliant man."

Angela smiled at the professor. "I'll tell him you said so. He'll be very pleased. Writers like my father exist on delayed gratification."

"What does *that* mean?" Eve couldn't help blurting out her question. It seemed to her that Angela was really trying to get in good with Professor Hellman.

"It's simple, Eve." Angela gave her a perfectly innocent smile. "My father writes historical fiction. They call it faction because he sets his books in historically accurate periods. His characters are fictional, but he has to do a lot of research to make sure the facts are right. It takes him three or four years to write a book, and it's another year before it's published. He lives in a void for five years before he gets any feedback from his readers."

Eve nodded. What else could she do? Professor Hellman was smiling at Angela, and it was clear she'd made points.

"You said you came from a family of writers." Professor Hellman looked interested. "Is your mother a writer, too?"

"My mother is Heather Adams."

"Of course! She's a political reporter." Professor Hellman glanced around the group. "I'm sure some of you have seen her show. It's called *Face the Press*."

Scott and Ryan nodded, and Eve noticed that Ryan looked very excited. And then Professor Hellman asked Angela another question.

"What are you planning to write, Angela?"

Angela laughed. "My family will probably disown me for this, but I'd like to try my hand at a murder mystery. I've always loved to read them."

"That's fine." Professor Hellman smiled. "How about you, Ryan?"

Ryan stood up. "I'm Ryan Young, and I'm interested in writing historical fiction, just like Angela's father. I've read all of his books, and I hope that'll help."

"Good." Professor Hellman then turned to Eve.

Eve was nervous as she stood up. She'd planned to write a series of articles on fashion and makeup, but Ryan wouldn't be impressed with that. She had to do something different, something that no one else had mentioned.

"I'm Eve Carrington." Eve thought fast. "And I'm going to write . . . a horror novel about vampires."

Angela raised an eyebrow. "That sounds very interesting, Eve. Are you trying to be another Anne Rice?"

"Not at all." Eve shook her head, even though she'd never read any of Anne Rice's books. "I'm just trying to be Eve Carrington."

Professor Hellman laughed. "That's fine, Eve. Ten different students, ten different projects. This should be a very interesting workshop. I'll come in every Thursday at four and collect your pages. I'll read them that night, and I'll get back to you on Friday afternoon with my critique."

"I have a question, Professor." Angela raised her

hand. "Would it be all right if we read each other's work?"

"Of course."

"I was thinking about Ryan's project in particular." Angela smiled. "I might be able to help him. I proof all my father's manuscripts before they're published, and he says I'm his best critic."

Ryan looked absolutely delighted, and Eve started to frown. Ryan was her boyfriend, and she didn't want him to spend long hours working with Angela.

"Excuse me, Professor Hellman?" Eve managed to look perfectly innocent. "It's really nice of Angela to offer to help, but . . . isn't this supposed to be an *individual* workshop?"

"That's right, Eve. But all of you might benefit from peer criticism. It's perfectly all right for you to compare notes and read each other's material before I collect it."

"Great!" Angela clapped her hands. "Why don't we have a group meeting every night? We can all take turns reading what we've written, and then we can discuss it."

Professor Hellman looked pleased as he put his papers in his briefcase and stood up. "That's an excellent idea, Angela. And it could be very helpful. I'll let you get started on your work now, and I'll be back on Thursday to collect what you've written.

After Professor Hellman left, everyone gathered around Angela again. Even Cheryl and Tracie wanted to ask her questions about her famous parents and the life they led. Eve felt like an outsider, even though Ryan was standing right next to her.

None of his attention was focused on her. He was much too interested in listening to Angela.

"It must be terribly romantic, living with a mother who's a television star." Tracie's voice was breathless with admiration. "And your father . . . everyone thinks he's just wonderful!"

Angela shrugged. "It has its drawbacks. When I was growing up, my mother left for the studio before I even got up in the morning. Heather had to be in makeup at five a.m."

"Heather?" Beth exclaimed. "You call your mother by her first name?"

Angela laughed. "Why not? Everybody else does. And Heather doesn't want anyone to know she's old enough to have a daughter in college."

Ryan frowned slightly. "How about your father? He's always worked at home, hasn't he?"

"Yes. He converted the entire third floor into an office. It's huge."

Tracie looked envious. "It must be nice, having a dad who works at home. You must have spent a lot of time with him when you were growing up."

"Not really. When he was first getting started, he went on a lot of book-signing tours. And Heather was usually somewhere on assignment. Most of the time, I just had my nanny and the housekeeper for company."

"How about when you were in high school?" Ryan was clearly enthralled by Angela's sad story.

"Sometimes they were home, sometimes they weren't." Angela shrugged her shoulders. "It really didn't matter. I was away, too."

"Away where?" Tracie was clearly intrigued.

"In Switzerland. They sent me to a private school, and it was so gruesome, I ran away twice."

"What do you mean . . . gruesome?" Scott perked up his ears, on the trail of a good story. "What happened, Angela?"

"Promise you won't tell?"

"Our lips are sealed." Jeremy grinned at her. "We promise, Angela."

"All right. I'll tell you about it. Madame Jollette's Academy was in the Alps. It was very isolated, and Madame knew we were virtual prisoners. She used to lock us in at night. And then the howling would start."

"Howling?" Scott's mouth dropped open. "From what?"

Angela's voice lowered to a whisper, and everyone leaned closer to hear. "From her brother. He was totally insane. Madame chained him up in the attic during the day. She only let him out at night, when we were locked up in our rooms. He wandered the halls, howling and screaming, looking for missing pages."

"From what?" Scott's eyes were wide as he asked the question. "Tell us, Angela!"

"From my murder mystery! The one I'm going to write while I'm here."

Ryan was the first one to catch on, and he laughed so hard, he doubled over. "That was great, Angela! You got us!"

"I know I did." Angela grinned and then everyone started to laugh. Everyone except Eve. Eve just sighed and rolled her eyes.

"Actually, part of that was true." Angela smiled at

everyone. "I did go to Madame Jollette's Academy. It was in the Alps, but it was a regular boarding school. I was just demonstrating a point about writing."

"What's that?"

Ryan was all ears.

"Start with something you know and take off from there. It's called the 'Willing Suspension of Disbelief.'"

"I get it!" Ryan looked very excited. "If you write about what you know, it has the ring of truth. And then, when you start branching out, your readers will go right along with you."

Angela gave Ryan a thumbs-up signal. "Exactly! That's why I'm setting my murder mystery right here."

"Here?" Cheryl was fascinated. "You mean right here, in the Sutler Mansion?"

"That's right. If Scott's sources are right and it's really haunted, it should make a good setting. And I think I'll use all of you as characters . . . unless you don't want me to."

"You can use me." Tracie looked very excited. "I'd love to be a character in your book, Angela."

"Me, too." Ryan grinned. And then everyone else chimed in, telling Angela how great it would be if she used them as characters in her book.

Eve was silent. She had a very bad feeling about being a character in Angela's book. It was almost like tempting fate, especially since Angela was writing a murder mystery.

"How about you, Eve?" Angela asked. "Do you mind?"

Eve winced. She didn't want to say that she had a

bad feeling about this whole thing. They'd be sure to tease her about being superstitious. So she just shrugged "Okay. I guess it's all right with me, too."

"Great!" Angela started to smile again. "Since there's ten of us, I think I'll pattern my book after *And Then There Were None*. You've all read it, haven't you?"

Eve shivered. She'd read *And Then There Were None* when she was in high school, and it had frightened her. She didn't want to be a character in a novel where everyone got killed one by one.

"I haven't read it, but I've seen the movie," Ryan spoke up. "It's one of my favorites."

"I've never seen it," Scott said. "Maybe we should rent it and watch it together."

"That's a great idea!" Angela beamed at Scott. "We could watch it tonight, after we read our pages."

"I'll get started making some snacks," Cheryl said. "I want to try out a couple of recipes for my cookbook. My grandmother used to make wonderful caramel corn, and she had a great recipe for peanut butter fudge."

"Cut it out, Cheryl. You're making me hungry." Marc groaned. "Is anyone else hungry?"

Everyone nodded, and Angela spoke up. "Does everybody like take-out Chinese?"

"My favorite!" Tracie sighed. "I just love egg rolls! And the fortune cookies are so much fun. The last time I went out for Chinese, my fortune said I was going to be lucky in love."

Angela laughed. "I'm sure you will be, Tracie. I'll treat you all to an early dinner."

"I'll come with you," Ryan volunteered. "You'll need help carrying all those cartons."

Angela turned to smile at Ryan. "Thanks. The rest of you can start in on your projects, and Ryan and I'll be back just as soon as we can."

Eve frowned as Ryan and Angela went out the door. She'd been planning to discuss her project with Ryan, but Angela had stolen him away. Of course, that wasn't completely accurate. Ryan had volunteered to go. To make matters even worse, he'd left without even bothering to say good-bye to her.

CHAPTER TWO

There was no way she could write, not when she was this upset. Eve frowned at her computer screen, and then she glanced at the clock on her desk. She had another hour to finish her required pages, but she'd only gotten as far as the title. After typing and deleting at least seven, she'd finally settled for *The Vampire's Vacation*.

Angela and Ryan had been gone for over an hour. When they'd come back, they'd been laughing and talking as if they were old friends. Eve had fumed as everyone else had raved about the take-out Chinese. It had been good, Eve had to admit that, but the whole group had acted as if Angela had spent hours and hours over a hot stove, cooking it herself.

When the last fortune cookie had been opened, everyone had gone back up to their rooms to work on their projects. Eve had gone to her room, and here she was, an hour later, still struggling with the opening sentence of her book. Why hadn't she told Professor Hellman she was writing about fashion?

It would have been a lot easier. At least she knew something about fashion.

Eve took a deep breath and started to type. She'd fill up her pages even if they weren't very good. It was like homework. You had to do it. And maybe she'd feel more inspired tomorrow.

There was a frown on Eve's face as she described the setting and introduced her main character. A beachfront hotel, very exclusive, resort of the rich and famous. A beautiful woman, Rochelle Dubois, who'd gone on vacation to search for romance and excitement. It should have been fine, but it wasn't. Rochelle wasn't very interesting at all, and Eve couldn't figure out how to make her more appealing.

Describing Rochelle's clothes filled up most of the pages, and listing what she'd ordered for dinner took another whole page. Painting a verbal portrait of her hotel room took another three pages, and Eve smiled as she stopped in the middle of a paragraph. She was finished. She'd done the required number of pages, and she wasn't going to write another word. Rochelle Dubois could just hang there, half in and half out of her bubble bath, until tomorrow!

Eve gave a sigh of relief and pressed the button that would print her work. She was done, and it wasn't a moment too soon! Now all she had to do was collect her pages from the fourth-floor printer and she'd be finished with her assignment for the first day.

As Eve walked down the hallway, she noticed that everyone else was still working. Beth was staring out her window, her forehead furrowed in concentration, and Eve wondered just how hard it was to write a poem. She could do one right now, but she doubted that Beth would want to use it. It would be about the workshop and the students who were here.

Eve grinned as she thought of one. *Roses are red, fuchsia is pink. Angela Adams makes this workshop stink!* She could write a poem about Ryan, too, one that he wouldn't appreciate. *Ryan Young is really dumb if he thinks Angela Adams is such a plum.*

Tracie was working, her fingers typing busily at her keyboard. There was a soft, almost longing expression on her face, and Eve knew she was writing about the hero of her romance. He'd be rich, and handsome, and powerful. And the woman in Tracie's story would fall head over heels in love with him.

Cheryl was working, too. As she wrote, she munched on a plate of cookies next to her keyboard. Eve watched while Cheryl ate one and then reached for another. Perhaps writing a cookbook wasn't good for Cheryl. She was bound to gain weight if she kept sampling her recipes.

Angela's door was open and Eve peeked in. The room was deserted, the desk was tidy, and the bed was neatly made. Angela must have finished her work and gone downstairs.

When Eve pulled open the door to the stairwell, she paused. She'd planned to go up to the fourth floor to retrieve her pages from the printer, but she didn't really want to go up there alone. She was still a little nervous about the creaking noises she'd heard and the idea of going up to the fourth floor after dark made her shiver.

Ryan would go with her. He had to pick up his pages, too. Eve headed down to the second floor and opened the door to the hallway. Jeremy was still working at his computer. As Eve passed by his open door, he laughed at something he'd written. Eve hoped it was as funny as his laughter indicated. They'd all have to listen to it tonight.

Scott's room was across the hall and he was working, too. So was Marc, although he'd already printed out and was proofreading his pages. Dean was playing his keyboard, earphones on his head. He looked strange, moving to the music he was playing, when Eve could hear nothing but silence.

Ryan's door was closed and Eve knocked softly. When Ryan didn't answer, she knocked again. After several more attempts, Eve opened the door and peered in to find that Ryan's room was empty.

Where was Ryan? And where was Angela? Eve frowned. Could they be together?

Quickly, Eve went down the steps to the first floor. There was no one in the kitchen or the laundry room. The dining room was deserted and so was the library, although someone had filled a cooler with soft drinks and set it on the table. Eve walked to the lace curtains and pulled them back slightly to peer out into the courtyard.

There they were, sitting on the bench, turned toward each other. As Eve watched, Angela threw back her head and laughed at something Ryan had said. Ryan laughed, too, and he looked very pleased that Angela had found his comment so amusing.

Eve's eyes narrowed and her blood began to boil. Ryan had that same look on his face, that same sappy, adoring expression she'd noticed when she'd first seen him with Angela. But Ryan was supposed to be her boyfriend, not Angela's. If he looked at anyone that way, it should have been her. And if Angela thought she could get away with stealing Eve's boyfriend, she was dead wrong.

Eve turned away from the window with a determined expression on her face. Her green eyes glittered with icy displeasure, and her lips were set in a straight, disapproving line. Angela wouldn't play games with Ryan for very long.

Eve would make sure of that. . . .

There was total silence when Eve finished reading her pages. The silence lasted for almost a minute, and then Cheryl spoke up. "I like the beachfront hotel, Eve. It's a great setting."

"Me, too," Tracie agreed. "And Rochelle's clothes are incredibly romantic. I especially like the gown she wore to dinner."

Ryan looked a little disturbed, but he nodded. "You did a great job with the clothes, Eve. When is the vampire going to appear?"

"I'm not sure." Eve shrugged. "Whenever he wants to, I guess. Does anyone know where a vampire sleeps?"

Scott spoke up. "In a coffin. It's usually in a basement or underground, so that the light can't reach him. Legend has it he'll turn into dust if he's in direct sunlight."

"Nope." Eve giggled and shook her head. "Any other guesses?"

Scott looked puzzle, but he shook his head. "Where do you think he sleeps, Eve?"

"Anywhere he wants to!" Eve laughed, and so did everyone except Angela. She was frowning, and Eve turned to her. "What's the matter, Angela? Didn't you get the joke?"

"I got it. But I am a little concerned, Eve."

"About what?" Eve faced her squarely.

"About your attitude. You don't seem to be very serious about the workshop, and that disturbs me. Take your main character, Rochelle Dubois. What's her motivation?"

"Motivation? Come on, Angela. Rochelle's on vacation and she's out for a good time. She doesn't really *have* any motivation."

"That could be the problem. You haven't spent enough time fleshing out your main character. We have to know her, to understand her, to care about her. We need to know her dreams, her hopes, her fears. Don't you see, Eve? We have to be able to identify with Rochelle. If we don't, it won't be frightening when she encounters the vampire."

"Really, Angela!" Eve couldn't help laughing. "I'm not going for the Nobel Prize in Literature here. I'm just trying to write some chapters of a book . . . for a class."

Now it was Ryan's turn to frown. "I can't believe you said that, Eve. Don't you want your work to be good?"

"Of course I do!" Eve backtracked quickly. She'd forgotten that students in the workshop were supposed to be very dedicated to the art of writing. "But I think my chapters have to be fun, too. I'm not writing serious literature. I'm writing a novel."

"That's a good point, Eve," Angela said. "You're

right, in a way. Novels should be fun, and we sometimes lose sight of that. But you do have to figure out your character and her motivation before you start. Why don't you give this some thought tonight and rewrite your first chapter? I'm sure it'll be much better when you read it to us tomorrow night."

Eve waited for someone to say something. Angela was acting like their teacher, and she wasn't. But everyone just nodded, including Ryan, and Eve felt her temper flare again.

"How about your chapter, Angela?" Eve hoped her grin wasn't too nasty. "Are you going to read it to us?"

"Of course. I'll be happy to read it. But remember, Eve . . . I'm a beginning writer, just like the rest of you. I'm just lucky I had the chance to pick up a lot of pointers from my parents."

Eve managed to keep a pleasant smile on her face as Angela began to read her pages. And despite herself, she began to get interested in the words that Angela was reading. Angela was a good writer, a very good writer. Even Eve had to give her that much. Eve wanted to find something she could criticize, but she listened and listened as Angela read, and she couldn't find anything wrong.

When Angela had finished, Tracie started to clap. "That's fantastic, Angela! I can hardly wait to hear the next chapter."

"Thank you, Tracie. "Angela smiled at her. "How about the rest of you? What did you think?"

Everyone was full of praise for Angela's writing, but Angela turned to Eve. "How about you, Eve? I criticized you, and turnabout's fair play. Now it's your turn to criticize me."

Eve winced. And then she decided to be honest. "I don't know enough about writing to criticize you. I thought it was really good, Angela."

"Thank you, Eve!" Angela looked perfectly delighted. "I just hope I can keep it up. A novel patterned after *Ten Little Indians* isn't easy to write. It's a complicated plot and you have to deal with ten different characters. You'll see what I mean when we watch the movie."

"We've all read our chapters," Ryan said. "Let's go into the living room and watch it right now."

"I'll get the snacks." Cheryl jumped to her feet. "Remember the section I read you tonight about Grandpa Al and the homemade pretzels? I made caramel corn and peanut butter fudge, but I also made pretzels!"

Angela laughed. "It's a good thing none of us have false teeth. Your grandmother revised that recipe, didn't she Cheryl?"

"Sure, right after they paid off the dentist. They're *soft* pretzels now."

Eve was slightly mollified as Ryan walked her up to her room. He'd sat next to her and held her hand, all through *Ten Little Indians*. Eve could understand why Ryan was so fascinated with Angela. Her father was one of his idols. But that didn't mean that Eve had to like her.

"Good night, Eve. I'm really glad you're here." Ryan placed a light kiss on Eve's forehead. And then he looked at her with something bordering on admiration. "You know, Eve . . . I was really happy about what you did tonight."

"What did I do?"

"I thought you were going to rip Angela apart, after she'd read her chapter. But you didn't. You told her you liked it."

"I did like it. Angela's a good writer, but that doesn't mean I have to like *her*."

Ryan laughed. "That's true. But I think you'll like her if you get to know her. Give her a chance, Eve . . . please?"

"Don't worry, Ryan. I'll give her a chance." Eve smiled sweetly and turned away, so Ryan couldn't see her face. She'd give Angela a chance. A chance to hang herself.

Ryan pulled Eve into his arms. "She had a rough childhood, Eve. She told me all about it, and maybe we're lucky we don't have world-famous parents."

"Maybe." Eve snuggled up to Ryan. "Let's not talk about Angela. Let's concentrate on us. Do you want to come to my room and listen to some music?"

Ryan looked tempted, but he shook his head. "I can't. I promised Angela I'd write another five pages tonight. My next chapter's really going to be exciting, Eve. My main character's all set to meet George Washington. It happens during the French and Indian War, when Washington was serving in the British army."

"That sounds fascinating." Eve smiled, even though she felt more like frowning. At any other time, Ryan would have jumped at the chance to spend time alone with her. Now he was more interested in going back to his computer, and that was all Angela Adams' fault!

"Is Angela going to work with you?" Eve's eyes narrowed as she pictured Angela and Ryan, alone in his room.

"No. She's helping Tracie tonight. They're down in the library, doing character sketches for Tracie's romance. After that, she's going to listen to some of Jeremy's jokes to help him decide which ones he should use in his book."

"So she's working late?" Eve felt a little better. If Angela was that busy, she wouldn't have time to spend with Ryan.

"I guess!" Ryan looked impressed. "She told me she wouldn't be free until breakfast tomorrow morning. That's when she's going to read my pages."

"If Angela's so busy helping everyone else, when does she have time to do her own work?"

"Beats me." Ryan shrugged. "She helped Scott right after we ate lunch, and she gave Cheryl some advice before dinner. Angela even went over one of Dean's songs with him. He said she was really helpful."

Eve mentally added up all the people Angela had helped, and then she asked her question again. "So when did she have time to write her own work?"

"I don't know, but she's managing somehow. Her chapter tonight was great, wasn't it, Eve?"

"Yes. It really was."

"Good night, Eve." Ryan gave her a kiss on the forehead and turned to leave. "I wish I could stay, but I've got to get to work. See you in the morning."

Eve stepped into her room. She'd just learned

some very interesting news, but she wasn't quite sure what to make of it. Angela's chapter had been very good. It had read exactly as if a professional writer had written it. But Angela hadn't had much time to work if she'd helped Scott, and Cheryl, and Dean before their meeting. So when had Angela written her chapter?

The night was hot and muggy. Eve changed to a light silk nightgown and opened the French doors to her balcony. There was a gentle breeze blowing, and Eve stepped out, keeping as far away from the rail as she could. She was terrified of heights, but she was fine as long as she didn't lean over and look directly down at the ground below her. Of course, she'd never admit that to anyone. It was a sign of weakness.

There was a lounge chair on her balcony, and Eve sat down to stare out at the courtyard garden. It was paved with bricks and there were potted trees and flowers everywhere. The house was L-shaped and all the bedroom windows looked out on the courtyard, but only Eve and Ryan had the luxury of balconies.

As she looked out, Eve saw someone walk across the courtyard. It was Cheryl, and she set a baking dish on one of the white, wrought-iron tables. Since the light was still on in the kitchen, Eve realized that Cheryl was probably testing another of her grandmother's recipes.

Eve's mouth began to water as the breeze carried the scent of cinnamon up to her. Perhaps she should go down to see exactly what Cheryl had baked. A piece of spice cake or a cinnamon roll, straight out of the oven, would be great. Eve was about to stand up and do just that, when someone else came out of the kitchen to join Cheryl.

It was Angela. Eve recognized the silvery laugh that floated up in the warm night air. Then Cheryl laughed, too, and they sat down at the table together.

Eve watched as Cheryl took something out of the pan. She handed it to Angela, and then she served herself. There was silence for a moment, and then Angela's voice rang out.

"This is incredible, Cheryl! I'm so glad you invited me to share it. Do you think we should take some upstairs to the rest of the group? Eve's light is still on. She might like some."

"No way." Cheryl laughed. "Let's just sit here and pig out. I'll bake more tomorrow, but this pan is ours."

A frown furrowed Eve's forehead. When Cheryl had baked at the sorority house, she'd always knocked on Eve's door with a sample. She'd told Eve that baking was fun if she shared it with her best friend. It was clear that Cheryl had a new best friend and Eve couldn't help feeling hurt.

"Did you finish your chapter for tomorrow, Angela?" Cheryl reached for another helping.

"Yes, I'm all through." Angela helped herself to another piece, too. "I'm reading Ryan's chapter at breakfast, tomorrow, but I'm free in the afternoon if you want me to help you with yours."

"Thank you, Angela. That would be wonderful!"

Eve's frown grew deeper. How could Angela have finished her second chapter when she'd been so busy helping everyone else?"

As Eve watched the two girls eat, she thought about it. After they'd all read their chapters, they'd watched *Ten Little Indians*. When the movie was over, at ten-thirty, Angela had helped Tracie and Jeremy. She was with Cheryl now, and it was shortly before midnight. If helping Tracie and Jeremy had taken an hour of Angela's time, she would have had only fifteen minutes to write her second chapter.

That was impossible. No one could work that fast. There was something strange going on, something that wasn't quite right. And before the workshop was over, Eve was going to get to the bottom of it.

CHAPTER THREE

It was over a hundred degrees in the shade and everyone was miserable. They were all sitting in the front of the television, listening to the noon weather report, hoping that the heat wave would break soon.

"Bad news on the weather front." The anchorman sounded very serious. *"Our Channel Seven weatherman, Stormy Raynes, will give you the details right after these messages from our sponsors."*

Angela laughed. "Stormy Raynes? That can't be his real name!"

"It's not." Ryan's face was perfectly innocent as he turned to her. "His real name is Will Frieze."

Angela cracked up and so did everyone else. And then she turned to the screen again, where Stormy Raynes was standing in front of a weather map, smiling. "How can he smile in weather like this?"

"It's simple." Eve shrugged. "He's in an air-conditioned studio."

"Everyone told me they were really miserable last night," Angela said. "It's hard to work when it's so hot, and it doesn't really cool down much at night."

"They're calling this the mother of all heat waves." Stormy Raynes pointed to a red area on the map. *"We broke the record yesterday, and today our temperatures are expected to rise even higher. Here's the five-day forecast, folks."*

Eve gasped as she read the numbers. They were all above a hundred degrees. It was going to be a miserable week.

Stormy Raynes sighed. *"There's no relief in sight and the national weather bureau just issued a heat wave warning. Here are some of their recommendations."*

Everyone leaned closer to the screen as a list of warnings appeared. They were exactly as Eve had expected.

"Stay inside during the hottest periods of the day." Stormy Raynes pointed to the first warning on the list. *"If you must go out, make sure you take along water and protection from the sun."*

They all listened as he read the other warnings about leaving children and animals in cars, turning off lights when you weren't in the room, limiting strenuous physical exercise, and drawing drapes and blinds to keep out the heat of the day.

"Remember, folks." Stormy Raynes pointed to the last item on the list. *"Conserve electricity during peak heat periods. If everyone turns on their air conditioners at once, we could be faced with a city-wide power failure."*

"At least we don't have to worry about that." Eve gave a sarcastic laugh. "We couldn't turn on our air-conditioning if we wanted to!"

"Let's look on the bright side," Ryan said. "At

least we've got the courtyard. It's cooler out there with all those big shade trees."

Angela stood up and switched off the television, and then she glanced at her watch. "I've got a surprise for all of you, and it should be here any minute."

"What is it?" Ryan started to grin. "A big block of ice?"

Angela shook her head. "No, but it's something to help us cool off."

There was a rumble outside, and they all rushed to the window. As they watched, a big truck came around the corner and parked in front of the mansion.

"It's here!" Angela looked very excited. "Come on, everybody. We've got to decide where to put it."

Angela raced out to the truck and everyone followed her. Two burly men got out of the cab, and one of them opened the door at the back of the truck.

"Sign here, lady." The older man handed Angela a clipboard. "Where do you want us to set it up?"

"Bring it around to the courtyard. We'll decide where to put it and meet you there."

"Where to put *what?*" Eve asked the question that was on everyone's mind as they followed Angela to the courtyard. "What is it, Angela?"

Angela laughed. "A portable swimming pool. I ordered it this morning. They promised me they'd have it set up in an hour, and then we can all cool off."

"That's fantastic!" Cheryl gave Angela a hug. "You're wonderful, Angela! Isn't she wonderful, everybody?"

Eve watched while everyone congratulated Angela

and thanked her for her gift. The swimming pool was a wonderful gift. Eve knew that. But she couldn't help feeling that Angela was using her money, trying to impress everyone else.

But she'd done that, too . . . hadn't she? She'd used her money to pay for parties and redecorate the sorority house. At the time, it hadn't seemed wrong, but perhaps that was because she'd been the one who was doing it.

Eve picked up her pages from the printer and smiled. She was the only one who'd worked this afternoon, and it had been no easy task. Everyone else had been too busy enjoying their new pool, splashing and laughing right below her balcony. It had been impossible for Eve to concentrate, but she hadn't wanted to complain. If she'd complained about the noise, it would have made her the most unpopular member of the workshop. She'd shut her balcony doors and suffered the hot, stuffy air in silence.

She'd done exactly what Angela had said and rewritten the first chapter of her book. Eve had thought about her heroine, and she'd finally come up with a motivation. Rochelle Dubois was Tracie in disguise, a woman who kept searching for romance in all the wrong places. Just like Tracie, Rochelle was sometimes foolish, and her dream of the tall, handsome stranger guided every aspect of her life. But just like Tracie, Rochelle now had a sweetness about her, an innocent quality that made her appealing.

Eve's vampire had changed, too. He was no longer

a he. Her vampire was a woman, a rich, evil woman who enticed her victims with her wealth and beauty and killed them when they were most vulnerable. Eve's vampire was modeled after Angela, and Eve had named her Adonna.

As Eve turned to leave the fourth-floor hallway, she felt strange, as if someone were watching her. She whirled around, but no one was there and the doors to the servants' quarters were all tightly shut. She shrugged it off. Her book was scary, and she'd managed to scare herself. There was no one here. The fourth floor was off-limits. But she hurried down the stairs, just in case.

The third floor was deserted. Everyone was still in the courtyard, laughing and talking after their swim. Eve wished she could have gone swimming, but she hadn't brought her suit. Jumping in the pool in a T-shirt and cut-offs just wasn't her style. She'd go shopping for a new, fashionable swimsuit, and then she'd join the group around the pool.

Eve stacked her pages on the desk in her room, picked up her purse, and went downstairs. Cheryl was in the kitchen, and Eve smiled at her. "Hi, Cheryl. I'm going to run out to the mall to get a swimsuit. Do you want to go along?"

"No thanks, Eve." Cheryl shook her head. "I'm making dinner and I still have to write my pages. I just don't have time."

Cheryl had never turned down the chance to go shopping before. Eve headed out to the pool to ask the other girls, but no one wanted to go. Eve was just heading for the front door alone, when the telephone rang. She picked it up and got the surprise of her life.

It was the president of the college, and he asked her to gather everyone around the speaker phone in the library.

It didn't take long to get everyone together. A summons from the president of the college was important. Eve swallowed hard and then she spoke. "We're all here, President Graham."

"I'm afraid I have some bad news for you." President Graham sounded upset. "I'm here at the hospital, and they've just taken Professor Hellman to isolation."

Everyone exchange puzzled glances, and then Ryan moved closer to the speaker. "Excuse me, President Graham. It's Ryan Young. Is Professor Hellman sick?"

"I'm afraid so." President Graham cleared his throat. "I'll let Dr. Fischer speak to you. Listen carefully and do exactly as he says."

There was a moment of silence and then Dr. Fischer came on the line. "We've run some tests, and Professor Hellman has an unusually virulent strain of infectious hepatitis. I understand he was with you yesterday?"

"That's right," Ryan answered. "Is Professor Hellman going to be all right?"

"He's doing very well, considering the seriousness of his illness. Do you have enough food to last for the next ten days?"

Ryan turned to Cheryl. She knew the contents of the kitchen better than anyone. Cheryl nodded, and Ryan spoke into the speaker again. "Yes. We've got enough food."

"Good. You're all under quarantine for ten days.

No one is to leave the workshop for any reason. If you need supplies you can have them delivered, but tell them to drop off the packages outside the front door. I don't want you to come into contact with anyone who's not a member of your group."

"Excuse me, doctor." Eve spoke up. "Does this mean we could get infectious hepatitis, too?"

"There's a slim possibility that Professor Hellman was still in the infectious phase when he met with you. It's unlikely, though. This is just a precaution."

"Oh, great!" Eve sighed. "What are we supposed to do if one of us gets sick?"

"We'll send out a team dressed in protective gear to transport you to the hospital. I want you to call me immediately if anyone shows symptoms."

"What are the symptoms?" Ryan took out a pad of paper and started to take notes.

"Fever, nausea, and a change in skin color. Check the whites of your eyes every morning. They're the first to change color. If you have the disease, they'll turn slightly yellow."

"Wonderful!" Jeremy started to laugh. "We get hot, we toss our cookies, and our eyes change color. It sounds just like one of our frat parties!"

Eve couldn't help it. She cracked up. There were times when Jeremy was actually funny.

"Excuse me, Doctor." Angela spoke up. "There were two delivery men here this afternoon. Should we notify them?"

"That's not necessary. If some of you did contract the disease, you won't be in the contagious phase for at least three days. And remember, I'll be happy to answer any questions you might have. All you have to do is pick up the phone and call me."

"Oh, sure," Jeremy said to Eve in an undertone. "Have you ever tried to call a doctor? All you get is their answering service. By the time the doctor gets your message, your relatives could be holding your memorial service."

Ryan turned to them. "Quiet! President Graham wants to talk to us again."

"I've assured Dr. Fischer that you're all responsible adults, and I expect you to follow his restrictions. You're not to leave the Sutler Mansion for any reason. Is that clear?"

Ryan answered for all of them. "It's clear, sir."

"Good. This is a very unfortunate circumstance, and I want all of you to know that I'm very concerned about your welfare. Continue with the assignments that Professor Hellman has given you, and call Dr. Fischer if you have any medical problems. You can contact me at my office if there's anything else you need."

"Thank you, sir. Good-bye." Ryan hung up the phone. And then he turned to the rest of the group. "Is anybody having any symptoms?"

They all shook their heads, and Ryan turned to Cheryl. "Are you sure we have enough food?"

"I'm sure."

"Maybe we'd better call in a grocery order, just in case." Angela spoke up. "I've got an account at Appleton's Market, and they'll deliver if I ask them. It'll be my treat. If we can't go out, at least we can have our favorite foods in the house."

Ryan smiled. "That's really nice of you, Angela. What does everyone want?"

As the group gathered around Angela, Eve sighed and turned away. Angela was trying to buy friends again, and from the smiles on the faces of her fellow workshop students, she was succeeding. Angela was the center of attention again, just as she'd been this afternoon when the pool had been delivered.

"Eve? Don't you want anything special?" Angela smiled at her, her pen poised over the grocery order.

"No thanks." Eve tried to be pleasant, but it was difficult. "Whatever's here is fine with me."

Eve went up the stairs to her room. Everyone probably thought she was upset at being quarantined, but that wasn't it. She didn't really mind the isolation and the fact that they couldn't leave the grounds. It would have been fun to be separated from the rest of the world with Ryan. What really made Eve furious was that Angela was quarantined with them. What Eve had told Angela was true. She didn't want food. What she wanted was some time alone with Ryan. And now that they were all quarantined with Angela, Eve couldn't even suggest that the two of them get away for a romantic evening together!

CHAPTER FOUR

Wicked stood at the printer as the pages dropped into the tray. No one else knew that the printer had such a big memory. It was possible to print out the previous hundred pages and that's exactly what Wicked had done. It was very important to read what everyone had written, and Wicked was planning to do that right now.

There was a furnished room on the fourth floor that no one else knew about. The technician who'd hooked up the computers had let Wicked in, several days before the rest of the students had arrived. Wicked had chosen this room because it was an excellent place to read. It was also an excellent place to keep an eye on everything that was happening in the Sutler Mansion.

The fourth-floor room was set up exactly the way Wicked wanted it. It had a comfortable chair, a reading lamp, and a small desk. The fire escape ladder was right outside the window, and Wicked had discovered that there was an excellent vantage place on the roof. One of the former Sutler servants had built a covered roof garden, and that was where Wicked kept an eye on the other students.

Of course, this wasn't Wicked's only room. There was the other room, downstairs, where Wicked slept and used the computer, just like the rest of the workshop students. The fourth-floor room was Wicked's special hideaway, where it was possible to think without interruptions and plan out exactly what to do to accomplish the goal.

Wicked took out the key and unlocked the door. It had been a simple matter to replace the existing padlock with a new one. No one had noticed the new padlock since the fourth floor was off-limits to everyone except Wicked.

Tracie's romance was taking shape. Wicked smiled, reading the pages quickly. Angela had helped her, and now it was very good. Jeremy's humor book was better, too. Angela had done an excellent job coaching him. The jokes were funny, the situations were hilarious, and Wicked had to be careful not to laugh too loudly. Someone might hear, and Wicked couldn't let anyone know about the room on the fourth floor or the plan to make the workshop such a huge success, everyone would be talking about it for years to come.

Scott's work was next, and Wicked read it with a smile. He'd written about the Sutler Mansion ghost story, and Wicked found it fascinating. But Wicked noticed that Scott was relying too much on his thesaurus program. Using a multi-syllabic word when a simple word would do was an affectation that turned most readers off. Perhaps Angela would notice and correct Scott's error. She was an excellent critic.

Beth's poetry was good. Wicked grinned at her choice of phrase. *The night was blue serge*, was an excellent line. It was much more original than the usual, *The night was blue velvet*. Perhaps Beth should get together with Dean. Wicked hoped that someone would suggest it. The problem wasn't with Dean's music. It was excellent. Wicked had heard Dean strumming his guitar, late at night, when he thought no one was listening. Dean would go far with his music, but his lyrics weren't very original.

Marc's sports book was interesting, although basketball wasn't Wicked's favorite sport. His characters were strong, and there was humor in the fact that a guy who was only five-feet-five-inches tall wanted to play hoops for the Lakers. Marc knew a lot about sports and that wasn't surprising, considering his father's choice of career. And Marc had managed to convert his sports knowledge into an interesting setting for the reader.

And then there was Ryan. Wicked was delighted with the historical time period Ryan had chosen. It was a rich tapestry, and Ryan had worked very hard on his writing. Perhaps Professor Hellman would choose Ryan's work. Wicked just wasn't sure. There was another book that was coming along fabulously, and that was Eve's.

Wicked was surprised. Eve hadn't shown much promise with her first chapter, but she'd rewritten it and now it was a fine piece of work. It was almost as good as Angela's, and that was saying a lot.

Angela. Wicked sighed. Angela had it all. She was beautiful, intelligent, and incredibly talented. She had only one flaw and Wicked hoped she'd correct it. Angela tended to treat everyone as if they were her social and intellectual inferior. Perhaps it was true, but Angela had to learn to be more accepting and less critical of the other students in the workshop.

It was always easier to see other people's faults. Wicked sat for a moment and thought about it. Wisdom came with age, and it was difficult to step outside oneself, to see what others saw in you. Of course, that was no longer difficult for Wicked. The split hadn't been a bad thing. Although it was difficult to juggle two personalities, Wicked had managed to do it without being detected.

Memories of childhood flickered across Wicked's mind. Wicked's parents hadn't noticed the split, and that was good. They might have become very concerned. Most unenlightened people thought it was abnormal to have two personalities sharing the same body.

Of course they were wrong. Wicked knew that. Everyone had a bright side and a dark side, and Wicked's two sides were separated very nicely. When the dark side was out, the bright side stepped back and went to sleep. Wicked's bright side was completely unaware of what the dark side was doing, and that was exactly the way Wicked wanted it. If there was no awareness, there could be no interference, nothing to keep Wicked from the goal.

Wicked stood up and flicked off the light. It was time to slip into the second persona, the bright side, and go down to dinner as a member of the group. No one knew who Wicked was, and no one, not even the bright side, would ever guess.

Tracie looked completely amazed as Eve finished reading her pages. "That was totally incredible, Eve! I can't believe you wrote it!"

"Thanks, Tracie." Eve grinned at her. She was relieved that Tracie hadn't recognized herself in the character Rochelle Dubois. Perhaps it was true that people never recognized unflattering portraits of themselves.

"It was really great, honey!" Ryan reached out to squeeze Eve's hand. But then he turned to Angela with a smile. "Thanks, Angela. Your criticism last night really helped Eve a lot."

Eve managed to keep the smile on her face, but she was burning up inside. She'd worked like a dog all afternoon, rewriting her chapter. And now Ryan was giving all the credit to Angela!

"Your chapter was wonderful, Eve." Angela turned to smile at her. "I'm not sure my criticism helped, but if I did, I'm really glad."

Cheryl laughed. "You're being too modest, Angela. You heard Eve's chapter last night. She never could have done such a good job rewriting it if you hadn't told her exactly what to do."

Eve's smile faltered. What was Cheryl talking about? Angela hadn't helped her!

"But I didn't write it." Angela turned to Eve. "Eve wrote those pages herself. She deserves every bit of the credit. Good job, Eve. You're turning into a very good writer."

"Thank you, Angela." Even though Eve was fuming inside, she did her best to be polite. Why was it that Angela's compliment felt more like an insult? Angela was saying the right words, but Eve was willing to bet she wasn't sincere. Angela was an actress, playing the role of someone who was gracious, and sweet, and utterly charming. And everyone else believed that role was real, everyone except Eve.

"We saved the best for last." Cheryl gave Angela an adoring smile. "Come on, Angela. We're dying to hear your next chapter."

Angela looked a little concerned. "I don't know if you'll like it, Cheryl. I'm afraid my next chapter might upset you."

"I'm the first to get murdered?!" Cheryl looked absolutely delighted, just as if someone had given her a prize. "Go ahead, Angela. I can hardly wait to hear all the horrible details!"

Eve frowned as Angela began to read. As usual, her work was very good. Eve found herself holding her breath as Angela read about the woman in the kitchen and how she'd been brutally stabbed with a butcher knife. And then Angela's chapter was over and everyone, including Cheryl, started to applaud.

"That was fantastic!" Cheryl leaned over to give Angela a hug. "I just loved that part where you had me take the cookies from the oven and drop them!"

Angela hugged Cheryl back and she looked very relieved. "I'm glad you're not upset, Cheryl. Remember, it's just fiction."

"I know." Cheryl giggled. "But I'm going to be very careful when I bake Grandma's chocolate cookies tonight. I think I'll hide all the butcher knives, just in case."

Everyone laughed, and then Scott spoke up. "Who's going to get killed off next?"

"I'm not sure." Angela shrugged. "I guess we'll all have to wait until tomorrow night to find out."

"I think it should be a guy next time." Ryan smiled at Angela. "You can kill off my character if you want to."

Angela shook her head. "I can't kill you off. You have to stick around because you're going to try to save my character. And that's all I'm going to say about my plot. It's a lot more fun if it's a surprise."

"Are you going up to work now, Angela?" Ryan looked concerned.

"No. I guess I'm like my father. I'm much more creative in the middle of the night. Did you need some help, Ryan?"

"If you can spare the time. I'm having some trouble with my outline for the next chapter."

"No problem."

"I'll see you later, honey." Ryan squeezed Eve's hand, and then he got up. "Come on, Angela. Let's grab a couple of Cokes from the refrigerator and go out in the courtyard. It's cooler out there."

Eve managed to keep the smile on her face as Angela and Ryan left the library. She'd been hoping that she could spend some time with Ryan tonight, but it was clear that wasn't going to happen. Ryan was tied up with Angela. Again. And Eve was left out in the cold.

"Does anyone want to watch a movie?" Eve asked the rest of the group.

Beth sighed. "I'd love to, but Dean and I have to work. Angela thought it would be good if we did some lyrics together."

"I'm working, too." Scott stood up. "Sorry, Eve."

"How about you, Jeremy?" Eve turned to him with a smile. Jeremy wasn't the type to spend long hours at his computer.

Jeremy looked tempted, but he shook his head. "I can't. Angela said she'd go over my next chapter with me if I finish it tonight."

"Me, too." Marc got up to leave. "I've got a breakfast meeting with her tomorrow, and she wants to see ten new pages."

"Tracie?" Eve was beginning to get frustrated. Didn't anyone want to watch a movie with her? "I've got a couple of new romances I know you haven't seen."

Tracie sighed and shook her head. "I'd love to, but I have to work. Maybe we can do it tomorrow night, Eve."

"And I have to bake." Cheryl stood up. "Sorry, Eve. I've got three new recipes to try tonight. If I don't get started, I'll be up until midnight."

Eve sat there, stunned, as everyone left. She didn't feel like working, but there was nothing else to do. She could see Ryan and Angela through the lace curtains, lounging by the side of the pool. They looked very serious, and they were huddled together, their heads almost touching, over the outline Ryan had written.

Thanks to Angela's influence, everyone was turning into a bunch of workaholics. This workshop was even worse than Eve had anticipated, and it was all Angela's fault.

CHAPTER FIVE

Cheryl felt absolutely marvelous. Her lemon cake had come out of the oven light and fluffy, exactly the way her grandmother had said it would, and her dill bread smelled so wonderful, she could hardly wait to cut it and try a piece. The only recipe she had left was the one for her grandmother's chocolate fudge cookies. Cheryl hoped they'd turn out to be as delicious as she remembered.

As she dropped four squares of unsweetened baker's chocolate in the double boiler on top of the stove, Cheryl thought about her grandmother's chocolate cookies. Everyone in the family had loved them, and Granny had sent them to all her grandchildren on their birthdays. It didn't seem like a birthday without Granny's chocolate cookies, and Cheryl planned to keep right on with her grandmother's tradition. If her cookies were as good as Granny's, she'd give them to her friends for their birthdays.

Cheryl frowned as she remembered whose birthday was next. It was Eve's. Eve was a sorority sister and she was supposed to be a friend, but Cheryl had decided she didn't really like Eve. She'd been on the receiving end of Eve's sarcastic tongue one too many times in the past. Eve could be very nasty if things didn't go her way.

It didn't take long for the chocolate to melt over the boiling water. Cheryl lifted the top pan from the double boiler and carried it to the walk-in cooler. Granny's recipe said the chocolate should be cooled while the other ingredients were mixed. There were six eggs in the recipe, and if the chocolate was too hot, it would cook the eggs and make the cookie dough lumpy.

Cheryl put the chocolate on one of the shelves and went back into the main part of the kitchen to mix up the dough. She loved the walk-in cooler. It was a luxury most people didn't have and didn't really need, unless they were serious cooks. The cooler was exactly like a room-sized refrigerator, and Cheryl wished they had one at the sorority house. Even though their refrigerator was large, there was never enough room on the shelves.

A smile flickered across Cheryl's face. Perhaps she should mention it to Eve. Eve had already spent a lot of money trying to buy everyone's vote for president, and she'd be sure to order a walk-in cooler if she thought it would make her more popular.

Eve thought she could buy everything with money. Cheryl frowned as she cracked open the eggs and put them in the mixing bowl. That just wasn't true, and Eve should be more like Angela. Angela had lots of money. The pool she'd bought for them proved that. But Angela didn't demand anything in return. She was an incredibly nice person who liked to share her good fortune with her friends.

Cheryl measured the sugar and mixed it with the eggs until they were fluffy. Then she sifted the flour with the salt and the baking powder and added it to the dough. Granny's recipe said to add the melted chocolate next, and then the nuts and the chocolate chips. Cheryl set the bowl on the butcher block counter in the center of the kitchen and went into the walk-in cooler to see if the chocolate had cooled enough to use.

There were footsteps in the hallway, and Cheryl looked up with a smile on her face. She hoped it was Angela. They'd had so much fun last night, sitting at the table in the courtyard, sampling Cheryl's cinnamon rolls. But no one appeared in the doorway. She was almost sure she'd heard footsteps, but perhaps she'd been mistaken.

Another sound, a slight rustling, made Cheryl jump. She turned to look at the kitchen doorway, but there was absolutely no one in sight. Perhaps it was just her imagination working overtime, but Cheryl couldn't help thinking of the chapter Angela had read to them tonight, and how her character had been killed in the kitchen.

That was fiction. This was real. Cheryl knew she was being silly, but she stepped out of the cooler, rushed to the counter, and hid the big butcher knife in a drawer.

Cheryl was embarrassed as she went back to the cooler. She wouldn't tell anyone what she'd done. But Angela was such a good writer that her book had seemed real, and even though Cheryl had denied it, tonight's chapter had frightened her. Perhaps she should have invited someone to keep her company tonight. Tracie loved chocolate. She would have come down to the kitchen to watch her bake. Beth and Dean might have come, too, if she'd asked them. They could have worked on their lyrics right here at the kitchen table. Or Scott, or Jeremy, or Marc. Or Angela and Ryan. When they'd finished going over Ryan's outline, they could have come into the kitchen.

But she hadn't asked anyone, and she was alone. Cheryl sighed and decided, from now on, she'd ask for company in the kitchen. The way she felt right now, even Eve would have been welcome. Angela's chapter had unnerved her much more than she'd realized.

The chocolate was almost ready. Cheryl was about to give it a final stir, when something totally unexpected happened.

The kitchen lights went off.

"Hey!" Cheryl whirled around, dropping her spoon with a clatter. "Who turned off the . . ."

But Cheryl never got a chance to finish her question as something sharp and heavy punched her skull.

Cheryl crumpled to the floor of the walk-in cooler without a sound. The pan of chocolate dropped from her hand and splattered in a sticky mess. Rivulets of chocolate ran into Cheryl's hair, but she didn't notice the mess. Cheryl Frazier was incapable of thought because all the life had left her body and she was quite dead.

Angela shook two aspirin out of the bottle. She had a terrible headache. But she always had problems if she took aspirin on an empty stomach and there was no food in her room.

She'd have to go down to the kitchen. Angela sighed as she put on a robe and slippers. They'd stocked up on plenty of snacks, and there would be something she could eat. As she stepped out into the hallway, Angela remembered what Cheryl had said. She'd been planning to try three new recipes tonight, and Cheryl was an excellent cook.

Cheryl had said she was baking a lemon cake, and that was one of Angela's favorite desserts. The second recipe had sounded good, too. A slice of crusty, warm dill bread slathered with butter would be wonderful. But the third recipe was the one Angela really wanted to try, and her mouth started to water as she walked toward the stairs. Cheryl had described her grandmother's chocolate fudge cookies, and they'd sounded incredibly delicious.

Everyone on the third floor was sleeping. As Angela passed the other bedrooms, she noticed that there was no light seeping out from under anyone's door. It was late, almost two in the morning, but she'd been hoping that someone was awake. She felt like company in the kitchen. It wasn't much fun, raiding the cupboards, if no one else was there.

Angela checked the second floor to see if any of the guys were up, but their rooms were dark, too.

It was strange, being the only one awake in the huge, four-story mansion. It was almost creepy, and Angela shivered as she went down the stairs to the ground floor.

The library was deserted, and so was the living room. Angela hurried through the darkened rooms. She almost wished she'd knocked on someone's door and invited them to come along. Any of the guys would have come, Angela was sure of that. They all seemed to like her, and so did the girls, everyone except Eve.

She really should have a talk with Eve. It was clear Eve thought she was trying to steal her boyfriend, and that simply wasn't the case. Although Angela enjoyed Ryan's company, she wasn't interested in him romantically. Once Eve understood that, they might be able to be friends.

The lights were off in the kitchen. Angela stopped at the door, and a puzzled expression crossed her face. They'd all agreed to leave the light on over the sink, in case someone wanted a late-night snack.

For a moment, Angela was actually frightened. This was exactly like the chapter she'd read this evening. When Cheryl's character had been murdered, the killer had turned off the lights in the kitchen.

Angela told herself she was being foolish. Cheryl had probably forgotten their agreement and turned the lights off when she'd left to go up to her room. There was nothing wrong, nothing at all. But Angela's hand was shaking as she pushed open the kitchen door.

There was a dim light shining in through the

window, from the porchlight on the corner. Angela waited until her eyes had adjusted to the near-darkness, and then she stepped into the kitchen to feel around for the wall switch.

There was a combination of scents in the air, and Angela began to smile. She could smell lemon, and dill, and chocolate. Angela could hardly wait to sample a little of everything.

Under the delicious aroma of freshly baked goods was another scent, one that wasn't pleasant. It was almost metallic in nature. What was it? Had Cheryl burned something?

It took a moment for Angela to find the switch in the dark. She flicked it on and gave a deep sigh of relief as the overhead lights glowed brightly. And then she saw it, something on the floor, half in and half out of the walk-in cooler.

Something that looked human.

Something that was covered with blood and chocolate.

Something that had once been Cheryl!

Angela's mouth opened in a silent scream. She was rooted to the spot, too horrified to move, too paralyzed to do more than stare. And then her silent scream built up to an audible whimper and finally burst out as a terrified shriek.

Eve tossed and turned on her pillow. Her eyelids flickered, and her arm thrashed out to thump against the mattress. She was dreaming about something so horrible, she simply had to wake up!

She was trapped in a small, dark place, unable

to move or even cry out. She was buried alive, and no one could save her because no one knew where she was.

Eve reached up to push at the barrier that covered her, that threatened to suffocate her if she couldn't fight her way out. But the barrier wouldn't lift. It was too heavy and thick, like a slab of unmoving concrete.

Her legs were cramping, but she couldn't move them. And her arms were so tired, they were shaking. But she couldn't rest or she would die. She had to get out!

There was a voice, far off in the distance, some-one calling her name. "Eve Marie Carrington! You've been a wicked girl, and you have to be punished!"

But what had she done to be punished this way? It must have been something horrible. Tears started to pour from Eve's eyes, and she began to sob. "It wasn't me. It was her! Margo did it, not me!"

"Margo?" The voice laughed. "There is no Margo. You did it, Eve. I saw you! And it won't do you any good to blame it on Margo this time! You're the one who's wicked . . . wicked . . . wicked. . . ."

Eve pushed out with all her strength. She had to get out of here! And then there was a crash as the glass of water by the side of her bed tipped over and soaked her face.

Eve sat up and shook her head. What a horrible nightmare! She switched on the light and drew a deep breath of relief as she saw her familiar room.

Fragments of the nightmare began to come back as Eve got up to get a towel. Margo had been her imaginary playmate, and Eve hadn't thought about her in years.

Lonely children often had imaginary playmates. Eve had learned that in one of her psychology classes. And children often blamed those imaginary playmates for things they had done. Eve's had been Margo, and Margo had been very wicked. When Eve had torn her clothes playing, or broken one of her mother's vases, she'd always claimed that Margo had done it. Her nanny had thought it was cute at first, but one day she'd decided that Eve had to take responsibility for her own actions. She'd locked Eve in a closet for writing on the wallpaper with a crayon, and Eve still remembered how terrified she'd been, all alone in the dark. The punishment had worked. Eve had never mentioned Margo again. She'd forgotten all about her until the nightmare she'd had tonight.

Her pillow was wet and Eve flipped it over. Then she changed her nightgown and crawled back into bed. It took several minutes of tossing and turning, but at last she went back to sleep. And that's when she started to have another nightmare. Someone was screaming, over and over. Doors were banging open and shut, and people were shouting and running down the hallway in a panic.

Eve sat up and flicked on the light, but her dream still went on. This was no nightmare. It was really happening. Someone was screaming, down on the ground floor, and everyone was running down the stairs.

Her robe was on the chair and Eve reached for it with shaking hands. She stepped into her moccasins, grabbed her purse, just in case it was a fire and they all had to leave the house, and then she rushed into the hallway and ran down the stairs to see what was the matter.

"Oh, my God! Should I call for an ambulance?" Eve's face turned pale when Marc shook his head. "Is she . . ."

Marc got up from the floor and sighed. "She's dead."

"But how would you know that?" Tracie started to cry. "You could be wrong, couldn't you?"

Marc shook his head. "I'm a sports medicine major, and I've taken emergency care classes. I'm sorry, Tracie, but she's dead."

"Does anybody know what happened?" Beth swallowed hard.

"I think Cheryl fell and hit her head on the edge of this steel table." Scott looked sick as he examined the table. "It's sharp, and it could have done that kind of damage."

"But why did she fall?" Eve turned away so she wouldn't have to see the chocolate in Cheryl's hair. Cheryl had always been proud of her lovely red hair. Even though Eve knew it was crazy, she had the urge to wash it so it could be pretty again.

"There's some water on the floor." Jeremy joined Scott for a closer look. "Cheryl must have slipped. At least that's what it looks like to me."

Angela was sobbing quietly and Ryan was holding her. For the first time, Eve wasn't a bit jealous.

Angela had been the one to find Cheryl, and it must have been a horrible shock.

"Come on, guys." Jeremy motioned for Scott and Marc. "Let's get out of here. We can't do anything for Cheryl, and we shouldn't touch anything."

"Good idea," Ryan said. "I'll call the police. Eve? Help me with Angela. I think she's in shock."

"Come on, Angela." Eve hurried to take Angela's arm. "Let's go. You'll feel better in another room."

Angela was trembling so much, she could barely walk. Eve supported her on one side while Ryan helped on the other. They half-carried her down the hall and got her settled on the living room couch. Eve sat next to her with her arm around Angela's shoulders, and Ryan hurried to the phone on the desk.

Everyone was silent as Ryan picked up the receiver. He clicked the button several times, and then he turned to them. "This phone's not working. I'll use the one in the library."

But the phone in the library wasn't working either, and Ryan was clearly upset when he came back. And although they checked every phone in the house to make sure none of them were off the hook, they couldn't get a dial tone.

"Somebody has to drive to the police station!" Tracie's voice was high and scared, and it was clear she was on the verge of panic.

Eve shook her head. "We can't leave the house, Tracie. We're quarantined, remember?"

"But . . . but there's no phone! We've got to do something!"

"Don't worry, Tracie. We will." Ryan tried to

soothe her. "Let's all try to relax for a minute and think about what we can do."

But there was nothing they could do. They couldn't call out, and they couldn't leave. They couldn't even shout out the window to one of their neighbors because the surrounding houses were all vacant.

"Do you think we could flag down a car?" Beth sounded very tentative. "One of us could stand out in the street with a big sign. As long as the driver didn't come too close, we wouldn't be breaking the quarantine."

Everyone else started to look very excited, but Eve just sighed. "That's a great idea, Beth, but it won't work. We're on a dead end, and there isn't any through traffic. The only cars I've seen on the street are ours."

"Relax, everybody." Scott gave them all a reassuring smile. "All of our friends have this number. They'll call, and when they can't get through, they'll report it to the phone company. Somebody'll come out to repair it. We just have to be patient."

Eve sighed. "That's true, but we'll still have a problem if there's something wrong with the wiring inside the house. We can't let the repairman in."

"This is all my fault!" Angela started to cry. "I wrote about Cheryl's death, and now it's . . . it's happened!"

Ryan shook his head. "That's crazy, Angela. Think about it for a minute. The murder weapon in your book was a knife, and Cheryl wasn't stabbed. She fell and hit her head on the table. Her death was an accident, not murder."

"I . . . I guess you're right." Angela looked slightly

reassured. "But what shall we do with . . . with Cheryl?"

Eve thought about it for a minute, and then she spoke up. "We'll just stash her body inside the walk-in cooler. It's probably as cold as the morgue."

"That's just awful!" Tracie glared at Eve. "How can you be so casual when Cheryl was your friend?"

"It's simple, Tracie. I'm facing facts. Cheryl is dead, and there's absolutely nothing I can do for her now."

Tracie shuddered, and then she looked angry again. "You know what's wrong with you, Eve? You have absolutely no respect for the dead!"

"Yes, I do. But I have more respect for the living. And I don't think any of us should be forced to look at Cheryl's dead body every time we go into the kitchen!"

"Eve's right," Beth said. "I think we should put her in the cooler and cover her with a blanket or something, just like they do when someone dies in the hospital."

"We can't." Ryan looked upset. "The police will want to see exactly how Cheryl died and that means we can't touch anything or cover anything up."

Eve sighed. "Let's be practical. If the phone doesn't get fixed, the police won't know that Cheryl died for nine more days. We're going to need food from the kitchen, Ryan. And I don't want to be the one to go in and get it!"

"I've got an idea." Scott spoke up. "I brought my camera with me. Why don't I take some accident scene photos before we move her? That's what the police photographers do."

Ryan thought about it for a minute. "That's reasonable. Go get your camera, Scott. If we've got a good photo record, I don't see any reason why we can't move Cheryl's body."

"I'll help. There's an extra blanket in my room we can use." Eve turned to Tracie, who still looked upset. "Come on, Tracie. If you were really serious about respecting the dead, you can do one last service for Cheryl. I'm going to need help wrapping her up."

Tracie shuddered and shook her head. "Not me! I prefer to remember Cheryl just as she was."

"If you want to do something to help, stay here with Angela." Ryan turned to Tracie. "Do you think you can handle that?"

Tracie looked a little embarrassed. "Yes. I can do that. I'm sorry, everybody, but I just can't face seeing Cheryl again."

Eve didn't say a word as everyone told Tracie it was all right. Tracie was such a romantic, she couldn't stand a world that wasn't perfect. Romantics didn't get along in the real world, and Tracie was a prime example. Tracie was weak, and she wanted to be protected from anything unpleasant.

"I'll help you, Eve." Beth stood up. "And Dean will, too . . . won't you, Dean?"

"Sure. And I'll clean up the kitchen, after you're through. We're going to have to go in there eventually."

Eve turned to smile at them. Beth might be shy,

but she was showing a lot of courage. And Dean had just volunteered for a task that was bound to be gruesome. They seemed to have an inner strength, and Eve was glad they were members of the workshop. Beth and Dean were turning out to be real friends.

CHAPTER SIX

It was almost time for dinner, and Eve hesitated at the kitchen door. She'd been perfectly all right last night. She'd helped to wrap Cheryl's body in a blanket, and Ryan had told her that she'd been a tower of strength. But now that the shock had worn off, she really didn't want to go into the kitchen again.

Eve sighed. Today was her day to fix dinner. She gathered her courage and pushed open the kitchen door. She tried to avoid looking at the place where Cheryl had died, but her eyes seemed to have a mind of their own. They were drawn to that spot on the floor by the walk-in cooler, and Eve shuddered. Faint bloodstains still remained, although Dean had scrubbed the wooden floor with cleanser.

Eve stared at the bloodstains with horrible fascination. She couldn't help remembering how Cheryl's lifeless eyes had started up at them. They'd seemed wide and startled as if death had taken her completely unaware, and Eve fought down the urge to turn and run back out into the hall.

She'd never been a coward, and Eve braced herself for the task ahead. No one else had been in the kitchen all day. They'd all snacked on the chips and cookies they'd kept in the library. But chips and cookies weren't a meal, and Eve knew that everyone would be hungry soon.

"I know exactly how you feel, Eve."

Eve whirled around to see that Angela was standing behind her. "What do you mean, Angela?"

"I don't want to go in there, either. It feels too much like . . . like a crime scene."

Eve shook her head. "But it's not a crime scene, Angela. Cheryl's death was an accident."

"I know that. But it still feels like a crime scene. I can't help thinking about how awful Cheryl looked when I found her."

There were dark circles under Angela's eyes, and she looked as if she'd been up all night. Eve felt an unwanted twinge of sympathy for the girl she'd come to think of as her rival. "It must have been horrible, finding her like that."

"It was. And what made it even more horrible was that I wrote about it before it happened. I mean . . . I didn't describe it exactly, but it was close enough to scare me. Do you think everyone blames me, Eve?"

"Of course not! How could you know what was going to happen? It was just a coincidence that Cheryl died, right after you killed off her character."

"I guess, but it still makes me feel strange, almost like I predicted the future, or tempted fate, or something like that."

"That's totally crazy, and you know it!" Eve took

Angela's arm and led her down the hall. "You're dwelling on it, Angela. Just try to think about something else. Let's go out to the courtyard and see who's there."

Everyone else was lounging on the deck that ran around the pool. Ryan spotted them and he waved them over. "Hi, Eve. I'm glad you found Angela. We were about to go up and look for her."

"That's right," Jeremy said. "It's not good for you to be alone, Angela."

Angela sighed. "I would have come down sooner, but I didn't think I'd be very good company. I'm just too miserable about what's happened."

"That doesn't matter." Beth smiled at Angela kindly. "You know what they say. Misery loves company."

Dean pulled out a deck chair for Angela. "Beth's right. That's why we're all sticking together. We were just talking about how we've got to put this behind us and go back to our regular schedule."

"We'd be eating dinner right about now." Tracie glanced at her watch. "I'm getting hungry. How about everyone else?"

"I'm hungry and it's my turn to make dinner," Eve said. "We'll have pizza tonight. There's some frozen pizza dough in the freezer, and we've got pepperoni and cheese in the walk-in cooler."

"You're going in the *cooler*?!" Tracie sounded horrified.

"Of course." Eve hoped she looked more confident than she felt.

"But . . . you can't!" Tracie's face turned pale. "Cheryl's in there!"

"I know that, but so is our food. Somebody's got to go in and get it."

"'Atta girl, Eve!" Ryan started to applaud, and so did everyone else, everyone except Tracie who looked very upset.

"I still say it's wrong! If you go in there, you'll . . . you'll disturb her!"

"How can I disturb her when she's already dead? Don't be ridiculous, Tracie!" Eve got up and started for the kitchen. "I'll be back in forty-five minutes with pizza for everybody."

As Eve crossed the courtyard, she heard Tracie's voice. "I don't know about you, but I'm not going to eat any of that pizza. Eve has absolutely no feelings. She's . . . she's *horrible*!"

"This is great pizza, Eve." Ryan smiled at her as he took the last piece.

"Yes, it is." Beth reached out to pat Eve's shoulder. "I think you showed a lot of courage, Eve. I don't think I could have fixed dinner tonight."

Eve was surprised. "But, Beth . . . you and Dean washed the kitchen floor. That took courage, too."

"Not really." Dean shook his head. "We were still in shock, and that made it easier. If we'd taken the time to think about it, we probably couldn't have done it."

Ryan stood up. "Come on, everybody. Let's all help Eve load the dishwasher."

"You mean . . . you want us to go into the kitchen?!" Tracie was clearly shocked.

"Yes," Ryan said. "We can't avoid the kitchen forever. Let's all go together, in a group."

Jeremy stood up. "You're right. It's like riding a bicycle and falling off. If you don't get right back on again, you're letting your fear control you."

"But . . . but something could happen! Something awful!" Tracie's face turned pale. "Cheryl's spirit might want us to leave the scene of her death undisturbed."

Eve laughed. "Relax, Tracie. I made four pizzas in that kitchen. I even stepped over her body to get the cheese, and Cheryl's spirit didn't bother me."

"Come on, Tracie." Scott took Tracie's arm. "I must have checked out a hundred sightings, and I haven't seen a ghost or a spirit yet."

Tracie didn't look convinced, and she turned to Angela. "Are you going, Angela?"

"Yes." Angela picked up her plate and stood up. "There's nothing to be afraid of. And after we finish in the kitchen, I've got an idea that might help all of us cope with Cheryl's death."

Eve was smiling as they all sat down in the living room. She'd given Ryan a list of the movies she'd brought and they planned to watch one tonight. It would be wonderful to cuddle up on the couch with Ryan. It had been a long time since they'd been together, alone.

"I think Dean was right when he said we should

go on with our regular schedule," Angela said. "I know it's after seven, but I think we could all try to write a chapter and meet in the library at eleven."

Eve's mouth dropped open. Angela's suggestion was almost as ridiculous as Tracie's fear of Cheryl's spirit. "You mean you want us to work tonight?"

"I think it'll help." Angela smiled at all of them. "Have you ever heard of R.L. Stine?"

"He writes young-adult horror," Tracie said. "I've read some of his books."

"Well, the first time I met him . . ."

"You met R.L. Stine?" Tracie looked excited as she interrupted Angela. "Did you get an autographed copy of one of his books?"

"No. This wasn't a book signing, Tracie. It was a dinner party at my parents' house. Mr. Stine told me that he writes at least fifteen pages a day, no exceptions."

"Wonderful." Eve couldn't help being sarcastic. "But I bet R.L. Stine never got quarantined in a mansion with a dead friend in the walk-in cooler!"

Angela started to laugh. She didn't seem to realize that Eve was being sarcastic. "You've got a point, Eve. But if something like that happened to him, he'd probably write about it in one of his books."

"Write about your personal experiences." Eve rolled her eyes at the ceiling. "Is that what you're saying, Angela?"

"Exactly! That's why I think we should all try to write our usual chapters tonight. We can incorporate some of the feelings we have about Cheryl's death into our own writing."

"What a great idea!" Ryan smiled at Angela. "Even if it doesn't improve our work, it might make us feel better."

Angela smiled back. "Maybe we'll even learn something valuable about ourselves."

"Come on, Angela." Eve couldn't believe her own ears. "You sound like Dear Abby!"

Tracie turned to glare at Eve. "I think Angela's right. This is the first time one of my friends died, and writing about it might help me to cope with my loss."

"Oh, brother!" Eve snorted. "Jeremy's writing a humor book. What's he supposed to do? Undertaker jokes?"

Jeremy cracked up and Eve felt slightly better. At least one person recognized Angela's idea for the farce that it was. But then Jeremy started to look thoughtful. "You know . . . it might work, Angela. People joke to cover up their fears. It's almost like they need to laugh in the face of death. I could do a chapter on that."

"Perfect!" Angela smiled. "Okay. Let's all go up and get to work."

"How about tempting fate, Angela?" Eve asked. "Your next chapter is a murder, isn't it?"

"Yes." Angela was serious as she faced the group. "I was upset when I talked to Eve this afternoon. I know this sounds crazy, but I felt I'd tempted fate by killing off Cheryl's character. Eve convinced me that it was just a coincidence. She was . . . well . . . Eve was just wonderful!"

Ryan turned to smile at Eve. "Good for you, honey!"

"I've decided to go on with *Ten Little Writers*." Angela smiled at Eve. "Thank you, Eve."

Scott started to clap, and soon everyone was applauding. Eve managed to put a smile on her face, but she felt more like screaming in pure frustration. Angela had just cheated her out of her evening alone with Ryan.

"So who are you going to kill off next, Angela?" Eve kept the smile on her face. "Me?"

"No, Eve. I can't kill your character yet. I considered it because I knew you wouldn't mind, but it just won't work with my plot."

"How about me?" Jeremy asked. "I don't mind if my character gets it."

"No, it's got to be a female. I guess it's between Beth and Tracie."

Beth looked nervous, but she nodded agreeably. "You can murder my character, Angela. I'm not that superstitious."

"Thank you, Beth." Angela reached out to squeeze Beth's hand. "I'll think about it, okay?"

Tracie realized that everyone was looking at her and she squared her shoulders. "You can kill me, Angela. I'm not superstitious, either."

"Are you kidding?!" Scott started to laugh. "Come on, Tracie . . . you were afraid of Cheryl's spirit!"

Tracie looked very embarrassed. "I know, but I'm not afraid now. And Angela's got to promise that if she kills me off, I get to sleep in her room tonight. Okay, Angela?"

"Okay. If I kill off your character, you can sleep in my room. That's a promise." Angela smiled at Tracie. "And now . . . let's all go up and get to work!"

Wicked smiled as the pages rolled out of the printer. It had been a very productive night. Everyone had written their chapter, even Eve, and that was a pleasant surprise. Eve hadn't wanted to stay in her room and write tonight. But she had, and Wicked felt like applauding. And here were the chapters. Nine of them, since Cheryl was no longer with them. Wicked could hardly wait to read them to see who would die tonight.

CHAPTER SEVEN

Tracie made a few changes, and then she smiled in complete satisfaction. This was her best chapter yet! She'd written about death in a flashback, and she thought it was very good. Her main character had witnessed the death of her first boyfriend.

The flashback was scary, and Tracie shivered as she read what she'd written. Anastasia, her main character, had seen her boyfriend in the arms of another woman. Anastasia had watched them kissing through a lace curtain, and she'd vowed to get even. And then something horrible had happened. Right after Anastasia had taken her vow of revenge, her boyfriend had been killed in a boating accident. Was it fate? Or had she willed it to happen? Anastasia had to resolve her feelings before she could love again.

Tracie climbed up the steps to the fourth floor to get her pages. No one else was there, and it felt a little scary. She grabbed her pages from the tray and ran all the way back down to her room again. She didn't like going up to the fourth floor alone, and she wasn't quite sure why.

As she stuck her pages in her loose-leaf notebook, Tracie frowned. She hadn't bothered to check out an important part of her story. Could you really see through lace curtains? Tracie wasn't sure. And Angela had told them to be careful that the basic facts they wrote about were true.

There were lace curtains in the library. Tracie smiled as she remembered. She'd run down to check it out. She still had time to revise her chapter if her premise turned out to be false.

Tracie hurried down the hallway and pulled open the door to the staircase. But she'd only gone down three stairs when she thought she heard stealthy footsteps behind her. She whirled around, her eyes searching the shadows, but nothing was moving.

"Is someone there?" Tracie's voice was a frightened whisper. Of course no one answered, and Tracie felt very foolish. There was no one else in the stairwell. She was just jumpy because of Cheryl's death.

Even though Tracie knew she was being silly, she stopped and listened several times as she walked down the stairs. She felt very relieved when she reached the ground floor and opened the door to the hallway. The lights in the hallway were much brighter, and there weren't any dark shadows for someone to hide in.

There was no one else on the ground floor, but someone had come down earlier to set up the library for their meeting. There was a pad of paper in front of every chair with a sharpened pencil on top of it. Nine pads of paper and nine pencils. It made Tracie feel sad that there weren't ten.

The big red and white cooler sat on the library

table, almost like a centerpiece. Tracie walked over and lifted the lid. There was a variety of sodas inside, and she took out one of her favorites. She popped the tab, took a big sip, and carried it over to the French doors leading to the courtyard. There were lace curtains on the library doors and she needed to know if she could see through them.

The courtyard was dark, and all Tracie could see was her own reflection in the pane of glass behind the lace curtains. But the girl in her book hadn't been inside, looking out. She'd walked past the house and gazed in at the lighted interior. Tracie decided to go out in the courtyard and try it.

She opened the doors and stepped out, into the courtyard. It was dark, but she didn't turn on the lights. The girl in her book had been out in the darkness, several yards away from the window. Tracie crossed the courtyard to a spot quite close to the pool.

"Yes!" Tracie started to smile as she realized that she could see the red and white cooler on the library table. She wouldn't have to rush to revise her chapter. It was perfect exactly the way it was.

Tracie sat down in one of the patio chairs and sipped her soda. It was a hot night, but it was slightly cooler out here than it had been in the library. She closed her eyes for a moment and smiled as she heard several birds chirping sleepily in the trees. It was quiet and peaceful, and Tracie was glad she had this time to relax before the meeting.

Suddenly, a thought occurred to her, and Tracie's eyes flew open. She was out here alone, in the dark, and she wasn't really frightened at all. Angela had been right and Tracie could hardly wait to tell her. Writing about her reaction to Cheryl's death had helped her get over her fear.

Wicked stood at the deep end of the pool, watching Tracie relax in her chair. There was a redwood deck that ran all the way around the portable pool, with eight steps leading up to the deck. Although it was a large pool, it was shallow, with only six feet of water at the deep end. Since Tracie wasn't tall, that would be enough water for Wicked.

Tracie was a nice enough person, and Wicked liked her, even though she was sometimes silly and superficial. Her preoccupation with romance bordered on the obsessive, but Wicked thought she'd probably grow out of it in a year or two. Unfortunately, Tracie wouldn't live that long.

It was a pity, but it couldn't be helped. Tracie was the next victim in Angela's book. Wicked had to make sure that Angela's talent was appreciated, and there was only one way to do that. Angela's fiction had to be accurate, and that meant the real world had to parallel her writing.

It was time. Wicked moved quietly, inching along the redwood deck to the portable stereo that Scott had left on a small table near the edge of the water. They only had one set of batteries. Scott had told them that. And it was dangerous to run an extension cord up to the deck, where it might short out if it got wet.

Wicked clicked on the stereo and gradually increased the volume until it was audible. Tracie didn't react, and Wicked turned it up another notch. When Tracie heard the stereo playing, she'd come up here to shut it off. And that was when Wicked would kill her.

Tracie's eyes opened with a snap as she heard her favorite song on the radio. But who was playing music? And why was it so loud? Tracie turned to stare at the bedroom windows that bordered the courtyard. Someone must have a radio in their room. But then she realized that the music was coming from the deck behind her. And she remembered that Scott had brought his portable stereo out to the pool this afternoon.

They only had one set of batteries, and they couldn't go out to buy replacements. Tracie remembered how Scott had checked his stereo to make sure that it was turned off before he'd gone upstairs to work. But why was it on now?

Tracie sighed. The answer was very simple. Someone must have come down here to go for a swim. They'd turned on Scott's radio and they'd forgotten to turn it off when they'd left. Although it wasn't really her responsibility, Tracie got up from her chair. She'd turn off Scott's stereo to save the drain on the batteries. They couldn't go out for more until the quarantine was lifted, and everyone liked to hear music while they were lounging around the pool.

It was dark up on the deck, and Tracie thought about going back inside to turn on the courtyard lights. But that was silly. There was a full moon tonight, and all she had to do was shut off the radio. She headed for the steps and began to climb them. And then she heard a soft rustling up on the deck.

"Who's there?" Tracie called out, but no one answered. It was probably a bird, pecking at the crumbs from Eve's pizza, or a squirrel, rummaging for food. Tracie climbed up the second step, and then the third.

There it was again! Tracie stopped, her foot on the fourth step, but everything was silent. She told herself there was nothing out here to hurt her and she climbed another step. The rustling had stopped now and as she climbed the sixth step, a bird flew up into one of the trees that surrounded the courtyard. That must have been what she'd heard.

Tracie hurried up the remaining two steps and held on to the rail as she moved toward the table. She didn't want to slip and fall into the water. Scott's stereo was playing loudly, and she reached out to shut it off. But just as her fingers touched the on–off switch, she heard the rustling noise again.

"Is someone here?" Tracie's voice was shaking slightly. But no one answered, and she laughed at herself for being foolish. Who would be up here on the deck in the dark? Everyone was still in the house, working.

Tracie turned off the stereo and it was perfectly quiet, so quiet that she heard the sound of a distant train whistle from the tracks that ran past the far edge of the campus, over two miles away. Someone laughed inside the mansion. It sounded like Jeremy, and Tracie started to grin. He was probably reading over his chapter for tonight. Jeremy always laughed at his own jokes.

As Tracie stood there, listening, she heard another sound. It was very faint, and it made her shiver, even though the night was muggy and hot. It was a scrabbling noise, like fingernails scratching against a metal surface. It seemed to come from the kitchen, and Tracie drew in her breath sharply. Could it be Cheryl, clawing at the metal door of the cooler, trying to get out?!

"Cheryl's dead." Tracie spoke the words aloud, just to reassure herself. Marc had checked Cheryl's pulse and all of her vital signs. He'd pronounced Cheryl dead, and Tracie was sure that he'd been right. Marc was a sports medicine major, and he'd taken all the emergency care classes. Surely they would have taught him the difference between a live person and a dead one.

But what if Marc was wrong? Tracie shivered and tried not to think of all the stories about people who'd been buried alive. There was a handle on the inside of the walk-in cooler. If Marc had made a mistake and Cheryl was still alive, she could open the door to the cooler and walk right out . . . unless she was so badly injured, she couldn't walk.

Tracie shivered again. She couldn't help imagining her friend, Cheryl, clawing at the door with bloody fingers, using the last of her strength to try to stand up to reach the latch. But that was ridiculous, wasn't it? Eve would have noticed that Cheryl was breathing when she'd wrapped her in the blanket.

Eve. What if Eve had found out that Cheryl was planning to blackball her as sorority president? Would

Eve have taken advantage of the awful situation and left Cheryl in the cooler to die? Eve could be mean when she didn't get her own way. Tracie knew that. But was Eve capable of that kind of horrible cruelty?

No, it was impossible. No one could be that dreadful, not even Eve. Cheryl was dead, and she was just imagining things. She was even imagining that she could hear breathing, coming from the direction of the kitchen. It was raspy and labored, almost as if someone were trying to lift something heavy, and it was coming closer and closer.

Tracie whirled around, and she gasped as she saw a dark figure reaching out for her. The breathing was real! She hadn't imagined it! But before Tracie could open her mouth to scream, strong hands struck her in the small of the back and she was falling into the pool.

Tracie struck out at the hands that were holding her down. It was probably one of the guys, and she was going to absolutely kill him when he let her up for air. This was a nasty trick. Tracie hated to be dunked.

Tracie reached up to grab the hands, and that was when she realized that the person who'd shoved her was wearing gloves. Why would he wear gloves on a hot summer night?

She had to take a breath of air! Spots began to swirl before her eyes, and Tracie hit out with all her strength. But the hands just kept holding her head beneath the water. Tracie struggled frantically, her lungs screaming out for oxygen. And then her struggles began to cease. That was when an awful thought crossed Tracie's mind, the last rational thought of her life.

The hands were wearing gloves because they intended to kill her. . . .

Tracie was dead. Wicked held her down for another few minutes, just to be sure. Then Wicked stood up and hurried down the steps, leaving Tracie's body in its watery grave. They'd find her later, after the meeting, and another body would take its place in the walk-in cooler.

Would they blame Angela and ask her to stop writing? Wicked didn't think so. Everyone liked Angela's story, and they'd think it was just another coincidence. Only Wicked knew that it wasn't, and Wicked would never tell the group.

Wicked pulled up the hood of the raincoat and hurried down the steps. The raincoat was black, and no one would notice the shadowy figure, hurrying across the courtyard. Wicked discarded the gloves by throwing them over the wall. No one would find them because no one would think to look. They'd never suspect that Wicked had killed Tracie because Wicked would be one of the first to arrive at the meeting.

Of course, Wicked wouldn't be Wicked anymore, not at the meeting. That was when the bright side would take over, the one everyone knew, the trusted member of the group. The books called it an alter ego. That was the name for Wicked's other personality, someone they'd never suspect. And they would be right when they assumed that Wicked's alter ego was perfectly innocent. The bright side had no memory and no awareness of what Wicked had done. That was why Wicked and the bright side could share the same body without conflict.

Would the bright side be shocked if the truth were known? Wicked laughed silently, imagining what the bright side would say. There were times when Wicked thought about telling, about shocking the bright side so much that it would never recover. But that would be foolish, and Wicked knew it. It was best to go on this way until all the killing was done. Then there would be a day of reckoning when Wicked could claim full credit for accomplishing the ultimate goal. Life would truly imitate art.

CHAPTER EIGHT

Ryan looked up as Jeremy entered the library. "Hey, Jeremy. We were wondering what happened to you. You're five minutes late."

"Sorry." Jeremy looked apologetic. "I sent my pages to the printer, but when I went up to the fourth floor, the lights were flashing for a paper jam. I had to clear the jam and go back downstairs to send my chapter for the second time. And then I had to climb up to the fourth floor again, to get my pages."

Marc started to laugh. "I guess you don't need to buy a StairMaster! Right, Jeremy?"

"That's right. I got my workout for today."

Scott motioned to the vacant chair next to his. "Sit down, Jeremy. Tracie's not here yet and we were waiting for her, too."

"I wonder where she is." Jeremy frowned slightly as he sat down. "She wasn't printing out when I was up on the fourth floor, and I didn't see her on the stairs. Do you want me to go up to her room and check?"

Angela shook her head. "I think you've climbed

enough stairs for one day. And actually . . . I'd rather get started without Tracie. I'd like to read my chapter before she gets here."

"You killed Tracie off?" Eve started to laugh when Angela nodded.

"I didn't really want to, but I couldn't revise my plot. I know that Tracie said it wouldn't bother her, but I'm not sure that's true."

"Me, neither." Beth looked a little worried. "I think Tracie just said that because she didn't want us to know how scared she really was."

Angela winced. "Oh, dear! Do you think I should rewrite my chapter?"

"No way." Scott shook his head. "You can't rewrite something just because one member of the group doesn't like it. You should leave it, Angela. After all, it's only fiction."

"Scott's right," Ryan agreed. "Why don't you read your chapter for us? After we hear it, maybe we can put our heads together and figure out some diplomatic way to tell Tracie that her character got murdered."

"That's a wonderful idea!" Angela smiled at Ryan. And then she turned to smile at all of them. "You don't know how much I appreciate your support. I've been agonizing over this chapter all afternoon!"

Eve sat silently as Angela read her chapter. She wanted to find something to criticize, but she couldn't. It was a great chapter, and she didn't see any way that Angela could change it so that Tracie's character wasn't the victim.

"That was really chilling!" Beth clapped her hands when Angela was finished. "And I'm really glad that

Tracie didn't hear it. She probably would have given up swimming for life!"

"I'm going to think about that, the next time I go into the pool," Dean said. "Can you really electrocute someone by throwing a lamp in the water?"

"Absolutely," Marc said. "That's why they tell you to never touch an electric appliance when you're in the bathtub."

Eve looked thoughtful. "It might not bother Tracie as much as we think it will. After all, we don't have any lamps out by the pool."

"That's why I wrote it that way." Angela smiled at Eve. "I wanted to kill off Tracie's character in a way that couldn't possibly happen here. I thought that if she knew it couldn't happen, it might not upset her as much."

"Good thinking," Ryan said. "I'd like to read my chapter next, if that's all right with you."

Everyone nodded, and Ryan started to read. Eve listened carefully, and she was impressed by how he had incorporated death into his chapter. He'd killed off his hero's sister in a typhoid epidemic, and the way he described her death made Eve blink back tears. Ryan was a wonderful writer.

"Eve?" Ryan turned to her when he was through. "Why don't you go next?"

Eve started to read. She knew her chapter was good. She'd written about her female vampire's first victim, and she'd made it as frightening as she could.

"Great!" Scott started to clap when she was through. "I love the funeral scene, Eve. It's really sad. Aren't you glad that Angela suggested we write about death?"

Eve nodded, although she hadn't been following Angela's suggestion. Vampires killed their victims. Her book would have been nothing without a couple of deaths. Now Scott was giving Angela the credit for what Eve had been planning to write about anyway.

"Great chapter, honey!" Ryan gave Eve a little hug. "You did exactly what Angela told you to. Rochelle's someone we can identify with now. And Adonna's just perfect! You've managed to make your vampire sympathetic and frightening at the same time."

"Thank you." Eve tried to keep smiling. She'd worked very hard on her chapter, but everyone was giving Angela the credit for her work. Only one thing made Eve feel good. No one had recognized the fact that she'd patterned her bloodthirsty, scheming, bad-to-the-bone vampire after Angela. But they would. Eve was going to make sure of that.

Scott was next, and he read about the death of Mr. Sutler's wife. It was scary and Eve shivered. According to Scott, Mr. Sutler had bound and gagged his young, beautiful and unfaithful wife. He'd shut her in a little storage space at the back of the walk-in closet, and then he'd bricked up the door to the storage space, knowing that she'd die an agonizingly slow death.

"That's horrible!" Eve turned to Scott. "Is it really true?"

Scott shrugged. "Who knows? It's a local legend. That's all I know. And no one's ever checked to make sure."

"I'm glad I don't have a walk-in closet in my room!" Beth shivered.

"Don't worry, Beth." Scott grinned at her. "The closet Mr. Sutler used was supposed to be in the master bedroom."

"Which one is the master bedroom?" Eve was curious.

Scott took a deep breath, and then he gave Eve a sheepish smile. "It's the one with the balcony on the third floor. It's your room, Eve."

"Oh, my God! I've been hearing these strange scratching noises in the middle of the night. Now I know exactly what they are!"

Angela's face turned very pale. "Are you serious, Eve?"

"Absolutely." Eve bit back a grin. It was clear that Angela was afraid of ghosts, and it was fun, trying to frighten her. "But I think Mrs. Sutler's ghost got out of the closet. Every once in a while, I hear the floorboards creaking, up on the fourth floor."

Angela shivered, and then she reached out to take Eve's hand. "You can move in with me, Eve. You shouldn't stay there alone."

"I'm kidding, Angela!" Eve couldn't contain herself any longer and she started to laugh.

"Eve!" Ryan gave her a disapproving look. "That wasn't nice!"

Eve shrugged. "I guess it wasn't. Sorry, Angela. I just couldn't resist.

Jeremy read his chapter next, and everyone thought it was very good. He'd managed to find a lot of jokes that showed exactly how people coped with death by laughing at it. Then Dean sang one of his songs about two lovers who'd died in each other's arms, and they all agreed that it was the best he'd ever written. Beth read her poem next, and it was excellent, all about a childhood friend who'd died. And Marc's chapter was good, too. The basketball coach in his story was remembering a player he'd coached who had died on the court.

When everyone had finished, Jeremy spoke up. "I think we're all turning into better writers because of Angela. I don't know about the rest of you, but I was really worried when Professor Hellman got sick. I didn't think we could do it alone. But I was wrong. I think Angela is teaching us just as much as Professor Hellman could, maybe more."

As far as Eve was concerned, Jeremy was crazy. Angela was just hogging the show, and she hadn't taught anyone a single thing they couldn't have learned on their own.

Eve waited until the compliments had died down, and then she spoke up. "I hate to remind you, but it's almost one in the morning and Tracie still hasn't shown up. She probably fell asleep in her room or something simple like that. But she could be sick. After all, we're quarantined for an infectious disease."

Angela looked worried. "You're right, Eve. Let's all go up and check on Tracie to make sure she's all right."

"Thanks for reminding us, Eve." Ryan waited for Eve to gather up her pages, and then he took her hand. "You don't really think Tracie's sick, do you?"

"I don't know. She looked all right at dinner, but

she didn't eat very much. Isn't loss of appetite one of the warning signs the doctor told us about?"

"That's true. It's a good thing you said something, honey."

Eve was smiling as she climbed up the stairs with Ryan. She didn't think that Tracie was sick, but she'd managed to break up the admiring group around Angela. And now Ryan was with her, instead of with Angela, and that was *exactly* the way Eve wanted it.

"Tracie? Open the door!" Angela knocked on Tracie's bedroom door for the third time.

"If Tracie's sick, she might not be able to get out of bed." Eve turned the doorknob and opened the door. She stepped in and saw Tracie's empty bed. The quilt wasn't rumpled, and it was clear that Tracie hadn't slept in it. "She's not here."

They all stared at the deserted room for a moment, and then Beth spoke up. "But where is she?"

"I don't know." Eve was beginning to get worried. She'd been sure that Tracie was in her room. "I think we'd better try to find her."

"Let's split up in teams," Ryan said. "Scott and Jeremy? You check the fourth-floor hallway and the stairwell while Beth and Dean search the rest of this floor. Marc and Angela can check the second floor, and Eve and I'll go back down to the first floor."

"How about the grounds?" Eve asked. "We should search those, too."

"We'll all meet in the library in fifteen minutes. If no one's found her, we'll grab a couple of flashlights and check outside. Tracie's got to be here somewhere. She can't have just disappeared into thin air."

"Actually . . . she doesn't have to be here," Eve said. "She could have left in her car. Did anyone check to make sure it's still there?"

They all rushed to the window at the end of the hall. It overlooked the street, and Eve's heart was pounding hard as she looked out. But Tracie's yellow Toyota was right where she'd parked it, at the curb.

"That's her car." Eve pointed to the yellow Toyota. "At least Tracie didn't drive off somewhere."

"That's a relief!" Ryan exclaimed. "She's got to be somewhere in the mansion. Let's go find her."

As Eve and Ryan hurried down to the ground floor, Eve found herself shivering. She wasn't sure why, but it was odd that Tracie had disappeared on the night that Angela had killed off her character. She couldn't help thinking about Cheryl and how she'd died when her character was murdered.

"Are you thinking what I'm thinking?" Ryan asked.

Eve nodded. "Yes, but maybe it's just a coincidence. Tracie could have fallen asleep in the living room, watching television."

But Tracie wasn't in the living room and the television wasn't on. She wasn't in the formal dining room, although Ryan and Eve checked every nook and cranny, and they already knew that she wasn't in the library, where they'd held their meeting.

"The kitchen?" Eve stopped at the kitchen door. Now that it was dark outside, the kitchen seemed much more frightening. She didn't want to go in, but there was no way she'd let Ryan know that her courage had suddenly left her.

"Come on, Eve." Ryan took her hand. "I don't think Tracie's in the kitchen. She was really afraid to go in there earlier. But let's take a quick look around, just to make sure."

Eve held her breath as Ryan opened the swinging door and turned on the lights. Her eyes went directly to the spot where Cheryl had died, but there was no new body on the floor. "She's not here, Ryan."

"I hate to mention this, but . . . do you think we should check in the cooler?"

"Are you kidding? Tracie would never go in there. Remember how freaked she was about even setting foot in the kitchen?"

"You're right. How about the laundry room?"

But Tracie wasn't in the laundry room, or the little sitting room, or the first-floor guest bathroom. They checked every closet and even pulled open the doors to the linen cabinet, but there was no sign of Tracie.

"She's not down here," Eve said. "We looked everywhere, Ryan."

"I know. Let's head for the library, honey. Maybe someone else found her."

They'd only waited a few minutes when footsteps approached in the hall. Jeremy and Scott came into the library with disappointed faces. "No luck?"

"No," Scott said. "We even checked all the padlocks on the fourth-floor doors. Everything's locked up tight."

"Tracie's not up there," Jeremy said. "We're sure of it."

Angela and Marc came in next.

"She's not on the second floor." Marc dropped down, into a chair. "We checked everywhere."

"We even checked the bathroom." Angela sat down next to Marc.

"But that's the guys' bathroom!" Eve was surprised.

"I know," Marc said. "But Angela pointed out that if Tracie was on the second floor and she got sick, she might have ducked in there."

"Good point." Ryan smiled at Angela.

Eve fought down her sudden feeling of jealousy. This wasn't the time for petty emotions. Tracie was missing, and that should be their main concern.

No one said anything for a long moment, and then Beth and Dean came in. When Dean noticed that they were all looking at him hopefully, he shook his head. "Tracie's not on the third floor."

"We checked everywhere. We even looked under the beds." Beth looked worried.

"Then she's got to be outside." Eve pointed out the obvious fact. "I grabbed a couple of flashlights when we were in the kitchen. Let's go search the grounds."

Everyone started to leave, but Angela grabbed Eve's hand. "When you and Ryan were in the kitchen, did you check the walk-in cooler?"

"No. We were sure she wouldn't go in there."

"I wish I could be that sure."

Eve turned to stare at Angela. "What do you mean?"

"I know this sounds strange, Eve, but I keep thinking about what Tracie told me. It was more frightening than anything I could write."

Eve was intrigued. Angela wrote some pretty scary stuff. "What did Tracie say?"

"She said she wasn't sure that Cheryl was really dead, that maybe Marc made a mistake. She told me she couldn't sleep at all last night. She kept thinking about how awful it would be if Cheryl woke up."

"Woke up?" Eve gave a little laugh. "But that's impossible! I wrapped Cheryl in a blanket. I know she was dead!"

"But Tracie didn't even look at her body. She covered her eyes, remember? And because she didn't actually look at Cheryl, she started imagining things that couldn't possibly be true."

"I get it. Tracie thought Cheryl might be unconscious, she'd be all alone, locked in the walk-in cooler." Eve shivered. "That's scary! And it's also crazy. But I don't think you have to worry, Angela. Tracie would never go in the walk-in cooler alone. She wouldn't have the nerve."

"Maybe you should check, just to make sure. After all, you were in there this afternoon so it shouldn't bother you now . . . unless you've lost your nerve and you'd rather wait for the guys?"

There was a strange look in Angela's eyes. Angela looked different, much more confrontational, as if she were trying to pick a fight. She'd never actually challenged Eve before, but it was clear she was doing it now.

Angela's message came through loud and clear. Eve would be a coward if she didn't check the walk-in cooler. But Eve decided to turn the tables on Angela. After all, she'd brought up the whole thing.

"It won't bother me." Eve started to grin. "But will it bother you?"

Angela looked startled. "Me? I don't have to go in the cooler."

"I think you'd better. If you don't come along with me, how will you know I checked it? I could just say I did, and you'd never know the difference. Of course, you could always call one of the guys and ask him to go with me. All you'd have to do is say that you were afraid to go in there."

Angela sighed. "All right. I'll go with you."

"Come on then." Eve hid a grin. She'd managed to beat Angela at her own game, and she was very pleased.

Angela looked thoroughly freaked as they walked down the hall and went into the kitchen. Eve switched on the lights and headed for the cooler door. "Are you with me, Angela?"

"I'm right behind you."

Angela's voice was shaking slightly, and her face turned pale as Eve opened the cooler door. Of course Tracie wasn't there. Eve hadn't expected her to be. And Cheryl's body was right where they'd placed it, on the floor next to the back wall.

"She's not here." Eve turned to face Angela, who was hanging back slightly. "But I do notice something different."

"What's that?" Angela took a step closer to the door.

"It's Cheryl's body. I think Tracie's right. It looks like she moved slightly."

Angela's mouth dropped open and she turned to run for the door. That was when Eve started to laugh.

"Relax, Angela. I'm just kidding. Cheryl's body didn't move at all."

"That was mean!" Angela stopped just outside the cooler door to glare at Eve.

"I know. I was just paying you back for making me go in the cooler at night. That was mean, too."

Angela had the grace to look slightly embarrassed. "You're right, Eve. I'm sorry. Can we call a truce?"

"Sure. But how long do you think it'll last?"

Angela laughed. "I don't know. We really got off on the wrong foot, didn't we, Eve?"

"Yes, we did."

"Do you know why?"

"You bet I do!" Eve took a deep breath. She'd been waiting a long time for this moment. "You're trying to impress us with your money and your famous parents. It might work with the others, but it won't work with me."

"Anything else?"

"Yes. You've been trying to steal my boyfriend, and I don't like it."

"Is that all?"

Eve didn't like the tone in Angela's voice. She had the feeling that Angela was toying with her, the very same way a cat played with a mouse right before the killing blow. She was seeing another side of Angela, and that side was very disturbing. "That's about it."

"Good. Now that you've got that off your chest, you ought to feel much better." Angela gave Eve a perfectly innocent smile. "Come on, Eve. Let's go find the others."

Eve followed Angela down the hall and out into the courtyard, frowning. Her criticism had bounced right off Angela's back. Angela hadn't said she'd stop trying to buy their friendship or impress them with her famous family. And she hadn't said she was sorry for trying to steal Ryan. This wasn't a truce. It was just a temporary ceasefire before the hostilities started again.

"Did you find her?" Angela headed straight for Ryan the moment they got out the door.

"No. We started with the garage. It's filled with stuff so it took us a while, but there's no sign of Tracie. Where were you two?"

"We checked the walk-in cooler." Angela smiled up at him.

"You did? I know it probably didn't bother Eve, but that was really brave of you, Angela."

Angela shrugged. "It was no problem. Where are we going to search next?"

"The west side of the house. There's an old kennel and a dog run there."

"You think Tracie's in the dog run?" Eve asked.

"It's possible," Beth said. "Tracie told me she loves animals. If she heard a kitten or a puppy in the yard, she might have gone out to make sure it wasn't trapped behind the fence."

Eve thought they were grasping at straws. "I've got my own flashlight. You can check out the dog run, and I'll start searching in the courtyard."

"I'll go with you, honey." Ryan handed his flashlight to Angela. "Just call out if you find anything."

There was a smile on Eve's face as she took Ryan's hand and headed across the courtyard. Ryan had chosen to go with her, rather than Angela. But Eve's joy was short-lived.

"I'm so proud of Angela!" Ryan squeezed Eve's hand. "She was terrified to go in that cooler, but she did it. Thanks for going with her, Eve. That was very nice."

Eve didn't answer. She was too upset. She wanted to tell Ryan how Angela had goaded her into checking the cooler and how she'd been clever enough to insist that Angela go along. But Eve couldn't tell Ryan any of that. Everyone, including Ryan, thought that Angela was wonderful, and they'd never believe that she had a mean streak she'd kept hidden from everyone except Eve.

"Let's check the rose garden." Ryan took the flashlight from Eve's hand. "Tracie told me she thought it was beautiful, and she might have gone out to smell the roses."

"All alone in the dark?"

"It's possible." Ryan chuckled. "If a girl in one of Tracie's romances went out to a rose garden at night, Tracie would probably try it. She's an incurable romantic."

Eve turned to look at Ryan in surprise. Although he'd only known Tracie for a couple of days, he'd certainly figured out her personality. It was too bad he couldn't see through Angela and realize that she wasn't the nice person she seemed to be.

They went down the walkway through the rose

garden, holding hands. The flashlight wasn't very bright, and Eve concentrated on the thin yellow beam.

"What's that?" Eve caught a glimpse of something big out of the corner of her eye.

"Where?"

"Over there by that little stone wall." Eve pointed. "I thought I saw something."

Eve held her breath as they walked toward the object she'd seen. She couldn't help feeling that there was something very wrong. But when Ryan illuminated it with the flashlight, she started to giggle. "It's a big bag of fertilizer!"

"The gardener must have left it here." Ryan laughed. "And it reeks! You don't think we have to open it to check it out, do you, Eve?"

Eve laughed, too. "No way! Tracie wouldn't go anywhere near something that smells that bad. She doesn't even like it when we have Italian food at the sorority house. She says the whole place stinks of garlic and onions."

"That figures." Ryan chuckled and he took her arm to lead her away from the fertilizer. "How about you, Eve? Do you like onions and garlic?"

"I love them. You can't use too much onion and garlic to suit me."

"I know a little Italian place with red-checkered tablecloths and wine bottles with candles on every table. The same family's owned it for fifty years, and the walls even smell like garlic."

Eve swallowed. Her mouth was watering. She adored Italian food. "It sounds heavenly."

"It is. Do you want to try it when our quarantine's lifted?"

"I'd love to!" Eve smiled happily. "I wish we could do it right now. But you shouldn't have told me about it so early. We're stuck here for another eight days and now you've made me hungry for Italian food."

Ryan laughed. "I've made myself hungry, too. Maybe we could try to cook up some pasta tomorrow night. I make a pretty decent Alfredo sauce."

"That's a great idea! I can make garlic and Parmesan bread."

"I didn't know you baked bread."

"I don't." Eve laughed. "There's some packaged bread dough in the freezer. I'm no cook, but I think I can follow the directions on the package. There's only one problem. I put on a lot of garlic."

"That's no problem, unless . . . do we have enough?"

Eve laughed. "We've got plenty. There's one of those long braids on the back of the pantry door."

"Then what's the problem?"

"Tracie. She hates garlic and she'll probably run around with her bottle of perfume, spraying it in the air."

Ryan cracked up. "That's okay. She can spray the rest of the mansion, but we won't let her in the kitchen. So we'll make dinner tomorrow night?"

"Sure." Eve grinned at him. "It'll be fun."

They walked across the courtyard to the pool. The deck loomed above them and Eve shivered.

"What's the matter, Eve?" Ryan put his arm around her shoulders. "Are you cold?"

"No. I've just got a weird feeling, that's all."

"About what?" Ryan looked concerned.

"About the pool. And about Tracie. Remember the chapter that Angela read tonight?"

"Of course I remember. It was the scariest chapter that Angela's written. But it was just fiction."

"I know that, but Cheryl's character got murdered in the kitchen and that's where we found Cheryl."

Ryan put his arms around Eve and gave her a little hug. "Cheryl's death was an accident, honey. She wasn't murdered."

"I know, but we found her in the kitchen. And Tracie's character got murdered in the pool. I think we'd better go up there, Ryan."

"Come on, Eve. If it'll make you feel better, we'll check the pool right now."

It was very silent as they climbed the steps and stepped out on the deck. Nothing was moving and the surface of the pool was perfectly still. Ryan and Eve made their way around the deck and stopped at the deep end.

"I think the batteries are going on this flashlight." Ryan shook it. "I don't think it has enough power to see anything at all."

What Ryan had said was true. His flashlight was flickering and the circle of light was growing dimmer with each second that passed. "Maybe we should yell for Jeremy. He's got a new set of batteries in his flashlight."

Ryan stood next to the edge of the pool and pointed his flashlight directly into the water. "You're right, Eve. I can only see down a couple of feet."

"It's okay. It doesn't look like there's anything under . . ." Eve stopped, and her heart began to pound. She thought she'd seen a shape beneath the water. A human shape. "Shine it right in the middle, Ryan. I thought I saw . . . oh, my God!"

"What is it? I don't see . . ."

"Right there!" Eve's voice was shaking as she pointed to the spot. "It's Tracie! She's in there, Ryan! She's right there at the bottom of the pool!"

CHAPTER NINE

No one felt like going up to their rooms, not after the awful discovery they'd made. There was no question that Tracie was dead, and they'd wrapped her in a blanket and put her next to Cheryl in the walk-in cooler. Scott had made a photo record of everything they'd done. The police would want it when they came to investigate the tragedies that had occurred at the Sutler Mansion. Now they were gathered in the courtyard, sitting around one of the tables, trying to figure out what had happened.

"This is so weird." Eve sighed. "What was Tracie doing up on the deck without any lights?"

No one answered for a long moment, and finally Ryan spoke up. "Maybe she just wanted to look out, over the courtyard, and think about the chapter she was going to read."

"I think you're right." Angela placed Tracie's pages on the table. "I just read Tracie's chapter for tonight and there's a scene where the girl walks past her fiancé's house. She sees him through the lace curtains, kissing another woman."

Beth nodded. "I get it. Tracie might have been doing some research, checking to make sure she could see through the lace curtains into the library. That would explain why she didn't turn on the courtyard lights. But why was she up on the deck?"

"To get as far away as she could. The girl in her chapter was out on the sidewalk. Tracie probably figured that the deck was about the right distance."

Everyone nodded, everyone except Eve. There was still something that wasn't right about Angela's explanation. "That might be part of it, but there's still something that bothers me. Tracie could have tripped and fallen in the pool. I don't have a problem with that. But Tracie knew how to swim. Why didn't she just swim to the steps and climb out?"

"She must have hit her head on something that knocked her out." Jeremy suggested the obvious answer.

"No." Marc shook his head. "I checked for bruising, and there wasn't any. Tracie didn't hit her head when she fell."

"Maybe Tracie tried to swim to the shallow end, but she got a cramp," Dean said. "My leg cramped up once when I was in a pool and I almost drowned."

"That could be it." Beth didn't look convinced. "But I think we should drain the pool. Maybe there's something else in the water."

"Like what?" Eve turned to Beth.

"I don't know. Maybe something fell in the pool and Tracie got tangled up in it. We can't see all the way to the bottom unless we drain it."

"That's a good idea," Ryan said. "I'll hook up the hose right now and let the water drain out. We can

check it in the morning to see if there's anything there.
You've got enough film to take pictures, Scott?"

"No problem. I've got more than a dozen rolls up
in my room."

"It's a good thing you brought so much film." Eve
gave a bitter laugh. "If Angela keeps killing off her
characters, we're going to need it!"

Angela's mouth dropped open in surprise, and
then she began to look very hurt. When Ryan noticed the tears that were beginning to glisten in
Angela's eyes, he put his arm around her shoulders
to comfort her. "Don't mind Eve. She's just joking."

"Am I?" Eve couldn't help speaking out. "Maybe
no one else noticed, but Cheryl's character was
murdered in the kitchen and that's where we found
Cheryl's body. And Tracie's character was killed in
the pool. I don't know about the rest of you, but I'm
not going anywhere near the place where Angela
kills off my character!"

There was silence for a long moment, and when
Angela spoke, her voice was quivering. "You're
right, Eve. It's a . . . a horrible coincidence and I'm
going to stop writing my chapters."

"Don't be silly, Angela!" Ryan gave her a little
hug. "These were accidents, not murders. You have
to keep on writing."

Tears threatened to spill from Angela's eyes.
Most girls looked ugly when they cried. Eve knew
she did. Her complexion turned blotchy, and her
eyelids became swollen and red. Sometimes she
even got the hiccups and that was really embarrassing. But none of those things happened to Angela.
Angela's deep violet eyes took on a glow that was

almost luminescent, and her tears made them sparkle. Her skin remained perfect, no ugly splotches of color at all, and there was no sign of swelling or redness around her eyelids. As Eve watched, one perfect tear rolled down Angela's cheek and Ryan reached out to wipe it away. Eve sighed and shook her head. It just wasn't fair. Angela even looked beautiful when she was crying.

"It's okay, Angela." Ryan hugged her tightly. "Don't cry. Everything's going to be all right."

"But don't you see? I can't keep on writing! Right after I read my chapter about Cheryl's character's murder, Cheryl died. And right after I read about Tracie's character getting killed, Tracie died. I'm afraid to keep on writing, Ryan. Somebody else might die!"

"You're wrong, Angela." Ryan shook his head. "That's not how it happened."

"What do you mean?" Angela blinked her incredibly long eyelashes and another glistening tear fell.

"You read Cheryl's chapter, and then she died. That part is true. But Tracie died *before* you read her chapter."

"Are you sure?" Angela asked.

"I'm positive. Tracie was wearing her watch. It wasn't waterproof and it stopped at ten-forty-five. That was at least thirty minutes before you read your chapter."

"Thank you for telling me, Ryan!" Angela gave him a brilliant smile. "I don't want to stop writing. I really like the chapters I've written. But are you really sure you want me to go on with my book?"

Ryan turned to the rest of the group. "We're sure, aren't we?"

"Of course we are!" Jeremy smiled at Angela. "And I think you just proved what a good friend you are. You were really willing to stop writing, weren't you?"

"Yes, I was."

"Even though you knew you'd flunk the workshop if you didn't finish *Ten Little Writers*?"

"Of course," Angela said. "I'm beginning to think that Ryan is right, that's there's no connection between my chapters and the . . . accidents. But your friendship is much more important to me than my grade."

"That's what I thought," Jeremy said. "You're a really nice person, Angela. And we appreciate what you were willing to do for us. But we want you to keep right on with your book, and I'm volunteering to be the next victim."

"You are? Are you sure, Jeremy?" Angela reached out to take his hand, and when Jeremy nodded, she gave him a delighted smile. "After all that's happened, I can't believe you're volunteering! You're wonderful, Jeremy! And you're so brave!"

Eve felt like groaning. Jeremy wasn't brave; he was stupid. But he really seemed to be enjoying the attention he was getting from Angela. Angela had Jeremy fooled, along with everyone else. Eve was the only one who thought there was a connection between Angela's chapters and the lethal accidents that had occurred. And Eve was the only one who thought that Angela wasn't as sweet and nice as she appeared. Angela Adams was like a black widow spider, trapping everyone in her web. But Eve wasn't about to fall into her trap.

Jeremy was stretched out on top of his bed, frowning up at the ceiling. It was almost two in the morning, but he couldn't sleep. He'd tried to write a couple of jokes, but they hadn't turned out very well. That was probably because he hadn't been in a very humorous mood. No one else had been in a humorous mood either, not after they'd found Tracie's dead body in the pool.

Two members of their group were dead. Jeremy shivered slightly. It was a frightening thing, but they couldn't let it get them down. They had to get through the next eight days, and they needed a little levity in their lives. Laughter was good medicine. They'd all feel a lot better if they stopped walking around with tragic faces.

Jeremy sat up and pulled on his clothes. It was too hot to sleep, and he might as well do something to pass the time. He'd figure out some way to make the group laugh. A practical joke was in order. They might be angry with him at first, but they'd thank him for it later.

Jeremy got the bag of props he'd brought with him out of the closet. As he passed the mirror to carry the bag to the desk, he realized that he was smiling. He always felt good when he planned a practical joke.

Forget the whoopee cushion. Jeremy took it out of his bag and tossed it on the bed. Nobody'd fall for it and it wasn't very funny anyway. The dribble glass was out, too. And the rubber baked chicken that flopped around when you tried to cut it with a knife. He needed something that would really startle them and snap them out of their serious moods.

The fake spiders had definite possibilities. Jeremy took out a package and set them on his desk. This was an old house and there were probably spiders. Every girl he knew hated spiders and when they discovered his fake ones, they'd think they were real.

All he needed was something for the guys, and Jeremy examined the contents of his bag carefully. Scott had seen the talking toilet seat at the frat house, and Jeremy never liked to repeat a practical joke. But he'd just ordered a special showerhead that exploded with rubber snakes when you turned it on. That would be perfect for the guys.

Everyone was sleeping as Jeremy tiptoed out into the hallway. He hurried to the bathroom and installed the exploding showerhead in just a few minutes. Then he climbed the stairs to the third floor and hesitated as he opened the door to the hallway. Where should he put the spiders?

It would be simple to put them in the girls' bathroom, but not as effective as hiding them in their rooms. Jeremy grinned as he imagined Beth waking up to find rubber spiders on her pillow. She'd scream. Jeremy was sure of it. And then she'd laugh when she realized that they were made out of rubber. He'd taken a class with Beth last semester and she had a good sense of humor.

Would Eve scream? Jeremy thought about it for a moment. Probably not. Eve wouldn't let anyone know she'd been frightened. She'd be angry though, and Eve's wrath was really something to behold. Her dark green eyes would snap as she glared at him and she'd put her hands on her hips, just daring him to apologize. Eve was quite a woman. He'd even asked her for a date last year, but she'd called his jokes childish and turned him down flat.

And then there was Angela. Jeremy sighed softly. Angela had the perfect name. She was an angel, a kind, sweet beautiful woman who'd call him brave and reached out to touch his hand. Jeremy didn't really want to put any spiders in Angela's room, but it would look strange if she was the only one he didn't try to scare.

Could he sneak into their rooms without waking them up? It was a real test of Jeremy's ability to set up a practical joke. It would work if they were sound sleepers, but if any one of them woke up and saw him, she'd tip off the others. He had to think of some excuse in case he got caught.

Jeremy's mind raced through a list of possible excuses and he finally settled on one. He'd heard a noise on the floor above, and he was just checking to make sure they were all right. It wasn't perfect, but it would do.

Beth's room was first and Jeremy opened the door. Beth was sleeping and he walked silently to the edge of her bed. He placed several spiders on her pillow and then he tiptoed out and shut the door behind him. One down and two to go.

Angela was sleeping, too. And she had the covers pulled over her head. Jeremy didn't see how she could sleep under the covers on such a hot night, but it was a lucky break for him. Angela didn't even move as he dropped the spiders on her pillow, and he was grinning as he left her room and went on to Eve's.

Eve's face was turned away from the door as Jeremy tiptoed across the room. She made a sound, mumbling something in her sleep, and Jeremy stopped in his tracks. He stood there poised, one foot forward and one foot back, for what seemed like hours. But she settled down and he moved forward again to dump the rest of the spiders on her pillow.

Jeremy breathed a deep sigh of relief when he was back out in the hallway again. He'd done it! It was the perfect setup and he could hardly wait for morning to arrive. Who would be the first to discover the practical jokes he'd played? Jeremy wasn't sure, but it would be great to find out.

Was it enough? Would his spiders and his exploding showerhead snap them out of their gloom? Jeremy was thoughtful as he went down the stairs and back to his room. Perhaps he should play one more joke, a really big one that they wouldn't discover until later. He'd sleep for a couple of hours, and then he'd concentrate on playing the biggest and best practical joke of his life.

Eve waited until she heard Jeremy go down the stairs, and then she turned on the light by her bed. She made a face when she saw the fake spiders. She'd expected something like that. Jeremy was up to his old tricks again, but Eve had a plan to put an end to his practical jokes. They were irritating, and they weren't funny at all.

It didn't take long to pull on a pair of shorts and

a halter top. Eve had raided Cheryl's closet this morning and borrowed some of her hot-weather clothes. She'd do the same with Tracie's closet tomorrow. The sorority had an unwritten law: share and share alike. Eve had shared. She'd paid for their parties and redecorated the sorority house. And although Tracie and Cheryl had been Eve's sorority sisters, they'd never shared anything with her. Eve needed cooler, more casual clothes, and she couldn't go out to buy them. This was one last favor that Cheryl and Tracie could do for her, and Eve felt perfectly justified.

Beth was sleeping when Eve opened the door to her room. Eve was about to wake her, to tell her about the spiders and explain how they were going to make sure Jeremy's practical joke backfired. She reached out to shake Beth's shoulder, but then she reconsidered. There was really no need to wake Beth.

Eve picked up the spiders and carried them out of Beth's room. Jeremy would be waiting for their reaction in the morning. When he didn't hear screams, he'd be very upset. It served Jeremy right. Eve was going to retrace his steps and undo every trick he'd done.

Angela's room was next. Eve hesitated with her hand on the doorknob. She really wanted to leave Jeremy's spiders on Angela's pillow. But teaching Jeremy a lesson was more important than frightening Angela. Eve opened the door, retrieved the spiders, and hurried back out again.

What else had Jeremy done? Eve thought about it for a moment, and then she decided he wouldn't leave the guys out of his joke. Eve crept down the stairs and went into Ryan's room. Ryan was sleeping peacefully, but there were no spiders on his pillow. Jeremy must have done something else to the guys, but what?

The bathroom. The moment Eve thought of it, she headed straight for the bathroom at the end of the hall. There was nothing on the sink, nothing in the medicine cabinet, and nothing attached to the toilet. Whatever it was, it must be in the shower.

Eve stepped into the small cubicle, and then she began to smile. There was a washer on the floor, the kind that fit into a showerhead. Jeremy had changed the head on the shower.

It didn't take long to take off Jeremy's showerhead. It simply screwed out. Eve found the original showerhead in the laundry basket and reattached it. Then she carried the evidence of Jeremy's practical jokes back to her room.

Eve was smiling as she went back to bed. When morning came, Jeremy would be holding his breath, waiting for them to react. But no one would scream, or laugh, or yelp. Jeremy would wait and wait until he finally gave up and came down to breakfast. That was when she'd hand him the bag with the spiders and the showerhead and tell him, in no uncertain terms, to grow up and stop playing these stupid practical jokes.

CHAPTER TEN

Wicked was up very early, just as the sky was beginning to lighten to a thin, pale shade of grey. The printer had activated several times during the night, and the pages had dropped into the tray. Several students had worked before the sun had come up, and Wicked pressed the button to duplicate the pages.

The first chapter was Eve's, and Wicked read it as it came out of the printer. It was very good, all about the vampire Adonna's first appearance to Rochelle. Of course, Wicked recognized the vampire. She was modeled after Angela. Angela hadn't noticed. People never realized that a character was patterned after them. Perhaps that was because they never saw the negatives in their own personalities. It was almost impossible to see yourself as others saw you.

Ryan's chapter was next, and Wicked thoroughly enjoyed it. Ryan was an excellent writer, and he deserved to be one of the students that Professor Hellman submitted to his editor. Three out of ten. That was what the professor had decided. Ryan should be one, and Eve should be the other. And of course Angela should be the third.

Angela. Wicked smiled and stood by the printer, reading the work Angela had done. Angela's chapter was superb, so frightening that even Wicked shivered. It was all about Jeremy's murder, and it was extremely graphic. Jeremy had climbed up on the roof to fix the television antenna, and someone had pushed him to his death.

Of course they didn't have a television antenna. Wicked knew that. The Sutler Mansion had cable, but that didn't really matter. Wicked knew what Angela was trying to do. She was writing about Jeremy's death in a way that couldn't possibly happen. And now Wicked had to make sure Jeremy's very real death was accomplished in a similar manner.

The alarm went off at six in the morning, and Jeremy almost turned it off to go back to sleep. But then he remembered what he'd done last night, and he got up with a smile on his face. He had to think up the best and biggest practical joke of his life, one that would target all of them, especially Eve.

Jeremy grinned as he went through his bag of jokes again. Eve had never reacted to any of his practical jokes. The others got mad, or they cracked up with laughter, but Eve just stared at him as if he'd done something incredibly stupid.

So what could he do to really get to Eve? Jeremy tried to decide where she might be most vulnerable. It was clear she really thought there was a connection between Angela's story and the accidents that had happened to Cheryl and Tracie. That was a good place to start. Eve blamed Angela for the fatal accidents. Of course they weren't Angela's fault. Jeremy knew that. After all, he was Angela's next victim and he was still alive and kicking.

There must be a way to make Eve stop picking on Angela. Jeremy thought about it for a long time, and then he began to smile. He'd play a joke that would make Eve look like a fool. She'd fall for it. Jeremy was sure of that. Everyone was freaked about the accidents, and every one of them would fall for his joke.

He'd brought his expensive tape recorder with him and Jeremy began to rig it on a timer. It was lucky that he was so good at impersonating voices. He'd do Cheryl and Tracie, speaking out from the grave. They'd say they'd been murdered. That would give everyone goose bumps. And then they'd accuse Eve of reading Angela's pages and arranging accidents to duplicate the murders in *Ten Little Writers*. They'd say that Eve had wanted to get Angela in trouble, to make her stop writing so that she'd flunk the class. But Eve had gone too far and they had died. They'd call Eve a murderer, and they'd vow to get revenge.

Jeremy chuckled. Anyone who'd had a run-in with Eve might believe it for a second or two. Eve had a nasty temper, and she wasn't above pulling a dirty trick to get even with Angela. Of course she wouldn't go as far as murder, and everyone would realize that when they took time to think about it. But Eve would have a few anxious moments when everyone eyed her with suspicion.

He'd let it go on for a moment or two, and then Jeremy would admit that it was only a joke. He'd show them how he'd rigged his recorder, and everyone would have a good laugh. Everyone except Eve. She'd probably slap his face for setting her up, but it would be worth it.

Jeremy did his best to keep a straight face as he impersonated Cheryl and Tracie on the tape. He'd set the recorder to go off at ten-fifteen, when they were all gathered in the library. Of course he'd be there and no one would suspect him of setting his recorder on a time delay. They would totally freak when they heard Cheryl and Tracie's eerie voices.

Where would the voices come from? Jeremy thought about it for a moment, and then he remembered that there was a fireplace in the library. They hadn't used it because the weather was so hot, and it was the perfect place. He'd carry his recorder up to the roof and tape it inside the chimney. The voices from the grave would come from above, echoing off the walls of the brick chimney. It would be absolutely chilling!

Jeremy put his tape recorder in a backpack and hurried down to the laundry room, where he'd noticed a long extension cord. He stuffed it in his backpack and climbed the staircase to the fourth floor. All he had to do was pick the padlock on the room next to the fire escape, plug in the extension cord, and trail it up to the roof.

The padlock wouldn't present much of a problem. Jeremy's older sister had padlocked her bike when he was a kid, and he'd learned how to unlock it. Jeremy was grinning as he climbed the stairs. If he could pull this off without a hitch, it would be the best practical joke he'd ever played!

Wicked was still trying to think of a way to get Jeremy on the roof when there was the sound of footsteps on the stairs. Three students had worked, and there were three chapters in the printer tray. The person climbing up to the fourth floor would be Eve, Ryan, or Angela.

Wicked picked up the duplicate pages and turned to find a place to hide. Heavy floor-length drapes covered the window at the end of the hallway. Wicked ducked behind them and stood perfectly still. Would anyone notice that the drapes were a little bulkier on the left side of the window? Wicked didn't think so, not if the person coming up the stairs was only here to collect a chapter from the printer.

But it wasn't Eve, Ryan, or Angela. Wicked took a quick peek and gasped as Jeremy appeared. What was Jeremy doing here? He hadn't written his chapter yet. As Wicked watched, Jeremy headed down the hallway, straight for Wicked's other room.

He was picking the lock! Wicked swallowed hard. What would Jeremy think when he saw the furniture? Would he realize that Wicked was using the room?

It took a few minutes, but Jeremy knew exactly what he was doing. He grinned as the padlock clicked and popped open. He hadn't lost his touch.

You never knew when knowing how to pick a lock might come in handy.

Jeremy was smiling as he let himself in the room, but he stopped short as he realized that it was furnished. There was a desk, and a lamp, and a cushioned armchair. It looked as if someone was using this room. Of course, that was impossible. The servants' quarters were off-limits, and the room had been locked. This furniture must have belonged to one of the former servants who'd left it behind for some reason.

As he walked toward the window, Jeremy happened to glance down and he stopped in his tracks again. There were footprints in the dust. Someone had been here recently.

For a moment, Jeremy was thoroughly freaked. Was it possible that someone was living up here, someone they didn't know about? But then Jeremy remembered that a technician from the computer lab had been up on the fourth floor to hook their workstations to the printer. They'd probably given him the keys to the padlocks so that he could run wires down to the rooms below.

The explanation made sense. Jeremy drew a deep breath of relief. For a second there, his imagination had been working overtime. He'd conjured up visions of criminals hiding out from the law, or homicidal maniacs who'd found a deserted house to live in.

Jeremy plugged his extension cord into the socket by the window. Then he opened the window and stepped out onto the fire escape, unrolling the cord as he climbed up to the roof. He was almost there when he thought he heard something behind him and turned back to look. But there was no one else on the fire escape.

He always got nervous when he rigged a big joke. Jeremy laughed at his fears and continued to climb. He stepped out onto the flat surface of the roof and gasped as he saw the view. The Sutler Mansion was taller than the surrounding houses, and he could see all the way across the campus to the football field on the other side.

Someone had built a roof garden, and Jeremy walked over to examine the potted plants. They were all dead now, just dry sticks poking up from the dirt, but it must have been pretty at one time. The garden was partially covered by wooden slats and half was in the shade. Jeremy was sure the owners of the house hadn't built the garden. The Sutlers had been rich, and there was no way they would have climbed up a fire escape to the roof. It had probably been the servants' hideaway, a place where they could relax after the Sutlers had retired for the night. They'd even brought up some patio furniture to sit on so they could enjoy the view.

Jeremy perched on the edge of an old chaise longue and looked out, over the city. The sun was shining brightly, but there was a nice cool breeze up this high. The view was incredible, and that made Jeremy smile. The Sutler servants had enjoyed a much better view than the Sutlers. That was an irony that pleased Jeremy very much.

His parents were working-class people, and Jeremy tended to dislike the rich. Most of them thought they were better than anyone else, just because they had money. Eve was like that. The only exception Jeremy had found was Angela Adams. Angela was a regular person even though she came from a rich and famous family. If all rich people could be more like Angela and less like Eve, it would be a much better world.

Jeremy stood up and walked to the chimney. It was time to rig his joke. He took a roll of duct tape from his backpack and taped his recorder to the inside of the chimney. He checked his watch and set the digital timer for the current time, and then he plugged the timer into the extension cord.

There was a smile on Jeremy's face as he turned on the recorder and bumped the volume up all the way. When the clock on the timer reached ten-fifteen, electricity would flow to the recorder and it would begin to play. Cheryl's voice would seem to come from the heavens, accusing Eve of causing her death. Cheryl would be followed by Tracie, saying that Eve had killed her, too. And when they were through talking, the recorder would shut itself off because it had reached the end of the tape.

Of course Jeremy would be right there in the library, sitting at the table next to Angela. No one would suspect him of rigging the joke since he'd be there with them. It would be fantastic. Jeremy could hardly wait to see their expressions. He'd let it go on for a couple of minutes, and then he'd lead them all up here to show them the source of the ghostly voices.

One final check and the deed would be done. Jeremy added one more strip of duct tape and then he stepped back to admire his work. He was feeling

very proud of himself when he thought he heard
stealthy footsteps behind him.

Before he could turn to look, a shadow loomed
over him, arms extended, and Jeremy gave a startled
yelp. But that was the last sound Jeremy would ever
make. Something hit him in the middle of his back,
knocking him off his feet. And then he was falling
over the edge of the roof, his mouth open in a silent
scream, plunging down four floors through the early
morning air to the unyielding ground below.

Wicked put the padlock back on the door and
smiled. No one had seen Jeremy fall and there would
be another search when he didn't come down for
breakfast. Wicked loved searches. It was almost like
playing hide-and-seek. The bright side would take
part, not knowing what Wicked had done. And
Wicked could sit back and watch, taking malicious
pleasure in the bright side's horror as Jeremy's body
was found.

CHAPTER ELEVEN

"Good work, Eve!" Ryan was laughing so hard there were tears in his eyes. "I can hardly wait to see the expression on Jeremy's face when he comes down to breakfast."

"Me, too." Eve grinned. She'd just finished telling everyone what she'd done to cancel the practical jokes that Jeremy had attempted to play on them.

"Thanks, Eve." Beth turned to Eve with a smile. "I'm so glad I didn't wake up to those spiders! I know it's silly, but I'm really afraid of them."

"Do you still have that showerhead you took out of our bathroom?" Scott was curious.

"Sure." Eve reached in the bag she was carrying and handed it to him.

Scott looked at it for a moment and then he shrugged. "I wonder what it does."

"Let me see it." Marc reached out for the shower-head and examined it closely. "I think it breaks apart somehow."

Dean took the showerhead and started to loosen the part that should have adjusted the flow of water.

Instead of stopping at the last setting, it screwed all the way off.

"What's in there?" Ryan peered over Marc's shoulder to look.

"It looks like . . . snakes. Rubber snakes all curled up. It's a showerhead that explodes when the water hits it and snakes come out."

"Wonderful." Eve rolled her eyes at the ceiling. "Just what you guys needed, first thing in the morning."

"Thanks for taking it off, Eve," Ryan said. "I was the first one in the shower this morning."

"Are you afraid of snakes, Ryan?" Beth looked very sympathetic. "I am."

"Not really, but I'd rather not take a shower with one. I probably would have yelled bloody murder if they'd all come out of the showerhead at once."

"And that's exactly what Jeremy's waiting for," Eve said. "He's probably sitting in his room right now, waiting for one of us to scream."

Ryan grinned at Eve. "Thanks to you, we won't. It's going to drive Jeremy crazy, waiting for us to react."

"How long do you think it'll take him to come down?" Angela glanced at her watch.

Eve shrugged. "I don't know, but I wish there was something we could do to him. He loves to play these stupid practical jokes. Maybe we should show him what it feels like to be on the receiving end."

"Good idea!" Scott exclaimed. "What should we do?"

Eve sat back and let her mind wander as everyone suggested various ways of getting even with Jeremy.

At least they were no longer puzzling over Tracie's death and trying to come up with a reasonable explanation for her drowning.

They'd all gone out to the pool this morning, hoping that something would give them a clue. But there had been nothing in the bottom of the pool except a few leaves and several dead bugs. Scott had taken pictures and then they'd swept out the bottom and filled the pool with water again. Tracie's death was still a mystery, and Eve doubted that even the police could solve it.

When Beth spoke, Eve tuned into the conversation again. She sounded very excited.

"I know what we can do to Jeremy! I've got a huge old armoire in my room."

"A what?" Marc looked puzzled.

"It's like a chifforobe." Beth explained, but Marc still looked puzzled. "You know, a huge, free-standing closet."

"Oh. One of *those*! There's one in my room, too. Why didn't you say so in the first place?"

Beth looked a little embarrassed. "Sorry, Marc."

"That's okay. Poets have to know all those obscure words. Anyway . . . what did you want to do with your armoire?"

"I thought we could back it up in front of Jeremy's door. When he opens his door to walk out of his room, he'll see nothing but a solid board. He'll think we boarded up his doorway because we were mad about his practical jokes."

"That's a great idea, Beth!" Eve started to laugh.

"But Jeremy might hear us moving the furniture and that'll tip him off."

"That's true. Is there some way we can block his doorway without making noise?"

"Yes!" Eve clapped her hands as she got an idea. "We'll sneak up there and take off his outside door-knob. When Jeremy tries to open his door, the inside knob will come off in his hand and he'll have to call us to let him out."

Ryan gave Eve an admiring glance. "Beautiful! I'll go up and do it right now."

"I'll go with you." Angela jumped up. "I'd better peek through the keyhole to make sure he's there. Our joke won't work if he's not."

Eve frowned as Angela left with Ryan. Why hadn't she thought to say that? Then she should be the one who was going with Ryan. Angela had gotten the best of her *again*.

Scott looked surprised when Angela and Ryan came back to report that Jeremy wasn't in his room. "But where could he be?"

"He's probably rigging another practical joke." Marc offered a possible explanation. "You know Jeremy. He's not happy unless he's playing a joke on somebody."

Eve started to nod, and then a very unpleasant and frightening thought crossed her mind. She turned to Angela and blurted out a question. "Did you write your chapter yet?"

"Yes. I couldn't sleep so I worked late last night."

"And did you kill off Jeremy's character?"

Angela looked a little worried. "Yes, but . . ."

"How did you do it?" Eve interrupted.

"I had Jeremy's character fix the television antenna. The killer followed him up to the roof and pushed him off the edge."

"Thank goodness!" Beth looked very relieved. "We've got cable so Jeremy couldn't possibly have done that!"

Eve shuddered. The thought of someone falling from that height terrified her, but she hid her fear. "That's true, Beth. But we didn't have a lamp by the pool, and Tracie still died there. And Cheryl wasn't stabbed with a butcher knife, but we found her body in the kitchen."

"Wait a second, Eve," Ryan said. "Are you saying Jeremy might have fallen off the roof?"

"I'm willing to bet on it. I hope I'm wrong. I really do. But I think we'd better go out and check the grounds."

Eve sighed as she took her place at the library table. Of course they'd found Jeremy's body, and they'd put it in the walk-in cooler with Cheryl and Tracie. Ten students had enrolled in the workshop and now there were only seven, the exact number of writers that were left in Angela's book.

Everyone thought it was a coincidence, everyone but Eve. As they all took their places, Eve glanced at the empty chair and she thought about Jeremy. Jeremy had been a royal pain with his adolescent practical jokes. Perhaps he had been rigging another big joke, but he hadn't deserved to die.

At least one thing had turned out perfectly today. Eve smiled slightly. She'd made dinner with Ryan, and it had been delicious. Ryan's incredibly rich pasta dish had lifted everyone's spirits. And Eve had received nothing but raves for her Parmesan garlic bread. Cooking was fun if you did it with someone you cared about. It was exactly what Cheryl had always said, and Eve wished that there were some way to tell her that she'd been right.

It took almost an hour for everyone to read their chapters. They'd started early, at nine o'clock instead of ten. No one had felt like sitting around, and they'd hoped that the reading would take their minds off what had happened to Jeremy.

The clock had just struck ten when Eve finished reading. It had been very silent as she'd read her chapter, and Eve knew that everyone had liked it.

"Great job, honey!" Ryan grinned at her. "I think that's your best chapter yet."

Eve smiled. "Thanks. It's your turn, Angela. Read your chapter."

Angela looked a little nervous. "Do you really want to hear it? I mean . . . after everything that's happened?"

"I want to hear it." Eve glanced around the table. "How about the rest of you?"

"So do I," Scott said. "Come on, Angela. I want to hear what you wrote about Jeremy."

"But it's not about Jeremy." Ryan stepped in the defend Angela. "It's about Jeremy's character, and we have to be smart enough to recognize the difference."

Eve tried to keep silent, but she couldn't help it. She blurted out what she was thinking. "Maybe it's not about Jeremy, but Jeremy's character dies in Angela's chapter. And now Jeremy's dead. Three out of three, Ryan. Isn't that too many to be a coincidence?"

"Not necessarily." Ryan turned to Angela. "Go ahead, Angela. Read us your chapter."

Angela's voice was shaking as she started to read, and Eve found herself feeling a bit sorry for her rival. It was clear that Angela was upset about what she'd written. Eve had always believed that words couldn't translate to actions, but Angela's story was turning into a reality and that was truly frightening.

Of course Angela's chapter was good. She was one of the best writers in the group. Eve found herself holding her breath as Angela read about the killer who was stalking Jeremy. Powerful arms were reaching out for him, to push him off the roof. Angela stopped to take a breath, and then they all heard it, a wail that seemed to be coming from the ceiling above them.

"What was *that*?!" Angela's face turned very pale.

"I don't know." Eve's eyes widened as they heard it again. "I think it's coming from the fireplace!"

There was another wail, and everyone turned to stare at the fireplace. And then a voice started to speak, a voice that sounded very much like Cheryl.

"It's your fault!" The voice was accusing, resonating strongly in the cavern of the fireplace. *"Now I'm dead and it's all your fault!"*

Angela's mouth dropped open in surprise. "It's . . . it sounds like Cheryl!"

"That's impossible." Eve didn't think. She just

reached out to take Angela's hand. "Calm down, Angela. Cheryl's dead and dead people can't talk."

"But . . . but her voice could be coming from the grave!" Angela looked totally freaked.

"Don't be stupid, Angela." Eve gave a short laugh. "Cheryl's not even buried yet so she doesn't have a grave. Her body's still in the cooler, and the voice isn't coming from there."

"You killed me! Cheryl's voice spoke again. *"I know you didn't mean it, but I'm dead all the same. You were trying to get Angela to stop writing so she'd flunk the class. You're jealous because Ryan likes her, and this time you went too far. You killed me, Eve!"*

Eve's mouth dropped open in surprise.

"You killed me, too!" This time the voice sounded like Tracie's. *"You pushed me in the pool, and then you walked away. You knew I could swim and I'd get out, but I got a cramp and I drowned. It's your fault, Eve! You murdered me!"*

Everyone gasped, but Eve was calm. Dead people didn't talk, and voices didn't come out of thin air. Eve smelled a rat, and she walked over to the fireplace to peer up, into the chimney.

"Tracie's right. Give it up, Eve." It was Cheryl's voice, again. *"Confess what you did or we'll get revenge. And bring back my clothes! I don't care if we were sorority sisters, you stole them from me!"*

Eve frowned as she stood at the fireplace. Someone knew she'd taken Cheryl's clothes! And then she remembered that Jeremy had seen her coming out of Cheryl's room, and she started to laugh.

"This isn't funny, Eve!" Angela was shaking so hard, her teeth were chattering.

"Yes, it is! It's a trick, Angela. That's Jeremy. He got to us, one last time!"

"Jeremy?" Angela stared at Eve in utter disbelief. "What do you mean?"

Eve took a deep breath and turned to face everyone. "Look . . . Jeremy played one final joke, and this is it. He knew we were all freaked about Cheryl and Tracie, and he decided to take advantage of it."

"That sounds like Jeremy," Scott said. "But why did he accuse you of murdering Cheryl and Tracie?"

"Because I turned him down for a date last year. It was right after he put the dead lobster in our pool, and I told him I wouldn't even consider dating someone with such a childish sense of humor. Jeremy rigged this joke to get even with me."

"You think that's what Jeremy was doing, up on the roof?" Ryan began to look as if he believed her.

"That's right. The voices were coming from the fireplace. Jeremy must have hidden his tape recorder by the top of the chimney."

Scott looked thoughtful. "Eve could be right. I know Jeremy was good at impersonations. He always did them at parties. One time he called the frat house and pretended to be President Graham, and everyone believed it."

"But how could Jeremy play a joke on us?" Beth looked completely puzzled. "He's dead!"

Dean shrugged. "He could have set it up before he died. He probably hooked a timer to his tape recorder and it went off, right on schedule."

"Are you sure?" Angela shivered slightly. She still didn't look convinced.

"I'm positive," Eve said. "Let's go up to the roof

and look for Jeremy's tape recorder. That'll prove it was just a joke."

"Good idea." Ryan stood up. "Come on, guys. . . . We'll climb up the fire escape and check it out."

Ten minutes later, the guys were back with Jeremy's tape recorder. Ryan sat down next to Eve and put his arm around her shoulders. "Good for you, honey. The rest of us were basket cases when that tape started to play. You were the only one who kept a clear head and figured it out."

"I guess Jeremy got the best of us, one last time." Marc shook his head. "I wish he knew. He'd be laughing like crazy right about now."

Eve blinked back a tear. She'd never liked Jeremy's sense of humor, and she'd been furious at him when he'd put the dead lobster in their pool. His last joke hadn't been very funny, either. It had been a deliberate attempt to get even with her. If Jeremy had been alive, she probably would have slapped his face. But Eve's anger didn't stop her from feeling very sorry that Jeremy was dead.

"I . . . I don't think I can finish reading my chapter." Angela placed her pages face down on the table. "And I'm going to change the names in my story. It's like Eve said. It's just too much of a coincidence."

Ryan looked thoughtful. "Maybe it isn't a coincidence at all. I know you didn't mean for this to happen, Angela, but your chapters might have led to these accidents."

"How?" Angela's mouth dropped open. "I thought you said that my book didn't have anything to do with it!"

"That's what I thought, at first. But now I've

changed my mind. Cheryl listened to you when you read about her character's death. It didn't seem to bother her, but she could have been hiding how upset she really was. And hearing about her character's death could have made Cheryl so nervous that she slipped and fell in the kitchen."

"That makes some kind of sense." Marc didn't look entirely convinced. "But what about Tracie? She died *before* Angela read her chapter."

"That's true, but Tracie could have read it when it was in the printer tray. Angela printed out early, but she didn't collect her pages until right before our meeting. Tracie could have seen them when she went up to the fourth floor to pick up her own chapter."

"And they made her so nervous, she fell in the pool?" Eve wasn't convinced.

"It's possible. And when she hit the water, she got a cramp and she drowned."

"And you think Jeremy read Angela's chapter about him?" Scott didn't look entirely convinced either.

"It could have happened that way. If Jeremy read Angela's chapter before he went up on the roof, he might have been very nervous."

Angela frowned. "If Jeremy was so nervous about my chapter, why did he go up to the roof at all?"

"To rig his joke. Jeremy would have walked across burning coals to set up one of his practical jokes."

Everyone nodded. They all knew Ryan was right.

"And because Jeremy was nervous, he hurried. That's why he stumbled and fell over the edge." Ryan finished his explanation. "Does that make sense?"

Everyone nodded again, and then Angela spoke

up. "So what shall I do? I told you I'd stop writing and I meant it. I don't want anything else to happen to my friends!"

"You don't have to stop writing." Ryan reached out to take Angela's hand. "Just don't print out until you're ready to read your chapter to us."

Scott started to grin. "I've got a better idea. Angela should pick her next victim very carefully. She should choose someone who won't get nervous, someone with nerves of steel, a professional who's an expert at separating fact from fiction."

"Like you?" Eve asked.

"Yeah, like me. I'll even read the chapter ahead of time, and I can guarantee you, I won't wind up dead!"

"But . . . how can you be sure?" Beth looked very nervous, and Eve sensed that she was about to become an ally. "Isn't that taking an awful chance?"

"That's what investigative reporters do. They take chances and they ferret out the truth. I've been in a lot of potentially dangerous situations and I know how to take precautions. Nothing's ever happened to me."

"Nothing's ever happened to you *yet,*" Eve corrected him.

Scott dismissed Eve with a wave of his hand and he turned to Angela. "Come on, Angela. . . . Make me your next victim, and I'll prove your story has nothing to do with these accidents."

"I know what you're doing, Scott." Eve confronted him. "You're going to write about this whole thing and try to sell it. You figure it'll jump-start your career. Am I right?"

"You're right." Scott looked a little embarrassed, but he laughed. "It's a real scoop and it'll read even better if I'm one of the victims in *Ten Little Writers*. Come on, Angela. . . . You can work me in as the next victim, can't you?"

"Yes. It'll fit with my story line. But are you sure, Scott?"

"I'm sure." Scott grinned at all of them. "Thanks, Angela. You've given me the chance of a lifetime."

"Let's just hope it's not the *last* chance of your lifetime." Eve pushed back her chair and stood up. "You're letting your ambition get in the way of your good sense. I just want you to remember that I tried to stop you from being a fool."

Scott laughed, and it wasn't a nice laugh. "Thanks, Eve. I'll be sure to send you a copy of my article when it's published. And then we'll see who the fool really is!"

CHAPTER TWELVE

It was past midnight, and everyone was either sleeping or working in their rooms. Angela had finished her chapter. Wicked smiled as Scott picked up Angela's pages from the printer and took them back down to his room to read. Scott had convinced Angela to let him read her chapter tonight, and he'd promised to give it back in the morning for any last-minute changes. Of course, there wouldn't be any last-minute changes. Wicked would make sure of that.

When the sound of Scott's footsteps had faded away, Wicked rushed to the printer and hit the button to print out again. Wicked would read about Scott's murder tonight. That would allow plenty of time to plan Scott's death in a way that duplicated what Angela had written.

Their meeting tonight had been very interesting. Wicked's bright side had been there, and that meant that Wicked had been there, too. Everyone had been thoroughly freaked when Jeremy's tape had been played. Wicked had looked out through the bright side's eyes and watched Eve very carefully. Eve had been just as shocked as everyone else, but she'd hidden it well. And she'd recovered much faster than any other member of the group. Wicked couldn't help but admire her composure. It would slip, sooner or later, but at that particular moment, Eve had been simply magnificent.

Wicked carried the pages back to the small fourth-floor room and sat down in the reading chair. Eve was a force to be reckoned with, especially since she seemed to be winning Beth over. Beth was beginning to believe that the deaths had been more than simple accidents. If too many people started to believe that the accidents were connected Angela's chapters, it would be very difficult for Wicked to achieve the goal.

Ryan's explanation had gone a long way to calm everyone's fears. Wicked knew that what Ryan had said was patently ridiculous, but no one else had Wicked's insight, not even Wicked's bright side, who was still unaware that they were sharing the same body. In this case, the bright side's ignorance truly was bliss.

Wicked began to smile, imagining what would happen if they suddenly learned the truth. Ryan was a nice guy and a good writer. He'd be horrified if he knew that by trying to calm the rest of the group, he'd actually bought Wicked some time. Ryan had helped Wicked tonight. It was too bad that Wicked couldn't tell him that.

Poor Angela would be appalled if she learned that the content of her chapters was providing the fuel for Wicked's fire. Given a choice between causing more deaths and discontinuing her work on *Ten Little Writers*, Wicked was sure that Angela would choose to stop writing. That's why Wicked couldn't give her the choice. Angela had to keep on writing until her project was finished and Wicked had turned her words into segments of perfect reality.

Then there was Eve. Wicked smiled. What would Eve do if she knew the truth? Of course she'd be repelled, but she wouldn't be as shocked as Ryan or Angela. Eve was a person of action. She thought clearly, even when she was frightened. Eve might actually try to defeat Wicked.

Ryan, Angela, and Eve were all intelligent enough to figure it out if they had all the pieces of the puzzle. Wicked had to be constantly on guard around them. They were the leaders of the group. If all three of them put their heads together, they could keep Wicked from reaching the goal.

Of course that wouldn't happen. Wicked smiled again. There was too much competition between Eve and Angela and that got in the way. There was also jealousy, and Wicked was glad that Eve thought Angela was trying to steal Ryan's affectations. Ryan was smart enough to realize that Eve and Angela were rivals. Trying to placate both of them kept him so busy that he didn't have time to see the real threat.

And then there was Scott. Poor Scott. Wicked frowned slightly. Scott was nice, and Wicked was sorry that he'd offered to be Angela's next victim. Eve had been right. Scott was a fool, and he would pay for his foolish mistake with his life. The pen was mightier than the sword. Professor Hellman had pontificated about that. The professor thought it was only a cliché, but the professor hadn't known about Wicked.

Eve was out on her balcony when she heard a soft knock at her door. She crossed the room quickly and opened the door a crack. Ryan was standing there, looking very apologetic.

"Did I wake you, Eve? I thought I heard you out on your balcony, and I took the chance that you were up."

"You were right. It's just too hot to sleep. Come out on the balcony. There's actually a breeze." Ryan followed Eve to the balcony, but when he perched on the rail, Eve gulped. Because of her fear of heights, she was afraid for him, but she couldn't admit that. "You'd better sit in the chair, Ryan. Angela might write about somebody falling off a balcony."

Ryan looked very serious as he sat down. "That's why I needed to talk to you, Eve. Do you really think there's a connection between Angela's book and the accidents?"

"Yes, I do. And I'm really worried about Scott. That's why I tried to embarrass him into backing out of his offer to be Angela's next victim."

"But it didn't work."

"I know." Eve sighed. "Just in case you haven't noticed, I'm not the most tactful person in the world. I probably jumped on him too hard. I should have given him a graceful way to back down, but I didn't know how to do it."

"And that bothers you?"

"Of course it does!" Eve was shocked. "Look,

Ryan . . . I admit I was tactless, but that doesn't mean I don't care."

Ryan smiled. It was a teasing smile, the kind of smile that meant he liked her, and Eve started to feel very good. "You really care about what happens to Scott? After all the nasty things he said about you?"

"Scott was just saving face. I backed him into a corner and he had to say something." Eve stopped and took a deep breath. It was time to be completely honest, and that was very difficult for her. "I should have told Scott he was very brave to even think of being Angela's next victim. And then I should have insisted that Angela use me, instead."

"You're dreaming, Eve. Scott never would have gone for that."

"You're wrong. I was watching his face, and he would have caved in if I'd said that I trusted him to protect me. And then, if I'd offered to give him an interview about how it felt to be slated as Angela's next victim, Scott would have bought it completely."

Ryan thought about it for a moment. "You could be right. But I wouldn't have let you do something like that."

"Why not? Even if Scott fell down on the job, I'm a big girl and I can take care of myself."

Ryan shook his head, and when he answered, his voice was very soft. "I couldn't let you take that chance. I care about you too much."

"You do?" Eve held her breath. Was Ryan about to tell her that he loved her?

"I really do. I know you're a good person, Eve. And that's why I need to talk to you about Angela."

"What about Angela?" Eve was glad it was dark.

She turned her face away from the light spilling out of her room, and tried not to look as disappointed as she felt.

"Angela's pretty upset about her book. She blames herself for everything that's happened."

Eve didn't say a word. What could she say? As far as she was concerned, Angela was perfectly right in blaming herself.

"She thinks you're against her, Eve." Ryan's voice was very sincere. "That's why I want you to tell her that you've changed your mind."

"Changed my mind about what?"

"About her book. I think you should tell Angela that you don't think her book has anything to do with the accidents. Even if you don't mean it, it'll make her feel a lot better."

Eve thought about it for a long moment. If she did what Ryan wanted, he'd probably say that he loved her. But Ryan would be loving a lie. Eve couldn't do that. You could call it scruples, or conscience, or whatever you wanted, but there was no way that Eve Carrington could pretend to be something that she wasn't.

"No, Ryan." There were tears in Eve's green eyes as she faced him. Perhaps she loved him. Eve wasn't sure. But Ryan was asking her to sell out. He wanted her to tell a deliberate lie, and she simply couldn't do that.

"Why, Eve?" Ryan reached out to take her hand. "Do you hate Angela that much?"

"No. I hate some of the things that she does, but I don't hate Angela. She can't help the way she is."

Ryan smiled. "Now you're talking sense. If you got to know her, I think you'd like her. I really do."

"Maybe." Eve was willing to give Ryan the benefit of the doubt. "But even if I did, I wouldn't lie to her. Don't you see, Ryan? I can't tell Angela that everything's just fine when I don't really believe it."

"Eve, honey . . . I know you're disappointed because we haven't been spending much time together. It's just that Angela's upset and she really needs a friend so I've been trying to give her some moral support."

Eve nodded, although she wasn't sure that was all there was to it. Angela was gorgeous, and Ryan had certainly noticed that!

"I'd rather spend my time with you, Eve. That's why I want you to tell Angela that what she's writing can't possibly have anything to do with the accidents. Then she won't be upset any longer and she won't need me to continually reassure her. You can see that, can't you honey?"

"I guess that makes some kind of sense, but I can't do it, Ryan."

"Even though it'll mean that we can spend more time together?"

"No." Eve shook her head. "I'd like to spend more time with you, Ryan. You know that. But I can't lie about something that important, even for you."

Ryan squeezed her hand once more, and then he stood up. He looked very serious, and Eve found she couldn't really read his expression. "All right. I guess you've answered my question. Good night, Eve."

Eve blinked back tears as Ryan left. She felt like

calling him back, but what good would that do? No matter what he said, she wasn't going to change her mind. She sat on the balcony until her tears had dried, and then she went inside to go to bed. Ryan was probably with Angela right now. He'd fallen completely under her spell, and there was nothing that Eve could do about it. She'd blown it with Ryan, but you had to draw the line somewhere, and that's exactly what Eve had done. And if it meant that Ryan was no longer her boyfriend, then maybe she was better off without him.

Eve sighed as she crawled into bed. Her tears had started to fall again, and she wiped her eyes with the back of her hand. It had been the truth when she'd told Ryan that she didn't hate Angela. But now that she'd lost Ryan to her rival, Eve certainly had a score to settle. Even if it took her the rest of her life, she was going to prove that Angela's chapters had some-how caused the deaths of their friends.

Scott couldn't help feeling nervous as he read Angela's pages. She was a very good writer, and the scene where she'd killed off his character was really horrendous. It had happened in the laundry room. Scott had been doing his laundry when the killer had crept up on him. He'd hit Scott over the head and Scott had fallen to the floor, unconscious. Then the killer had stuffed Scott into the industrial-sized dryer. Scott had regained consciousness and died a horrible death in the suffocating heat as his body and his clothes had gone around and around.

Scott's hands were shaking as he put down the pages. The thought of whirling around in a hot dryer, barely conscious because of a blow to the head, was really horrifying.

Scott had always been claustrophobic, but he hadn't told Angela about that. No one knew, not even his roommates. Scott didn't like to discuss his private fears. It was embarrassing. But, somehow, Angela had managed to plug in to his worst fear.

"It's only fiction. It's only fiction. It's only fiction." Scott repeated it over and over, like some sort of magical mantra that could ward off evil. But the mantra didn't work. Scott's hands were still shaking as he crawled into bed and turned off the light.

There was no way he could sleep. Scott sighed and stared up at the ceiling. Every time he closed his eyes, he pictured his character in the dryer, mouth open in a soundless scream, hands beating at the round safety glass as he whirled around and around with his shorts and his socks.

Scott tried to think of something else, touch football on a sunny afternoon in the park, driving his car with the window rolled down and the air streaming past his face, Sunday barbecues at his older brother's house with spicy ribs and a keg of beer and his little niece and nephew playing in the yard. Nothing worked. The image of his body in the dryer was permanently etched on his mind.

With trembling fingers, Scott reached out and flicked on the light. The warm glow of the lamp chased away the horrible image, and Scott actually laughed at himself. It was strange how things seemed

much more frightening in the dark. It was almost as
if night unlocked the chains on his innermost fears
and made them grow strong and powerful. Everything was exaggerated, even the slightest sound.
Nothing was too horrible to contemplate in the dark,
and the black side of the imagination ruled.

Now that the light was on, everything seemed perfectly normal, and Scott wished he'd brought his
night-light with him. He'd told his roommates he
used it so he wouldn't stub his toe on the furniture
when he got up in the middle of the night, but that
wasn't the only reason. A night light was comforting.
Scott had always used one. It chased away the demons
of the dark.

Everyone said he was brave. Scott thought about
it for a moment, and then he grinned. He *was* brave.
He'd gone into deserted houses to investigate ghost
sightings, even though he'd been petrified with fear.
He'd spent three incredibly anxious days locked up
in a psych ward to interview a homicidal maniac.
He'd even gone skydiving to write about a couple
who'd gotten married in midair, and he'd been so terrified he'd barely been able to hold on to his camera.
People who weren't afraid couldn't claim they were
brave. Bravery was doing something in spite of the
fact that you were frightened out of your skin.

And now he was being brave again. Scott felt
rather proud of himself. He'd volunteered to be
Angela's next victim, even though he'd been more
than a little scared. He still was, but there was no
way he'd tell anyone that.

When he thought about it rationally, Scott knew

he didn't have any reason to worry. Angela had been true to her word, and she'd made sure that her chapter couldn't turn into reality. They didn't have an industrial-sized dryer, and no one could stuff a body in the small, apartment-sized model that the college had installed in their laundry room. And that meant Scott couldn't possibly suffer the same fate as his character in *Ten Little Writers*.

CHAPTER THIRTEEN

At the first sign that dawn was breaking, Eve got out of bed. She hadn't slept very well and her eyes felt swollen and hot. Her first sleepy thought was that she might be coming down with the flu, but then she remembered the events of last night and knew it was only the result of crying.

Eve hated to cry, and she vowed not to do it again. Ryan was gone, but she would get over it eventually. At least that's what everyone said. Broken hearts mended, and time healed all wounds. The words were clichés, but people wouldn't repeat them so often if there wasn't some basis in fact.

When she caught sight of her reflection in the mirror, Eve groaned. Her eyes were red, her skin was blotchy, and her whole face was puffy. She looked like death warmed over, and no amount of makeup could hide that.

Even though she was hungry, Eve decided she wouldn't go to breakfast until the swelling had gone down. She didn't want anyone to see her this way. They'd ask questions, and she might start to cry again. It might be different if she looked beautiful when she cried, but she didn't.

Angela looked beautiful when she cried. Eve glared at her reflection, imagining what she'd say if Angela were standing behind the glass. *You stole my boyfriend, your stupid book is causing all these accidents, and now I can't even go down to breakfast. You're trying to ruin my life, Angela!*

But she was the one who was letting Angela do it. She was a fool for letting Angela intimidate her this way. So what if she ran into Ryan and Angela, together at breakfast? They were all living here, under one roof, and she'd have to face them sooner or later.

Eve straightened her shoulders and marched to the shower. She turned it on full-blast and let the cool water rush over her face. Then she washed her hair, brushed it back, and got dressed in a pair of Cheryl's shorts and a tank top that had belonged to Tracie.

She was ready. Eve glanced in the mirror again and curved her lips up in a smile. She didn't look great, but she refused to let Angela and Ryan affect her life. If anyone asked her what was wrong, she'd tell the truth. She'd say that she'd broken up with Ryan and she'd been crying. If they couldn't understand, that was just too bad.

Eve opened her door and stopped cold as she saw what someone had left for her. It was a beautiful bouquet of roses in a glass vase and there was an envelope taped to the glass. Eve picked up the bouquet and carried it back to her room. Who had left her flowers? And why?

Eve's fingers were trembling slightly as she

opened the envelope. The flowers were from Ryan, but she didn't understand his message at all.

Good morning, Eve. The note said. *Meet me in the courtyard when you get up. I've got a surprise for you.*

There was only one way to find out what that surprise was, and Eve rushed down the stairs. She was breathing hard by the time she reached the ground floor. and she took a few moments to calm herself. Then she stepped out into the courtyard and walked to the big, round table where Ryan sitting.

"Hi, Eve." Ryan smiled at her. "Did you like the flowers?"

"They're beautiful. But why did you give them to me?"

"I'll explain everything. Sit down, honey."

He pulled out a chair and Eve sat down. She still didn't understand what was going on. Ryan had broken up with her, and now he was acting as if nothing had happened!

"I'm sorry I was so hard on you last night, Eve." Ryan looked very serious. "But I had to find out the truth and it was the only way."

"The truth?" Eve felt like Alice in *Alice in Wonderland* when she'd met the Mad Hatter. Although she understood every one of Ryan's words, she had no idea what he meant. "The truth about what?"

Ryan reached out to take her hand. "Angela told me you were trying to sabotage her work."

"Sabotage?" Eve was still feeling like Alice. She just didn't understand.

"That's right. Angela said you were jealous of the time I spent with her. And she was sure that was the only reason why you tried to convince everyone that there was a connection between her book and the accidents."

Eve still didn't understand.

"It's like this." Ryan put his arm around Eve's shoulders. "If you manage to convince everyone that there's a connection, Angela will have to stop writing. Then she'll flunk out of the program and she'll be out of your hair."

Eve's eyes widened as she caught on at last, and then she started to laugh. "That's ridiculous! If I wanted Angela out of my hair, I wouldn't play mind games with her. I'd just boot her out the front door!"

"That's exactly what I told her." Now it was Ryan's turn to laugh. "But Angela insisted that she was right, and she can be pretty persuasive. I just had to find out, for sure. And I did, last night."

Eve wasn't sure she liked being tested by Ryan. He should have trusted her from the beginning.

"I know what you're thinking, Eve." Ryan gave her a little hug. "I should have known you wouldn't do something like that, but . . ."

"But what?"

"Maybe I shouldn't say anything, but I've heard stories about some of the things you've done in the past. They weren't always very nice."

Eve sighed. She knew she had a reputation for being ruthless, and now her past was coming back to haunt her. "You're right, Ryan. I can see how you'd think I might pull a dirty trick like that, but I didn't. I've changed, Ryan. It was different before I met you. It was like I was at the center of the universe and no one else mattered. I never cared about other people's feelings before."

"And now you do?"

"Yes. I even care about Angela's feelings, and I really wish I didn't! She tried to break us up, Ryan!"

"I know." Ryan hugged her again. "But it didn't work and I'm glad. Are you glad, Eve?"

Eve turned to smile at him. "Yes."

"Good! Then I can give you my surprise." Ryan reached into his pocket and pulled out a small box. "Here, Eve. This is for you."

Eve opened the package with trembling fingers and lifted the lid. Inside was Ryan's fraternity pin, and Eve knew exactly what that meant. It was a custom that dated back to the turn of the century in Ryan's fraternity. A guy didn't give his fraternity pin to anyone except the girl he hoped to marry.

"Will you were wear it, Eve?"

Ryan looked anxious, and Eve threw her arms around his neck and gave him a big kiss. "Yes, I'll wear it, Ryan!"

Ryan, Eve, Beth, and Dean were all seated around the breakfast table when Angela came downstairs. If she noticed the fraternity pin that Eve was wearing, she didn't say anything about it. She took a piece of toast and spread it with strawberry jam. And then she sat down at the end of the table.

"Good morning, Angela." Eve smiled at her. Now that Ryan had given her his fraternity pin, Eve had decided that she could afford to be charitable. Ryan had made his choice, and Angela was no longer her rival.

"Good morning." Angela didn't meet Eve's eyes. "I was hoping Scott would be here. He's got tonight's chapter."

"That's not tonight's chapter?" Ryan motioned toward the stack of printed pages that Angela had placed on the table.

"No. I couldn't sleep so I decided to stay up and write tomorrow's chapter. I just printed it out a couple of minutes ago."

"Oh, oh!" Beth looked nervous. "Who's the victim for tomorrow night?"

"Marc, but don't tell him. I don't want him to get nervous. I took every precaution. I set it up so it can't possibly happen."

"How did you manage that?" Eve was curious.

"I had the killer murder him in the cupola. And we don't have a cupola."

Ryan nodded. "Very smart. But I think we'd better tell Marc. He's got a right to know."

"Well . . . all right." Angela sounded reluctant. "I'll tell him as soon as he finishes jogging."

"I don't understand why Marc jogs in this heat," Eve said. "It can't be good for him."

"He's used to it." Ryan smiled at her. "Marc jogs every morning, rain or shine. He says it keeps him in shape."

Dean nodded. "It must work. Marc's in great shape. Maybe I should try it."

"You're in great shape without jogging." Beth blurted it out, and then she started to blush. "I mean . . . well . . . you know what I mean."

Everyone laughed except Angela. She looked distracted, and Eve turned to her. What's the matter, Angela?"

"I don't know. I just feel uneasy, that's all. Has anyone seen Scott this morning?"

"I saw him," Dean said. "He was in his room, working at his computer, when I came down for breakfast."

"He wasn't nervous, was he?" Ryan looked concerned.

"No. At least I don't think he was. He told me he was going to take a shower and then he'd come down."

Eve gave a relieved sigh. At least Scott was all right. But she wished that Angela hadn't written a second murder. It was almost like tempting fate.

"What's the matter, Eve?" Ryan put his arm around her shoulders. "You shivered."

Eve thought fast. She didn't want to bring up her worries to the rest of the group. And perhaps she was just borrowing trouble. "It's just lack of sleep."

"Maybe you should take a nap." Angela's smile was perfectly innocent, but Eve thought she saw a hardness in her eyes. "You can't write well if you're tired, and you still haven't finished your chapter for tonight."

Eve's eyes widened. How did Angela know she hadn't finished her chapter? But Eve didn't want to confront Angela in front of Ryan so she just nodded and stood up. "Thanks, Angela. That's a very good idea. I think I'll go up to my room for a while and relax."

"I'm going to take a quick dip in the pool." Ryan stood up, too. "Does anyone want to join me?"

Beth shook her head. "I've got to work on my poem."

"Not me." Dean looked disappointed. "I'd like to go swimming, but I have to write another song."

Angela shook her head. "I'd love to, but I've got some proofreading to do. Who's making lunch?"

"I am," Beth said. "We've got everything we need for a chef salad. Is that all right?"

"A chef salad sounds great, but it's a lot of work," Eve said. "Do you need any help, Beth?"

"No thanks, Eve." Beth smiled at her. "Dean's going to help me, and he's promised to make some muffins to go with it. Let's meet in the courtyard at one o'clock, and we'll eat on the deck around the pool."

Eve wore a bemused smile as she climbed the stairs to her room. She'd never offered to help in the kitchen before, and it felt good.

Five minutes later, Eve was in bed, her alarm set for twelve-thirty. There was a slight breeze coming in through her open balcony doors, and Eve smiled as she nestled her head on the pillow. Ryan had given her his fraternity pin. Life was truly wonderful. Eve sighed in perfect contentment as she dropped off to sleep.

He was glad they'd all gone their separate ways. Scott walked down the hallway, hoping he wouldn't run into any of them. He just didn't feel like socializing yet. He had to check something out before he faced them. He'd been thinking about the murder that Angela had written and the size of the dryer in their laundry room. The best way to set his fears at rest was to go in and make sure that he was right.

There was no one in the kitchen, and Scott gave a relieved sigh. He didn't want to talk to anyone, not until he'd checked out the dryer. He walked quietly across the kitchen and opened the door to the laundry room. It was just as he'd thought. The dryer door was much too small to accommodate a human body.

"Yes!" Scott grinned as he shut the door behind him and walked closer. His head would fit in the dryer door, but that was about it.

Something was glittering in the bottom of the dryer. Scott leaned over to look. It was his grandfather's silver pocket knife with the etching of the pheasant on the handle. The knife was Scott's prized possession. His grandfather had given it to him, right before he died. It must have fallen out of his pocket when he'd washed his clothes yesterday afternoon.

Scott hesitated, his hand only inches from the dryer door. He remembered what had happened in Angela's chapter and he shivered slightly. Did he really want to open the dryer door?

Ryan was outside, by the pool. He could ask Ryan to open it for him. But then he'd have to offer some kind of explanation, and there was no way that Scott wanted to admit that Angela's chapter had scared him so much, he was afraid to even touch their clothes dryer!

He was being ridiculous. The clothes dryer couldn't possibly hurt him. Scott attempted to laugh at himself, but it was a very nervous laugh. He'd let Angela's story of his character's murder really get to him. It was affecting his judgement, and that wasn't right. There was nothing to be afraid of. He'd just open the dryer door, grab his knife, and get out of the laundry room.

Scott took a step closer and frowned. Someone had spilled water in front of the dryer. He'd mop it up, just as soon as he got his knife. Perhaps the hose on the washer was leaking. He'd check that out, too.

As Scott's fingers were about to touch the metal handle, he spotted a heavy-duty extension cord, coiled up on the floor. That was odd. But Scott didn't have time to wonder about the cord for more than a brief second. As his fingers touched the metal, a powerful zap of electricity jolted his body, electrocuting him on the spot.

Wicked smiled an evil smile. The deed was done. Scott was dead. Wicked stepped into the laundry room, jerked the extension cord from the socket before someone could throw the handle on the circuit breaker to turn the electricity back on, and hurried out to the trash with the evidence. There was still work to be done. While they were still confused about what had caused the sudden power outage, Wicked would make sure that Angela's next chapter became a reality.

Angela had given Wicked some cause for thought. Marc's character had been killed in the cupola. Wicked had gone to the unabridged dictionary in the library for an exact definition of the word. A cupola was a light structure on a dome or roof, serving as a belfry, lantern, or belvedere, and the Sutler Mansion didn't have anything like that. A second definition had been more promising. It had said that a cupola was a dome, especially one covering a circular or polygonal area. And a third choice had defined a cupola as any of various dome-like structures.

Wicked had explored the grounds and found the perfect thing. There was a dome at the Sutler Mansion that matched the description of a cupola. It was in plain sight, an abandoned greenhouse at the real of the rose garden, and that was where Wicked would kill Marc.

Marc was very sports-oriented. Wicked knew that. And Marc was also a physical fitness addict. He was in the habit of jogging three miles every morning, and now that they were all confined to the mansion, he did his laps around the grounds. Marc's route took him right past the greenhouse, and that was a lucky break. It would be laughably simple for Wicked to lure Marc inside and make certain that Angela's fiction turned into fact.

CHAPTER FOURTEEN

At first, Eve thought she was having another nightmare. Someone was shouting about losing something and a black screen. A door slammed shut, and then there were running footsteps, outside in the hallway.

Eve sat up and blinked as another door slammed. What was going on? She hurried to open her door and almost ran straight into Beth.

"We had a power failure." Beth looked very upset. "I think I lost my file!"

"It's all right, Beth. Ryan told me we have a battery backup. Your file's still there. The computer saved it automatically."

"That's a relief!" Beth began to smile. "I left my computer on, and when I came back upstairs, the screen was blank."

"Is everyone okay up here?" Ryan appeared at the end of the hall. He had a towel wrapped around his body, and he was barefoot.

"We're fine," Eve said. "What happened?"

"I guess we had a short, and it tripped the circuit

breaker. I heard Beth hollering up here so I jumped out of the pool and came right up."

"Sorry about that." Beth laughed. "I thought I lost my file, but Eve explained about the battery backup. Can you help me get back online, Ryan?"

"Sure, right after I check the circuit breaker."

"We'll go with you." Eve shivered slightly.

"What's the matter, Eve?" Ryan slipped his arm around her shoulders. "Is something wrong?"

"I hope not. But I can't help wondering . . . has anyone seen Scott yet?"

It didn't take long to find the circuit breaker and throw the switch back on. Everyone breathed a sigh of relief as the second hand on the kitchen clock started to sweep in its endless circles again.

But Scott didn't come down to see what was the matter, and neither did Marc. "I think we should look for Scott and Marc," Eve said.

"I'm sure they're perfectly all right." Angela looked very defensive.

"Marc's okay." Dean spoke up. "I saw him jogging past the rose garden, just a couple of minutes ago."

"He probably doesn't even know we had a power failure," Eve said. "Do you want me to catch up with him and tell him?"

"Don't bother. We'll tell him when he comes in. But I am a little worried about Scott. I haven't seen him since early this morning, and he always comes down to eat breakfast."

"Let's go look for him." Beth looked worried, too.

"I'll check his room." Ryan took charge. "The rest of you split up and check the other floors."

"I'll got up to the fourth floor," Dean said. "He might be printing out. Come on, Beth. . . . You can check the girls' floor. Scott might have heard you yelling about your file and gone up to your room."

"It's a good thing we don't have an elevator." Angela shivered a little.

Eve lifted an eyebrow. "That's where you set Scott's murder?"

"No, but I wish I'd thought of it." Angela gave a nervous laugh. "It'd be a perfect place, especially if the power went off and Scott and the killer were stuck between floors."

Beth swallowed hard. "That's scary, Angela!"

"I know."

Now it was Eve's turn to shiver. She'd always hated elevators. Perhaps it was because she didn't like heights and she always imagined what it would be like if the cable snapped, plunging her down to a certain death.

"We'll meet back here in fifteen minutes. Come on, everybody. Let's go." Ryan shooed them all out of the kitchen. "The sooner we find Scott, the better we'll feel."

Eve turned back to ask Angela exactly where she'd killed off Scott's character, but she changed her mind when she saw that Angela was still shivering. There was no reason to make Angela even more nervous. She'd bring it up only if their search failed and they couldn't find Scott.

* * *

Marc felt great as he jogged around the perimeter of the grounds. It was another sweltering day, but he'd brought his water bottle and he raised it to his lips to take a quick swig. Jogging was the ticket to good physical condition. Even his father had commented on how fit he looked.

His father's approval was something Marc had always craved. When he was younger, he'd tried to earn it by excelling at sports, but he'd failed miserably. Marc had earned the lowest batting average and the highest percentage of errors on the baseball team; he'd fumbled the football every time it was passed to him; and he'd missed more hoops than anyone else on the basketball team. But Marc loved sports and he'd conveyed that enthusiasm to every other member of the team. His high school coaches had discovered that they won more games if Marc was around, and they'd given him the position of student coach.

Marc had loved coaching. He'd read the rule books from cover to cover and turned into an excellent strategist. His high school coaches had been so impressed, they'd let Marc make up the rosters and call most of the plays. One of them had even managed to secure a college athletic scholarship for Marc.

Of course Marc hadn't played on any of the college teams. He didn't have that kind of ability. But he'd worked on the playbooks, compiled all the stats, and taken charge of the equipment. It was while he was helping the trainer one day that he'd decided what his career should be.

Sports medicine was a growing career, and Marc

was planning to concentrate on physical therapy. Perhaps he'd even go to medical school. He just wasn't sure. If he did, he'd need a source of income, which was why he was trying to write his sports novel. He knew his father would give him the money if he asked, but Marc wanted to earn at least part of it himself.

The sun was shining brightly, and Marc was on top of the world. Everyone thought his writing was good. Just last night, Angela had told him she thought he'd shown more improvement than any other member of the group.

Marc grinned as he thought about Angela. She was gorgeous, she was bright, and she was really kind to help him with his chapters. When all this was over, he really wanted to ask her for a date. His father would be really impressed if he found out that Marc was dating Angela.

Wicked was smiling at the way things had gone. They'd all split up to search for Scott in different places, and now that the bright side was alone, Wicked could take over their body. It was just in time. Marc's route would bring him past the greenhouse in a little less than a minute, and Wicked had to be ready for him.

The greenhouse wasn't locked and Wicked stepped inside. Various tools and re-potting equipment lined the shelves. Wicked chose a sturdy shovel with a flat back. Although Marc was strong, one well-aimed blow should knock him out. Then Wicked would finish the job with one of the heavy clay pots.

Marc was just coming around the corner of the potting shed. Wicked put on the bright side's expression and stepped out, into his path. "Hey, Marc. Come in here for a second, will you? I want to show you something strange."

"Sure." Marc smiled and stepped into the greenhouse. "What is it?"

"It's this!" Wicked swung the shovel and Marc went down. Another dozen blows with the clay pot, and his heart stopped beating forever.

Wicked stood up and sighed. Killing was really a lot of work. The bright side might wonder why their arms were so stiff, but they'd go for a swim in the pool later to take away some of the soreness.

There was only one thing left to do. Wicked grabbed the shelf with the rest of the clay pots and inched forward until it toppled. Several clay pots smashed, and Wicked grinned. Marc's death would look like an accident. They'd all think he'd come into the greenhouse for some unknown reason and the shelf had fallen on top of him. It was absolutely perfect, and Wicked was proud to have thought of it. Wicked's job would be easier if they thought Marc's death was accidental.

Wicked closed the greenhouse door and walked through the rose garden to the edge of the courtyard. It was time for the bright side to come out for the trip across the courtyard. Someone else could be there, and Wicked didn't want to be seen. There would be too much elation in Wicked's stride, too much joy in Wicked's eyes. The bright side was supposed to be searching for Scott, and that called for a serious, worried expression. It would look strange if any of them saw the blissful smile on Wicked's face. Timing was everything, and it was much too early to reveal that another victim in Angela's book had turned into Wicked's fifth victim in real life.

"He's got to be somewhere!" Eve turned to Angela. They'd searched the house and the grounds, but no one had come across Scott. "Where did you kill off Scott's character, Angela?"

Angela swallowed. She looked very nervous. "I . . . uh . . . I had the killer stuff in him in an industrial-sized clothes dryer. I thought that would be fine because ours is much too small."

"Did you check the laundry room, Angela?" Ryan looked very concerned.

"Uh . . . no. Since it couldn't happen the way I wrote it, I didn't see why I had to go in there."

"I'll do it." Eve walked to the laundry room door. Angela was a total coward. She'd written about Scott's death in the laundry room, but now she was afraid to go in and look. Eve took a deep breath, opened the door, and flicked on the light switch. And then she gasped and began to shudder at the awful sight that met her eyes.

"Eve?"

Ryan was calling her and Eve turned around in the doorway. She knew all the blood had left her face because she had to lean on the door frame to keep from fainting. The sight of Scott's blackened body had been so horrible, it had taken her breath away. She opened her mouth and tried to speak, but nothing came out.

"Eve? What is it?"

Eve's mouth was dry with horror, but somehow she managed to swallow. She had to tell Ryan.

"Yes, Ryan." Eve forced out the words. Her voice sounded strange, much too loud in the stillness of the room. "Scott's here. And he's dead."

CHAPTER FIFTEEN

No one felt like leaving the group and they sat at a table in the courtyard. Now there were four bodies in the walk-in cooler, Cheryl, Tracie, Jeremy, and Scott. The laundry room was off-limits. Ryan and Dean had nailed the door shut. There was something wrong with the wiring, and poor Scott had been electrocuted when he'd touched the metal door of the dryer.

Eve sighed. And then, quite suddenly, she began to laugh. When everyone turned to stare at her in astonishment, she laughed even harder.

"Eve? What is it?"

Ryan was frowning and that set Eve off again. She laughed so hard, tears came to her eyes. "It's the extra blankets. We've only got one left. We'd better make Angela stop writing before we run out of supplies."

"Eve!" Ryan looked shocked for a brief moment, but then he started to laugh, too. Dean joined in, and then Beth, all of them laughing so hard, they could barely catch their breaths.

The only one who didn't laugh was Angela, and she glared at them. "I think you're all horrible! How can you laugh at what happened to Scott?"

"We're not laughing at that." Beth was the first to recover. "Haven't you ever heard the phrase, *And if I laugh at any mortal thing, 'tis that I may not weep?*"

"Is that Shakespeare?" Ryan asked.

"No. George Noel Gordon wrote it. You probably know him as Lord Byron."

Eve reached out to take Angela's hand. Poor Angela really did look upset, and Eve felt a little guilty for joking. "The point is, laughter and tears are very close. They're both powerful emotions. We all feel terrible about Scott's death, but we're laughing instead of crying."

"I . . . I guess I understand." Angela didn't look entirely convinced.

"Eve's right." Ryan patted Angela on the back. "We're laughing to release the tension. What happened is horrible, and it's one way of coping."

"I see. But there's another way of coping, Ryan. Why don't we all go back to work? It'll take our minds of what's happened, and I think I could write another chapter." Angela began to laugh when Eve gasped. "I'm kidding, Eve. And you're right. I do feel much better, now that I've had a good laugh."

Eve wasn't sure that Angela really got the point. And then Angela said something that made Eve's blood run cold.

"How about Marc? He should be in from his run by now, shouldn't he?"

They all exchanged uneasy glances, and then Ryan nodded. "We'd better find Marc. We have to tell him what's happened. But this time I think we should all stick together."

"I know what you're thinking, but Marc's perfectly all right." Angela looked very positive. "I set his murder in the cupola, and there's no cupola here. I even looked it up in the dictionary, just to make sure I had the correct architectural term. A cupola is a dome-like structure on the roof, like a belfry."

They all looked up at the roof, but there was nothing even remotely resembling a dome-like structure. Eve looked very relieved as she turned to Angela. "You're absolutely right, Angela. There's no cupola on our roof."

"Let's go." Ryan looked resigned as he got out of his chair. "The last time anyone saw Marc, he was jogging. Let's go find him and give him the bad news."

It took them almost an hour, but they found Marc on the greenhouse floor, surrounded by shards of pottery. There was no doubt that he was dead and it was clear what had happened. Marc had gone into the greenhouse for some reason, and he'd been standing under the shelf of heavy clay pots when it had pulled loose from the wall. They'd wrapped Marc in their last remaining blanket, and now they were all out in the courtyard, trying to cope.

Eve was worried about Beth. Her face was very pale, her hands were shaking, and there were traces of tears on her cheeks.

"Come on, Beth." Eve patted her on the back. "You've got to pull yourself together."

Beth shuddered. "But . . . it's so awful! First Scott.

And now Marc. It's like Angela's book is cursed! She wrote about it, and now it's actually happened!"

"You can't blame my chapter this time." Angela was clearly upset. "We didn't find Marc in a cupola. He was in the greenhouse, and that's not the way I wrote it at all!"

"Were there any other definitions of a cupola in the dictionary?" Ryan asked.

"Yes. There were a couple of others, but I didn't bother with those."

"Maybe I'd better look it up." Eve got out of her chair.

Angela looked confused. "But why?"

"Well . . ." Eve wanted to say that it might give them a clue to why Marc had died in the greenhouse. But she bit back her words and settled for the first thing that popped into her mind. "I'm curious, that's all. I'll be right back."

A few moments later, Eve was back. She was carrying the heavy, unabridged dictionary, and she placed it on the table. "The greenhouse is a cupola. It fits the third definition."

"Let me see!" Angela pulled the dictionary to her side of the table and looked up the word. As she read the third definition, her face turned very pale.

"What does it say?" Dean was frowning as he faced Angela.

"It says a cupola is any dome-like structure. But I didn't know that!"

Ryan sighed. "Okay. Nobody's blaming you personally, Angela."

"Ryan's right," Eve said. "You tried to be as careful as you could. It just didn't work out, that's all.

But that doesn't change the fact that every murder victim that you've written about has wound up dead."

"It blows my theory," Ryan said. "Scott might have been so nervous about Angela's chapter that he was accident prone. But Marc couldn't have been nervous. He didn't know he was the next victim."

"I think victim is the operative word here." Beth sat up a little straighter and looked much more composed. "Are we really sure these were accidents?"

Eve winced. The same thought had occurred to her, but she'd decided not to voice it. "What do you mean, Beth?"

"We've all been in that walk-in cooler and we didn't fall and hit our heads on that table. And we've all used the washer and dryer and we didn't get electrocuted. We've had five accidents in a row, and everyone who died was a victim in Angela's book."

"You've got a point, Beth," Ryan said. "Five accidents in a row is just too much to blame on coincidence."

"Then you think someone is actually killing off the victims in my book?" Angela's hands started to tremble and she clasped them together to keep them from shaking.

"It's possible," Ryan said.

"But there's only five of us here!" Eve swallowed hard. "If there is a murderer, it's got to be . . ." Eve's voice trailed off, and Dean finished the thought for her. "It's got to be one of us."

"But . . ." Angela took a deep breath. "That's impossible, isn't it?"

"I think so," Ryan said. "And that leaves only one

other possibility. There's someone else here, someone who's reading your pages and acting them out."

"Oh my God!" Beth moved a little closer to Dean. "What are we going to do?"

Ryan took a deep breath. He looked very determined. "We're going on the buddy system. No one goes anywhere alone, not even to the bathroom. We're going to cook together, eat together, swim in the pool together, and watch television together. We're even going to sleep together."

Beth burst into laughter. "Excuse me?"

"I didn't exactly mean it that way." Ryan laughed, too. "We'll all sleep in the living room. There are three couches and you girls can have those. Dean and I'll sack out in sleeping bags on the floor. Are we all agreed?"

Everyone nodded, but Angela looked upset. "How are we going to work? Our computers are in our rooms."

"I think I know how to solve that problem." Dean smiled at her. "We can all work together in the library."

"But we can't use our computers down there." Angela still looked upset.

"Yes, we can. The guy who installed our workstations put a hook-up in the library. I'm sure it's linked to the whole system, and I noticed that there's a new phone jack right next to it. They were probably planning to use the library for a fax and modem line when they converted this place to offices."

"Does the phone jack work?" Eve held her breath, but Dean shook his head.

"No. I thought of that and I plugged in a phone, but it's not activated yet."

Ryan looked a little concerned. "We've got cable television. Are you sure the cable you saw is a computer cable?"

"I'm almost sure it is," Dean said. "Why don't you check it out? It's on the far wall, opposite the fireplace."

Ryan got up to look and when he came back, he was smiling. "Dean's right. It's a computer cable, and we can split it, five ways. We've got five extra setups. Dean and I can move them to the library and we can all work in there together."

Eve knew where the extra workstations had come from. They'd started with ten students in the workshop, and now five of them were dead. But she didn't mention that because she didn't want to get them all upset again.

"I'm so glad we can all work together!" Angela smiled at Eve and Beth. "I don't know about the rest of you, but I really didn't want to go up to my room to work. I know I'll write a lot better if I'm not nervous about being alone."

"Me, too!" Beth exclaimed.

Eve shivered slightly. She couldn't help wondering which victim's workstation she'd be using. And then she realized what Angela had said. "Wait a minute, Angela. Are you really going to go on with *Ten Little Writers*?"

"Of course I am." Angela looked surprised. "Why shouldn't I keep on writing? If we're all together, protecting each other, nothing can possibly happen."

No one said anything for a long moment, and then

Ryan nodded. "I guess that's true. Maybe I shouldn't bring this up, but who's going to be your next victim?"

"I'm not sure." Angela gave a little sigh. "I almost have to stick to my original plot. The story won't work if I don't. That means it'll have to be either Beth or Dean."

Beth shuddered, and Dean put his arm around her shoulders. "Make it me, Angela."

"All right." Angela gave him a brilliant smile. "You're very brave to volunteer, Dean."

Eve noticed that Dean didn't look brave. He looked terribly nervous. She turned to him with a question in her eyes. "Are you sure, Dean?"

"I'm sure." Dean gave Beth a hug. "I don't have a thing to worry about. I know you'll all watch out for me."

Beth hugged him back, but she didn't look happy. "I'm going to spend every second with you, Dean. You're never going to get out of my sight."

"He's not going to get out of anyone's sight," Eve agreed. "We're all going to stick to Dean like glue. And Angela's going to make his character's murder impossible to duplicate. Isn't that right, Angela?"

"Of course I will." Angela was very serious. "You don't have a thing to worry about, Dean. I'm going to write it so that it can't possibly happen."

WICKED

Ryan and the figures in his tale. "And I'll do thy bidding, Raven," he wou a change to your next victim."

"Do not slay, Angel," gasped Julia with a faint... have to stick to my original plot. The story won't work without being told her friend. "I'll have to do it then Julia told him.

"Fine," Angela grumbled.

"All right," Angela nodded as she bent and smiled. "You're very brave indeed, Dean."

I've noticed that Dean can indeed be very brave, he looked terribly nervous. She turned to him with a...

CHAPTER SIXTEEN

If he hadn't been so scared, Dean would have felt really good. When he'd volunteered to be the next victim in Angela's book, Beth had been very nervous. That meant she cared about him. And Dean had already realized just how much he cared about Beth.

Beth was bright, and pretty, and she understood his music. Dean smiled as he typed another sentence on his computer. He was attempting to write lyrics for one of his songs. That was the hardest part for Dean. The music was easy. His mind was continually filled with melodies. But his lyrics had always been weak.

Beth would help when she read through what he'd written. Dean smiled again as he imagined her pretty brown hair falling over her forehead as they worked at the table. She'd brush it back and then he'd catch a glimpse of her shy smile. Such a gentle smile, filled with goodness. Beth was the girl he'd always dreamed of, the girl he couldn't quite describe in his songs. She'd been a romantic illusion all of

Dean's life, but he'd finally met her. His dream girl was Beth.

Dean had surprised himself when he'd jumped in and said he'd be Angela's next victim. He'd always regarded himself as a physical coward, shying away from confrontations and situations that might lead to ugly scenes. He'd seldom fought back when he was threatened, and the few times he'd taken a stand, he'd ended up losing. Avoidance had been his pattern since grade school, but he'd taken a stand today.

The pride in Beth's eyes had made it all worthwhile. She'd looked up at him like he was some kind of hero, and Dean had felt on top of the world. And then the group had promised to protect him, and Dean was sure they'd do their best.

He'd done it for Beth. There was no way he would have let Angela make Beth her victim. He loved Beth, and he was willing to do anything, even give up his life, to protect her. He just hoped it wouldn't come to that.

Wicked smiled as Angela's words appeared on the computer screen. It had been simple to bring up her file. When Wicked had met the technician, he'd explained the whole system. The library hook-up was unusual. It was the place where they'd eventually install the master computer, capable of interacting with any one of the ten workstations on the second and third floors. The workstations could access the master computer for mailing addresses, copies of letters that the department secretary had sent out, and a line to the Internet although it wasn't working. Since the cable for the master computer was split, it was simple for Wicked to tap into their files to see exactly what they were writing.

There was a frown on Wicked's face as Wicked read Angela's chapter. She'd written another murder, and that was one too many, as far as Wicked was concerned. Killing was exhausting. It took an emotional toll as well as a physical one. Wicked wished that Angela would relax and take a day off, but Angela was a dedicated writer. And now Wicked would have to figure out some way to make her latest murder come true.

Poor Dean. Wicked sighed deeply. Dean actually thought that the group could protect him. Of course they couldn't. Wicked would find a way to outwit them. Dean had volunteered to become the latest victim in Angela's book, and that meant he had to die tonight.

There was one thing that Wicked found very amusing. Although Ryan had suggested that there was another person in the mansion, some kind of a homicidal killer that wanted to turn Angela's story into reality, the members of the group were still eyeing each other with distrust. It was clear they thought that Ryan could be wrong and that one of them might be the killer. The situation would have been laughable if it hadn't been so pathetic. People were social animals and they had to invest a certain amount of trust in each other. When their trust broke down, fear took hold. And fear was the tool that Wicked would use to kill Dean.

* * *

Eve had deliberately taken the workstation next to
Angela, and she nudged Beth as Angela pressed the
button to print. Beth waited a moment, and then she
stood up. "I have to go up to my room for a minute.
I forgot my rhyming dictionary."

"But what about the killer?" Eve looked concerned.

"I'll be safe. My character isn't the victim in
Angela's chapter. Isn't that right, Angela?"

"That's right. Dean's character is."

"I'm coming with you anyway." Eve stood up,
too. "Just in case."

Beth shrugged. "Okay, if it makes you feel better.
Ryan? Will you and Angela stay right here to protect
Dean?"

"Of course."

"But . . . I just printed out and I was going to
collect my pages," Angela said. "You said I should
get them right away."

"That's true, but a minute or two shouldn't make
any difference," Ryan said. "I'll go upstairs with you
when Beth and Eve get back."

Eve waited until they were on the stairs before she
let out a sigh of relief. "We did it, Beth!"

"Yes, we did." Beth gave Eve a smile. "Let's get
her pages and read them fast. We've got to find out
how she killed off Dean's character."

They stopped at the third floor so Beth could grab
her rhyming dictionary, and then they rushed up to
the fourth-floor printer. Angela's pages were in the
tray, and they read them as fast as they could, hand-
ing them back and forth.

When they were finished, Beth turned to Eve.

"Angela did it. She set Dean's murder in a red room on the ground floor. There is no red room, is there?"

"I don't think so, but we're going to check every inch of the ground floor, even the broom closet!"

"Who do you think it is, Eve?" Beth put her hand on Eve's arm. "A stranger? Or . . . or one of us?"

"I don't know. At first, I suspected Angela. I think she'd do anything to get ahead, and her book's bound to be published now. But I changed my mind this afternoon."

"Why?"

"I caught Angela crying after we found Marc. There was no one else around, and she didn't know I was watching her. Why would she cry if she was the one who killed him?"

"She wouldn't. You're right, Eve. It can't be Angela."

"It can't be you, either." Eve smiled at Beth. "You're even more upset than Angela is. And I saw your expression when Angela said that Dean would be her next victim. You were really scared!"

"That's true. How about Dean? Did you ever suspect him?"

"No. Dean's a nice guy, and I can't picture him as a killer. Besides, he wouldn't have offered to be the next victim if he was."

"Ryan?"

"No way!" Eve laughed. "Ryan doesn't even like to kill flies. He always opens a window and tries to shoo them outside."

"I've got a confession to make." Beth looked

embarrassed. "At first I . . . I thought you were the killer."

Eve's eyes widened with surprise. "Me?! But why did you think that?"

"Because Ryan was spending so much time with Angela and I knew you were jealous. And . . . well . . ."

"You don't have to say it." Eve interrupted her. "I know exactly what you thought. You heard about the nasty things I'd done in the past and you thought that I could be capable of murder."

"But I know I was wrong, Eve. You've really changed since you came here. You've even been nice to Angela, and I'm not sure that she deserves it."

"That makes two of us!" Eve gave a little laugh. "I don't think she's the killer, but Angela's still not one of my favorite people. Come on, Beth. Let's get back before they send up a search party."

Beth led the way, but she stopped as she opened the door to the stairwell. "Do you realize we just eliminated everybody from our group? That means the killer has to be a stranger."

Eve followed Beth down the stairs. She really hoped that Beth was right, but she felt very uneasy. Something was hovering at the edge of her consciousness, something frightening, something that would change her mind forever about a member of their group.

Angela didn't understand why she was so nervous. Perhaps it was because they'd tried to spend every moment together since they'd found Marc's body in the greenhouse. Angela liked her privacy. She'd always relished her moments alone. She'd managed to get away for a while, earlier, but she did have to admit that she felt safer when she was surrounded by the group.

They were watching a sitcom, two professional women who wisecracked continually and thought that they were hilarious. When the commercial break arrived, Angela got up. "Does anyone want anything from the kitchen? I'm going in to pop some popcorn."

No one responded and Angela started for the door. But before she could escape to the hallway, Ryan spoke up. "Hold on, Angela. Do you want me to go with you?"

"Why? I'm the author, not the victim. Nobody's going to mess with me!"

Ryan stared at her with surprise, and Angela realized she'd spoken too harshly. "I'm sorry, Ryan. I guess I'm a little jumpy. But what I said is true. I'm perfectly safe."

"Okay. But if you run into anything unusual, call out and we'll come running."

"Thanks. I'll do that." And then she stepped out into the hallway and breathed a big sigh of relief as no one followed her on her way to the kitchen. She needed some time to gather her thoughts and enjoy just being alone.

Eve wouldn't have been pleased if she'd known that she was mirroring Angela's thoughts, but she really needed some time alone. Watching television was a total drag. She was hot and tired, and she really needed to cool off. She stood up and stretched, and then she smiled at all of them. "I'm going for a swim. And don't feel you have to come with me. I'm not the victim for tonight."

"I'd like to go for a swim, too." Beth looked hopeful. "You don't mind company, do you, Eve?"

Eve took one look at Beth's face and she relented. They'd all been watching Dean like hawks, and it was clear that Beth needed a break. "Come on, Beth. Get into your suit and meet me in the pool. Ryan can stay with Dean."

Ryan and Dean watched the end of the sitcom, and Ryan started to surf the channels. He went through three times, and then he handed the control to Dean. "Here, Dean. You find something you want to watch."

"There's nothing on," Dean said. "Tonight's television is lousy."

Ryan grinned. "You said it! Why don't we go in the library and read? There's a whole music section in there if you're interested."

"Really? That sounds better than watching the tube."

Ryan smiled. "You can read, and I'll work on my next chapter. Come on. Let's go."

The lights in the library flickered on, and Eve smiled. She was sitting on the edge of the pool with Beth, and they were dangling their legs in the cool water. "Look at that, Beth. The guys got bored with television, too. Dean's reading and Ryan's working on his computer."

Beth turned to look, and just then the mansion plunged into darkness. Beth gasped and grabbed Eve's arm. "What's happening?!"

"It must be another short." Eve did her best to remain calm. "But we don't have to worry, Beth. The library's paneled in dark wood. It's not a red . . . oh my God!"

"Eve! What's the matter?!"

Beth's voice was shrill, but Eve didn't stop to explain. She just raced across the courtyard and barged into the library through the French doors.

"Ryan? Dean?!"

There was a groan from the far corner of the library and Eve ran to the chair where Dean had been sitting. And then she heard the sound of someone racing across the floor and out, into the hallway.

"Dean? Dean?!" Eve felt her way to the fireplace mantle and grabbed the long matches that were there. She struck one and gasped as she saw Dean sprawled in the chair. "Are you okay, Dean?"

And then Beth was there, cuddling Dean in her arms. And Ryan was standing in the doorway. And Angela was right behind him, wearing a shocked expression.

"He's all right!" Eve couldn't see Beth's expression, but her voice was joyful. "I can hear him breathing. Dean is alive!"

"I'm sorry I left you alone, Dean. " Ryan looked very apologetic as they sat around the table in the courtyard. "The power outage took me by surprise, and I wanted to get to the circuit breaker as fast as I could. I really thought you'd be perfectly safe. I was only a few feet away."

"I don't understand why Dean was attacked in the library," Angela said. "The walls have wood paneling and the doors and ceiling are green. The library's not red."

"Yes, it is." Eve sighed. "The library's filled with books and they'd been read. Don't you get it, Angela?"

Angela looked stunned. "But . . . that's not what I meant, at all! I was talking about the color red. They're even spelled differently."

Dean laughed. Except for a bump on the head and a bad scare, he was fine. "I guess the killer didn't know that."

"It's a good thing Eve thought of it in time!" Beth stroked Dean's forehead. "At least we know our killer's not a writer. He can't spell."

Dean winced a little. "You can't be sure of that. I'm supposed to be a writer, and I'm a lousy speller."

"The color red is R-E-D. And the past tense of the verb 'to read' is R-E-A-D," Beth explained to him.

"Thanks, Beth." Dean grinned at her. "I feel a *lot* better now."

Everyone laughed, even though it wasn't that funny. It was a good way to release the tension they all felt. Dean had come very close to becoming the sixth victim in real life.

Eve looked very thoughtful. "I still think the killer could be a writer. It was a clever pun, and a lot of writers love puns. Just look at Shakespeare's plays. He used a lot of puns."

"You're right, Eve," Angela said. "I'm going to have to be very careful with my next chapter. I can't let the killer turn anything I write into a pun."

Eve was shocked. "You're going on with *Ten Little Writers* after Dean was almost killed?"

"I have to go on. The story's not ended. You don't want me to flunk, do you?"

Angela's violet eyes took on a glow, and Eve shuddered slightly. Angela was actually looking forward to writing another murder! "No, Angela. I don't want you to flunk. But we don't want another murder attempt, either."

"But you managed to protect Dean from the killer. And now I have to rewrite the ending to his chapter. Dean has to wind up as a survivor."

"Are you upset that you have to do a rewrite?" Eve asked. Angela actually looked annoyed because she had to rewrite Dean's chapter.

"No!" Angela was clearly shocked. "It's just that . . . it'll be difficult, that's all. It means I have to change my whole plot. But I can do it, don't worry."

Eve glanced at Ryan. He looked thoroughly disgusted with Angela. "So who's the next victim? If Dean's a survivor, there's only three of us left."

"Well . . . it almost has to be a guy. And there's only one guy left. You don't mind, do you, Ryan?"

"I don't mind at all. As a matter of fact, I was about to suggest it."

"You . . . you can't!" Eve grabbed his arm. "The killer will try to murder you!"

"Exactly! And this time we'll catch him. Don't you see, Eve? It's the only way. We can't leave the mansion, and we're stuck here with no phone. There's no one to help us, so we have to catch the killer ourselves." Ryan turned to Angela. "I want you to start writing tomorrow morning. Set my character's murder in the living room. That's a good spot to set a trap."

"That's a wonderful idea! And it'll fit in with my plot perfectly."

Eve shivered and held Ryan's arm tightly. She knew exactly what he was doing. Ryan was using himself as bait, and somehow she had to stop him!

CHAPTER SEVENTEEN

No one slept very well that night, and when they got up, storm clouds loomed on the horizon. The air was so muggy, it carried an oppressive weight that seemed to sap their energy. Eve felt as if she'd been in a sauna far too long, and she craved a breath of cool, fresh air.

"This is horrible weather!" Angela complained. "The humidity must be a hundred percent. And that makes it feel like it's even hotter than it actually is."

Eve laughed. "It's pretty hot. It's over ninety degrees. And it's going to get a lot hotter before this day is over."

"How about a swim?" Ryan suggested. "We could cool off in the pool."

A swim was a wonderful idea. They all agreed to change to their bathing suits and meet on the deck.

Eve hesitated at the foot of the stairs. She wanted to take a dip in the pool, but she had work to do. Instead of climbing the stairs with the others, she headed for the library and her workstation. She had a chapter to write, all about a horrible murder.

She was writing Angela's next chapter, and the victim wasn't going to be Ryan.

Beth was clearly surprised when she passed the library door and noticed that Eve was working. "Aren't you going to swim with us, Eve?"

"I'll be there in a couple of minutes." Eve smiled at Beth and managed to turn down the contrast on her screen before Beth could catch a glimpse of what she'd written. "I just feel like working for a while."

"Okay. It should be all right as long as you open the French doors to the courtyard. That way, we can keep an eye on you from the pool."

"But Angela hasn't started writing her chapter yet. And she chose Ryan for her next victim. I'm perfectly safe, Beth."

"I know, but it'll make me feel better." Beth gave a little laugh and walked over to hug Eve. "It's ridiculous, but I can't stop worrying."

Eve laughed and hugged Beth back. "You're a mother hen, Beth. When you were a kid, I bet you saved every homeless kitten and puppy on your block."

"That's true. I spent all my allowance on pet food. It used to drive my parents crazy. They never knew how many pets they'd find in the house when they came from work."

"And you found homes for all of them?"

"Oh, yes. My parents used to call our house an animal way station. They didn't seem to mind, though. They understood how happy it made me."

"You must have had wonderful parents. Mine

would have killed me if I'd brought a pet home. It would have interfered with their perfect lives."

"That's too bad, Eve." Beth looked very sad. "But now that you're on your own, you can have a pet if you want to."

"And you've got just the pet for me?"

"As a matter of fact, I do." Beth walked over to the French doors and opened them. "I found a puppy a couple of days before the workshop started. She was half-starved, and my roommates are taking care of her for me. She's half German shepherd and half yellow Lab, and she's got the most beautiful eyes. She'd fit right in at your sorority house."

Eve's sorority sisters would never allow a puppy in the house. "They won't go for it, Beth. We just re-carpeted the whole house, and they'd worry about the mess. But I'll take her. I'd like to have a dog."

"How can you do that?" Beth looked puzzled. "Won't you have to vote on it?"

Eve shook her head, and then she said something that had been on her mind for the past few days. "I'm moving out. I'd rather have my own place."

"You would?" Beth's eyes widened. "But I thought you were going to be the next president!"

"I was, but it's just not important to me anymore. If you can keep the puppy until I find a new place, I'd really like to adopt her."

"Great!" Beth grinned. "You're going to love her, Eve. She's very affectionate, and she needs a good home. And she'll be great protection if you're going to live alone. And speaking of protection, don't work too long. I feel a lot safer when you're with us."

"You do?" Eve was surprised.

"Yes. I don't know how you do it, Eve, but you always manage to keep your head in a crisis. You never panic like I do."

If Beth only knew that her composure was just an act!

"You know what they say about that, don't you, Beth?"

"No. What?"

"If a woman manages to keep her head when everyone around her is losing theirs, she probably just doesn't understand the problem!"

Ryan smiled as he watched Eve through the open doorway. She was working fast, her fingers flying over her computer keyboard. And Eve was so engrossed in what she was writing, she didn't even notice that he was only a few feet away, watching her.

Eve was so beautiful today. Ryan felt his breath catch in his throat. She'd always been beautiful, but there had been something a little off-putting about her before the workshop. Every time he'd seen her, her long, black hair had been perfectly curled and she'd been wearing expensive clothes that looked as if they'd been especially designed for her. For the first few weeks they'd dated, Ryan had been almost afraid to touch Eve. She'd looked like a doll in a showcase, or a glamorous model on assignment, and he hadn't wanted to risk smearing her perfect makeup, or rumpling her perfect hair, or wrinkling her perfect clothing.

She was different now, and Ryan was glad. Eve was much more natural and relaxed. He could tell that appearances no longer mattered quite as much to Eve. As he watched, a lock of hair fell over her forehead and Eve brushed it back impatiently. It happened a second time, and Eve picked up a rubber band from her workstation, pulled her hair back in a casual ponytail, and secured it without even going to a mirror to see if the style was attractive on her.

Her clothes were different, too. Eve was wearing a pair of denim shorts and a tank top that was much too large for her. Ryan thought she looked great, but it was a far cry from the designer outfits she used to wear. Eve was approachable now and even her attitude had changed. She'd always been cool, and aloof, and perfectly poised, not the sort of person who'd give anyone a spontaneous hug or a friendly pat on the back. When Beth had gone into the library a couple minutes ago, he'd seen Eve hug Beth quite naturally and the two of them had laughed together. Eve had changed. She was a much friendlier person now. And Ryan loved her even more than he had before.

As he stood there and watched Eve work, Ryan thought about his own life. He'd always been a loner, just like Eve. Perhaps that was one of the things that had attracted him to her.

Ryan sighed, and a sad expression crossed his face. He'd never had a real family. He'd lived with a succession of relatives when he was growing up, but he'd never felt that he was a real part of their lives. He was poor Ryan, the kid whose parents had died in an auto accident, and they'd done their duty by taking him in.

The fantasy had started when he was in grade

school, living at his uncle's house. Uncle George was a minister, and Ryan had attended the parochial school next to the church. His classmates had avoided him. No one had wanted the minster's nephew for a friend. Lonely, Ryan had invented a friend, a boy who'd been daring and mischievous, the way Ryan had wished he could be. He'd named his friend Tom and they'd held long conversations, alone in Ryan's room.

When Ryan had graduated from parochial school, his uncle had sent him away to a church-run board- ing school. By that time, Ryan had outgrown the need for Tom, but he was still a very private person. Although he'd shared a room with three other boys, Ryan had kept to himself. He'd been the kid who'd always had a book in his hand, the teachers' favorite student. The other boys had tolerated him because he'd helped them study for tests, but no one had really regarded Ryan as a friend.

It was while he was in boarding school that Ryan had developed a love of history. He'd read every history book in the boarding school's library and taken pleasure in studying the campaigns of famous military men. History had become his escape, and he'd received such high grades in his history classes, he'd earned an academic scholarship to college.

In his freshman year, Ryan had enrolled in every history class he could find. He'd been a loner on campus, spending all his time between classes in the college library, and that was where he'd met several fraternity members who'd been cramming for a history test.

Ryan had helped them study, and several weeks

later, he'd been asked to join the fraternity. Ryan had accepted, hoping that his frat brothers might become the family he'd never had. Life in the frat house had been good, but Ryan had never felt the closeness that the other frat brothers seemed to feel.

Last semester, Ryan had taken a seminar in the history of psychology, and that was where he'd met Eve. They'd studied together several times, and Ryan had found himself falling in love, despite the advice of his fraternity brothers. They'd warned him that Eve would break his heart, but that hadn't happened. Perhaps Eve had sensed some need in him that only she could fill. He'd sensed that about her, too. They were both struggling to be accepted, each in their own way. Ryan tried to do it by being amiable, tutoring his frat brothers whenever they asked and never saying no to any of their requests. Eve was different. She was like an Old West gunfighter, stepping out with both barrels blazing and demanding that everyone accept her exactly as she was.

Some people would say that they were both emotional cripples, but Ryan didn't think that was the case. It was a matter of building a strong base, of feeling safe enough to reach out to others. As a couple, they'd done each other a lot of good. Eve had influenced him to assert himself, to say no to something he really didn't want to do, even if it meant being rejected by the person who'd asked. And he had softened Eve. She was friendlier now, less confrontational, more willing to make compromises.

A smile flickered across Ryan's face. They were making new friends as a couple. Beth and Dean were examples. And now that they had two new friends, they'd make others. They'd have their own circle of people they truly cared about, almost like an extended family. Ryan knew it would work out just as long as they all could survive until the quarantine was lifted.

Low thunder rumbled overhead, and lightning flashed in the distance as Eve typed her final sentence. It was a good thing that she was a good speller because there was no time to run the spelling program. If the lightning struck a power line, it could knock out the whole system and she wouldn't be able to print out.

Eve pressed the button that sent her work to the printer, and then she leaned back and stretched. She'd done her best to copy Angela's style and write a truly chilling murder. If the killer thought that Angela had written the chapter, everything would work out perfectly. Since Ryan wasn't the victim in Eve's chapter, he would be safe.

Thunder growled in the darkening sky. It sounded like some sort of prehistoric monster, and Eve shivered. The storm was rolling in, the storm she'd written about in her chapter. It would be a dark and stormy night, a perfect night for a murder.

What would Angela say when she found out what Eve had done? Eve thought about it for a moment, and then she gave a short, sarcastic laugh. Angela wouldn't see the big picture, how Eve had tried to save Ryan's life. Angela had an ego that just wouldn't quit, and she'd be angry that Eve had written a chapter in her book.

Brave, but foolish. The phrase kept running through Eve's mind. Some people might say she was brave for trying to save Ryan from the killer. They could be right. Eve just wasn't sure. But others would say she was very foolish for taking Ryan's place and setting herself up as the next victim.

CHAPTER EIGHTEEN

There was a shocked expression on Wicked's face as Angela's newest chapter rolled out of the printer. It was a total surprise. Angela had changed her plot. Her newest victim wasn't Ryan. It was Eve!

Long moments passed while Wicked read. This chapter was very good, and the setting for Eve's murder was perfect. Of course it would present a huge problem, and Wicked would have to be very clever to make it all work the way that Angela had written it.

Wicked replaced the pages in the tray and headed for the stairs. It was time to go to the regular room and let the bright side out again. There would be time to plan Eve's murder later, and it would take some thought. Wicked wasn't entirely sure what would happen tonight, but it was bound to be an experience that no one would ever forget!

Everyone had gone up to change their clothes, and now they were all gathered out in the courtyard again, sitting around their favorite round table. Eve had joined them, and they were all watching the storm clouds roll in and the lightning flash across the sky.

Angela stood up. "I'd better get to work. I've got a whole chapter to write."

"That's not a very good idea." Ryan looked up as another lightning bolt flashed across the sky above them.

"But I have to work." Angela looked very upset. "I have to write my chapter before tonight!"

Ryan shook his head. "Not while there's an electrical storm going on. We could blow out the motherboard on the computer if lightning strikes while you're working."

"But how can you set a trap for the killer if I don't write my chapter? You've got to let me do it!"

Eve grinned. She was about to drop her bombshell, and she could hardly wait to see the expression on Angela's face. "You don't have to work, Angela. Your chapter's already written."

"What do you mean?!"

Angela's voice was high and shrill, and Eve reached out to take her arm. "Sit down, Angela. And calm down. I wrote a fake chapter, that's all."

"You wrote *my* next chapter?!"

Angela was glaring and Eve patted her arm. "Relax, Angela. And don't worry. I'll tear up my chapter and you can write the real one, right after we catch the killer."

"Come on, Angela. . . . Loosen up." Ryan draped his arm around Angela's shoulders. "Eve did us all a favor. There's nothing to get mad about."

"But . . . it's *my* plot. And it's *my* book!"

"You're absolutely right," Eve said. "And I know my chapter's not half as good as the one you're going to write. But I couldn't wait, Angela. The storm was coming, and I had to get it done."

Angela didn't look quite so angry. "You don't think your chapter's very good?"

"No. It's not very good at all. You're the best writer, Angela."

Angela gave Eve a small smile. She was obviously placated by Eve's compliment. "Where did you set the murder, Eve?"

"In the stairwell."

"The stairwell?" Angela looked amused. "Why did you do that?"

"Because I thought it might be a good place to trap the killer. We can split into two groups. One group can be at the top of the stairs and the other group can be at the bottom."

"Not bad. Of course, I wouldn't have set it there, but it might work. What floor is Ryan's character near?"

"I didn't say. But it's not Ryan's character, it's mine."

"Yours?" Ryan's mouth dropped open. "Eve! What have you done?!"

"Somebody's already read these pages." Ryan pulled Eve's work out of the printer. "They're upside down."

Beth's eyes widened and she shuddered. "The killer?"

"Who else?" Eve tried for a jaunty tone, but her voice was shaking slightly.

"Has anyone else been up here?" Ryan turned to the group. They shook their heads, one by one, and Ryan put his arm around Eve. "The killer's going to be after you, Eve. And I'm not letting you out of my sight!"

Even though Eve didn't regret her decision, she was beginning to get very nervous. "That's fine with me, Ryan."

"We're going to watch Eve, too," Beth offered. "Isn't that right, Dean?"

"Right. We'll help you protect her, Ryan."

"I'll help, too." Angela spoke up just as soon as she realized that everyone had turned to look at her. "That goes without saying. You must be terrified, Eve."

Eve tried for a brave shrug, but it didn't quite work. "I don't know if I'm terrified, but I'm certainly a little nervous."

"A little nervous?" Beth gave a shaky laugh. "If I were you, I'd be a basket case! But you don't have to worry, Eve. We're not going to leave you alone for any reason, and that's a promise."

"You'll have to leave me alone. The killer's got to have a chance to murder me. I'm the bait for your trap."

"Eve's right." Ryan looked sick, but he nodded.

"Come on. Let's go downstairs." Beth took Eve's hand and headed for the stairs. "Just knowing that the killer was standing right here at the printer is giving me the creeps!"

They gathered up flashlights, candles, and matches and then they all headed back out to the courtyard. It

made them feel better to be outside, even though the
storm was threatening.

"Okay." Ryan set their supplies in the center of the
round table. "We've got three flashlights and two
candles. Who wants what?"

Angela yawned. "I'll take a flashlight, and then
I'm going up to my room to take a nap. It's going to
be a long night."

"But aren't you nervous about leaving the group?"
Beth shivered a little.

"Of course not." Angela shrugged. "I've never been
a victim in any of my chapters. I'm perfectly safe."

Ryan looked very thoughtful when Angela left,
and then he turned to Eve. "Do you want a flashlight,
or a candle?"

"A candle. I was carrying one in my chapter—it'll
be more authentic."

"Oh, Eve!" Beth shivered. "I don't know how you
can be so brave."

"It's not bravery, Beth. I figure we're just going to
get one chance at this, and I want to do everything
right."

"Maybe we'd better read over the chapter one
more time." Dean looked concerned. "Eve's got a
point. We want to do everything right."

Ryan agreed. "I left it in the printer tray. I'd better
go back up and get it."

"We'll stay right here with Eve." Beth looked very
serious.

"That's a promise," Dean said. "If the killer tries anything while you're gone, he'll have to go through us."

* * *

Ryan's heart was pounding hard as he raced back up to the fourth floor. He hadn't left the pages in the printer. They were right on the table, under the box with the candles and the flashlights. But Angela had been very insistent about going to her room, and that made Ryan suspicious. She'd been upset that Eve had written her chapter and she might write a new one, even though he'd warned her not to use her computer during the storm. Ryan was going to disable the printer, just in case. He certainly didn't want to confuse the killer with more than one victim!

The printer was on a stand with wheels, and Ryan rolled it away from the wall. He found the cable that connected it to the workstations and started to loosen it when he noticed something strange. There was a telephone cord plugged into the back of the printer.

Ryan's heart beat fast as he traced the wire to a brand-new phone jack in the wall. The printer was set up to act as a fax machine, and fax machines usually had dedicated lines. If this wasn't the main line that ran into the house, it might still be active. And if it was, he could send a fax to the campus police!

Five minutes later, Ryan was hurrying down the stairs again. He'd typed in a message on Eve's workstation and sent the fax. The message had been short and to the point. *Writers' workshop quarantined at Sutler Mansion. Phone out. Five murdered. Send help!* As soon as Eve's monitor had indicated that the fax had been sent, he'd rushed back up to the fourth floor and disabled the printer.

Ryan made up his mind as stepped out into the courtyard. He wasn't going to tell them what he'd done. If he was wrong and the fax line wasn't active, he didn't want to get their hopes up. They might relax a little and let down their guard, and he wanted them all to be alert to protect Eve. If he was right, help would soon be on the way, and that couldn't be too soon to suit him!

The two officers were just going out the door when they heard the fax machine ring. The younger officer stopped, as if to go back, but his partner shook his head. "We'll catch it later. It's probably a message from the chief about wearing full uniforms to work. What we don't know won't hurt us."

"Right." The younger officer grinned. "I sure don't want to wear a tie on a night like this. It's got to be a hundred degrees out there."

His partner motioned him out the door and locked the office door. "What have we got for tonight?"

"Professor Ryskind wants us to check the animal lab." The younger officer glanced at his clipboard as they climbed into the squad car. "The storm's got her white rats freaked out."

His partner laughed. "Okay, but what are we supposed to do once we get there?"

"Give them extra food. She says it'll settle them right down."

"Oh, great!" His partner laughed. "What else?"

The younger officer glanced at his clipboard again. "We're supposed to check the back door to the men's gym. The coach says some homeless guy's been hanging around. They think he's been sleeping in the locker room."

"And they want us to arrest him for trespassing?"

"No." The younger officer grinned. "We're supposed to get him a blanket and a pillow from the coach's office. The coach says he's harmless and nobody should be out on a night like this."

"Are there any other poor souls we have to rescue?"

"Just one." The younger officer laughed. "We have to go over to Phi Delta Epsilon. Their cat's in a tree and they can't get it down."

His partner put the car into gear, and they drove away from the station. Lightning flashed across the sky and thunder rumbled overhead.

"We're in for a big one." The younger officer frowned slightly. "They're saying it's going to be the storm of the century."

"It sure looks that way. Let's get that cat down before it starts to rain."

The younger officer jumped as lightning struck a tree they were passing. It was followed, almost immediately, by a crash of thunder so loud that both officers winced. "At least we don't have to worry about any crimes. Nobody's going to go out tonight."

"That's true. But we never have any real crimes here. I've been a campus cop ever since I retired from the force, and the biggest thing that ever came down was some guy trying to sneak a bottle of booze into a football game."

"No real crimes?"

"Well . . ." His partner shrugged. "We did make one arrest about five years back, some guy trying to break into a car."

"But that's a real crime." The younger officer looked interested.

"Actually, it wasn't. It turned out to be his girlfriend's car, and she'd locked her keys inside by mistake. After she came down to the station and explained the whole thing, we let him go."

"Maybe we'll get a big case someday . . . like a murder."

"Here?" His partner laughed. "You've got to be kidding. This is a private college with good little rich kids. The biggest crime they'll ever commit is pocketing a salt shaker from the cafeteria!"

CHAPTER NINETEEN

It would be difficult to turn Angela's newest chapter into reality, but Wicked was the only one who was smart enough to do it. They were watching Eve, protecting her, and Wicked had to find a way to lure them away. It would take some careful planning, but Wicked could do it. The storm was a real help. The rain was coming down hard, splattering against the windowpanes with a loud drumming sound that would mask any noise that Wicked made. And since they'd all gone inside when the rain had started, Wicked's job would be even easier.

Jeremy had tried to fool them by using a tape recorder, and Wicked planned to use the same method. Wicked had taken Jeremy's tape recorder, and it was a perfect tool to lure Eve's friends away. The plan would work. Wicked was sure of it. Angela's newest chapter would turn into fact, and Eve would die tonight.

* * *

Eve sat in the middle of the couch with Beth on one side and Ryan on the other. Dean was across from them, in a wing chair he'd moved to a spot where he could watch the doors and windows. The storm was raging outside, and they'd all been thoroughly drenched as they'd dashed into the house. Ryan had started a fire in the fireplace, but Eve was still shivering.

"Do you want a blanket, Eve?" Ryan hugged her a little tighter.

"No. That's okay. I'm warming up now." Eve did her best to smile. There was no way she'd admit that she was actually shivering from fright.

"I wish Angela would come down." Beth sighed. "The more people we have to watch Eve, the safer she'll be."

Ryan shook his head. "Actually, we're probably better off without her."

"Why?" Dean looked surprised.

"Because Angela always tries to be the center of attention and we need to concentrate on Eve."

"You're right," Beth agreed. "If Angela were here, she'd just distract us. But I'm a little worried about her, upstairs all alone. I know she's not the victim, but what if the killer decides that Eve's too hard to kill? He might go after Angela, instead."

"He wouldn't do that." Ryan shook his head. "He's always followed Angela's chapters. Serial killers don't break their patterns. It's a part of their sickness."

"Maybe that's true, but I agree with Beth," Eve

said. "I think we should all go up to get Angela. I'd feel a lot better if she were here."

"But why?" Dean looked puzzled. "Maybe I'm wrong, but I got the impression that you didn't like Angela."

"You're not wrong. I don't like Angela very much, but I'm still concerned about her."

Just then there was a brilliant flash of lightning that lit up the whole living room as bright as day. It was followed by a mighty crash of thunder, and then a loud snap that plunged the room into darkness.

"Oh, oh!" Ryan groaned. "I think that one hit a power line. Grab your flashlights and candles. They're right in the middle of the coffee table."

Ryan turned on his flashlight, and Eve gave a sigh of relief. Things weren't quite as scary when they had a source of light. Then Dean's flashlight clicked on, and Eve felt even better.

Dean aimed his light at the table so he could pick up the candles and books of matches. "Beth? Here's your candle and matches. And Eve? Here's yours."

Eve tried to steady her hand as she struck a match, but she was trembling so much, she almost dropped her candle.

"Let me do it for you, Eve." Ryan struck a match and lit Eve's candle.

Eve smiled as she took the candle. "Thanks. I really hate storms like this!"

"So do I. They always remind me of horror stories where . . ." Beth's voice trailed off, and she gave Eve an apologetic glance. "I'm sorry, Eve. I don't want to make you more nervous."

Eve gave a shaky laugh. "That's impossible. I'm already as nervous as I can get."

Beth winced as a drop of hot wax fell on her hand. "I really wish we had holders for these candles. They're going to drip wax all over."

"There's a pair of silver candlestick holders on the piano." Dean got up from his chair. "Hold on a second. I'll get them."

They all watched the beam of Dean's flashlight as he crossed the room to get the candlestick holders. A moment later, he was back, and he handed one to Eve and one to Beth.

"Drip some wax in the bottom, Beth." Eve showed her how. "The bottom of the candle will stick in the wax, and it won't fall out if you tip . . ."

Eve's advice was interrupted by another crash of thunder. The storm was growing worse. And then there was a horrible sound that made them all jump.

"What was that?!" Eve swallowed hard.

Ryan reached out to take Eve's arm. "It was probably just a branch scraping against a window. The wind's blowing hard outside."

"Are you sure?" Eve was still worried. It hadn't sounded like a branch to her.

"I'm sure. The storm's making us all a little jumpy, and we're overreacting to . . ."

Ryan stopped in midsentence as they heard the sound again. And then again.

"That was no branch." Beth shivered. "It was a scream."

"You're right," Ryan said. "I think it came from upstairs."

"Angela!" Dean jumped to his feet. "Come on, everybody. We've got to make sure she's all right."

Ryan grabbed Dean's arm. "Hold it, Dean. This could be a trap. I'll go up first. Eve? I want you right behind me, one step down. And Beth? You get behind Eve. Dean'll bring up the rear."

"We'd better arm ourselves." Dean picked up a fireplace poker and handed it to Ryan. "I'll take a piece of wood. I can swing it like a bat."

They all nodded. It was a good plan. But Eve was very nervous as they started up the dark stairwell. Although the guys searched the shadow with their flashlights, it was still very frightening.

"It's so quiet." Beth whispered as they climbed up to the second floor. "It's really . . . eerie."

Eve didn't say anything. She was too busy straining her ears for the sounds of someone moving or breathing in the darkness.

They reached the second-floor landing, and Ryan stopped. "Okay. One floor to go. We'll take it slow, and if anyone hears anything, call out and stop dead in your tracks."

"Please don't say dead," Eve said, trying for a little humor, and everyone laughed nervously. And then they started up the stairs again, to the third floor.

It took at least five minutes to reach the landing, and Ryan made sure they were all ready when he opened the stairwell door. The sound of the storm assaulted their ears, and it was almost a relief from the eerie silence of the stairwell. Lightning streaked through the window at the end of the hallway and lit up the entire hall with flashes of brilliant light. It was almost like watching a giant strobe light, and Eve was afraid to blink for fear she'd miss some danger that lurked in a corner.

They stopped at Angela's door. It was closed, and Ryan pushed it open. "Angela? Are you all right?"

But Angela wasn't in her room. Her bed was rumpled, her quilt was on the floor, and there was a strange smell in the air. It was something familiar, but Eve couldn't quite place it. And then Ryan's flashlight illuminated a trail of dark red leading from the bed to the door.

"That looks like blood!" Eve's voice was shaking as she pointed to the trail. "Angela's hurt and the killer's got her!"

Ryan took Eve's arm. "We'd better split up to look for Angela. It looks like she's losing a lot of blood. I'll take Eve with me and we'll search the second floor. You guys check all the rooms on this floor and wait at the stairwell door for us."

Eve shuddered as they went down the stairs again. She didn't understand why the killer had targeted Angela, but this wasn't the time to ask questions. They had to find Angela fast, before she bled to death.

They'd just checked the last room on the second floor when they heard another scream. Ryan pulled Eve close to him and listened intently. There was another scream, a few seconds later, and Ryan pulled Eve toward the stairwell. "He's got her out in the courtyard!"

"Let's go!" Eve stepped through the door, but Ryan grabbed her arm.

"No, Eve. I'm going to send you back up to Dean and Beth where you'll be safe."

"I don't understand why I can't go with you. You might need some help."

Ryan shook his head. "I won't take you with me, Eve. It's too dangerous. Just do what I say . . . please?"

"Okay." Ryan was still concerned about protecting her, and that made her feel good. He didn't realize that she could hold her own in a fight, but this wasn't the time to convince him. Angela was in trouble, and there wasn't a moment to waste.

"Dean? Beth?" Ryan called out.

"We're here." Dean's voice floated down the stairwell. "Did you find her?"

"She's out in the courtyard, and I'm going down there. Stay right there, and I'll send Eve up to you."

Wicked smiled as Eve started to climb the stairs. Her face was illuminated by the flickering candle she carried, and she didn't look at all frightened. Wicked's plan had worked perfectly. Everyone had assumed that the killer was out in the courtyard with Angela.

Eve hesitated on the third step. That made Wicked feel good. Her candle was trembling in her hand. She was beginning to get a little nervous. Wicked knew she was remembering Angela's chapter and where her murder had taken place. Eve would die on the staircase, exactly as Angela had written it. Wicked would make her fiction turn into fact.

But Eve still didn't look nervous enough to give Wicked any real satisfaction. Wicked wanted to see the fear that would wash over Eve's features and make her beautiful face turn ugly with terror.

It was hard to wait, and Wicked gripped the knife

tightly. Patience was a virtue, and Wicked would wait until Eve rounded the bend in the staircase. That was when she would see Wicked. Her candle would illuminate Wicked's long, sharp knife, and Eve would gasp in horror. Very soon now, Eve Carrington would realize that she was all alone with her worst nightmare.

It was too quiet in the stairwell, and Eve found that her legs were shaking as she climbed up another step. The same strange smell that she'd noticed in Angela's room hovered in the stuffy air. Sour and sweet with a hint of spice. Eve wasn't sure what it was, but it seemed somehow ominous.

She didn't like this. Eve climbed up another step, and then she opened her mouth to call out for Beth and Dean. They could meet her on the stairs. But Eve didn't want them to know that she was frightened for no reason at all. The killer was out in the courtyard with Angela. He couldn't be two places at once. She was perfectly safe. All she had to do was climb up the stairs and push open the door, and Beth and Dean would be there.

Eve stopped and listened. Her imagination must be working overtime, because she thought she could hear the sound of faint breathing. It seemed to come from above, right past the bend in the staircase. But there was no one here, no one but her. And she only had a few more steps to go.

Ketchup. That was the smell. Eve began to smile as she recognized it. But who had spilled ketchup on the stairs? And why had she smelled it in Angela's room?

Eve climbed up another step, puzzling over the smell. Ketchup. They used it in the movies because it looked like blood. But if it had been ketchup in Angela's room, instead of blood . . .

Eve stopped cold. Something was wrong. Her mouth felt dry and she swallowed. Ketchup. Blood. Angela. The sound of faint breathing. Some instinct made Eve raise her candle high enough to see beyond the bend. And what she saw made her eyes widen in surprise.

"Angela?!" Eve gasped as she saw Angela's face. "We've been looking all over for you! Are you hurt?"

But Angela didn't answer. She just rose slowly to her feet. And then she smiled a terrible smile.

Suddenly Eve remembered what had been hovering at the edge of her mind. Angela had smiled this smile before, when she'd goaded Eve to go into the walk-in cooler. She'd seemed like a different person then, and Eve had realized that Angela had a mean side. But what if this wasn't just a mean side? What if Angela truly had a split personality? And what if Angela was the killer?

Eve didn't stop to consider whether she was right or wrong. She just started to back down the stairs. "Angela? Are you all right?"

"I'm not Angela. I'm Wicked. And you're the next to die!"

Angela lunged forward and Eve reacted instantly. She blew out her candle and pressed herself back, against the opposite wall. She heard Angela stumble in the darkness, but Eve didn't wait to see if she'd fallen. Eve just whirled and ran back down to the second floor. She had to get away from Angela!

A flash of lightning illuminated the hallway as Eve raced toward Ryan's room. She ducked in, shut the door behind her, and pushed a chair in front of it to wedge it shut.

She was safe! Eve's knees went suddenly weak, and she crumpled to the floor. Angela was a classic case of a split personality. One side of her was nice, trying to be friendly to everyone. And the other side was a maniacal killer.

Long moments passed in silence, and Eve began to take heart. Had she managed to elude Angela? But then Eve heard something that made her heart leap up to hear throat. It was the sound of Angela's footsteps, coming down the hallway, as sure and certain as death, itself. And Angela's voice, barely a whisper, speaking the words that made Eve's blood run cold.

"I know you're here, Eve. You can't hide from me. Wicked will find you. Wicked will kill you. Come out, come out, wherever you are."

CHAPTER TWENTY

Beth gave an unhappy sigh as she sat on the couch with Dean. "I still think Eve should have told us they changed their minds and she was going outside with Ryan."

"You're right. I'm glad Angela came up to tell us. It was funny about the ketchup, wasn't it?"

Beth laughed. "I never dreamed that Angela was the type to scream when she saw a mouse. And I still can't believe she got so scared, she dropped the ketchup bottle and climbed down the fire escape to get away."

"It's pretty incredible." Dean laughed, too. "Did she tell you why she had a ketchup bottle in her room?"

"For her sandwich. Angela's got some weird eating habits. I wouldn't put ketchup on a tuna fish sandwich, would you?"

Dean shook his head. "Not on a bet! Mustard

maybe, but definitely not ketchup. Did Angela say how long they'd be working out there?"

"Not exactly, but it's going to take a while."

"Maybe we should give that mouse a medal." Dean started to laugh. "If Angela hadn't climbed down the fire escape, we wouldn't have known about those clogged courtyard drains, and the whole house could have flooded."

"That's true. I feel kind of guilty about not helping, but Angela said to stay here and keep the fire going. They'll all need to warm up when they come in."

"I think we got the best job." Dean put his arm around Beth's shoulders. "At least we're not out there in the rain, getting soaked."

"I just thought of something. Angela wasn't wet when she came up to tell us they were all outside. Even her hair was dry."

"She probably had a raincoat." Dean pulled Beth a little closer. "Stop borrowing trouble, Beth. Everything's going to be just fine."

The younger officer made a dash to unlock the door and held it open so his partner could enter. They were both dripping wet, but they were still smiling.

"How did you know what to do with that cat?" The younger officer hung up his jacket to dry and plopped down in his desk chair.

"My sister used to have a cat that climbed trees.

When the girls said it'd been up there all day, I figured a bowl of food would do the trick."

"I guess that's all the excitement we're going to get for the night. We rescued the cat, bedded down the homeless guy in the gym, and fed Professor Ryskind's rats."

"Oh, I don't know about that." His partner motioned toward the fax machine. "Better check the fax that came in right before we left. Maybe we've got a serial killer on the loose."

"Right." The younger officer got up and walked to the fax machine. "The chief probably wants us to write out reports in triplicate instead of dupli . . . oh my God!"

"What is it?"

"It's from someone named Ryan Young at the Sutler Mansion. He says they've got five homicides over there!"

Eve held her breath as she heard another door close. Angela had checked three rooms and now she was heading straight for Ryan's. The doorknob rattled, and there was a muffled exclamation. And then Eve heard Angela's laugh.

"I've got you now, Eve!" Angela's voice was a hissing whisper. "You can't hide from Wicked!"

Eve shuddered. Angela was insane. That much was very clear. She was a classic case of a split personality, the kind that Eve had only read about. Wicked was the bad side, the violent side. And Wicked was out. Somehow, she had to bring Angela back.

"Angela?" Eve called out. "Where are you, Angela?"

There was silence from the other side of the door. And then a sweet, calm voice spoke. "Eve? What are you doing in Ryan's room?"

It was Angela. Eve breathed a sigh of relief. "I'm just sitting here thinking. Why don't you go down and make us both a cup of hot chocolate? When you come back up, we'll talk for a while."

"Yes. I can do that. Come with me, Eve. I don't want to be alone."

Eve was about to open the door when she reconsidered. Was this really Angela? There was only one way to tell. Eve knelt down and looked through the keyhole.

Just then another flash of lightning cut across the sky. It illuminated the hallway, and Eve gasped as she saw Angela's face. Angela was beautiful, but the creature who stood outside the door had blazing eyes and a mouth twisted up like a silent scream. Wicked was imitating Angela's voice, and she had a knife in her hand!

"Angela? I need you now." Eve stepped away from the door. "You've got to be strong and come out."

There was a sound from the other side of the door, a terrible struggle. Cries and moans filled the air, and then there was a strangled gasp of pain.

"Angela?" Eve drew in her breath sharply. "Angela! Are you all right?"

And then another voice answered Eve, a voice that sent shudders up and down her back. "You tried to trick me! And now Angela's dead! You killed my bright side, and I'm going to kill you!"

Eve's eyes widened as a mighty blow almost shattered the door. The chair she'd wedged under the doorknob wouldn't hold for long. Eve had to do something to escape. But what? There was only one way out, and that was the door. And if she opened the door, Wicked would kill her just like she'd killed the others. The only other way out of Ryan's room was . . .

The balcony! Eve rushed to open the French doors. Perhaps she could hide behind something. But there was nowhere to hide on Ryan's balcony. He didn't even have any patio furniture.

Eve stepped to the trail and looked down with a shudder. It was only a one-story drop to the courtyard below, but it still made Eve feel dizzy. She'd always been terrified of heights. The pool was directly below her, its surface dimpled with the falling rain. Eve knew it was possible to climb over the rail and drop down into the pool. But could she force herself to do it?

Eve turned as she heard the chair legs scraping against the floor. So what if she was terrified of heights? She was even more terrified of Wicked. Eve made her hands reach out and grip the rail. She had to gather the courage to jump!

There was a crash as the chair toppled. Wicked was in Ryan's room! Eve didn't stop to consider what might happen when she hit the water. She just forced her shaking legs to climb over the rail and she dropped out into space.

A strange thing happened when Eve hit the surface of the water. She thought she heard voices, lots of them, and sirens screaming in the distance. And then strong arms were pulling her from the water, Ryan's arms.

"Are you all right, Eve?"

Eve had read about what happened to some people who'd had a near-death experience. They heard the voices of the people they cared about, and they saw the faces of their loved ones as they went to meet them in the bright white light. This was Ryan's voice. Eve was sure of that. And she could see his face. And there was a strong white light beckoning them as he carried her from the pool.

"Eve?"

Eve tried to smile. "Ryan. Am I dead?"

"No, Eve. You're just fine. But just in case, we'd better let the paramedics check you out."

As Ryan set her on her feet, Eve caught sight of her reflection in the library window. Her hair was hanging in limp, wet strands, her blouse was torn from climbing over the rail, and her denim shorts hung on her like a pair of bloomers. She looked like a drowned rat.

She turned to Ryan. "Oh my God! Just look at me!"

"I am." Ryan smiled at her. "You look beautiful, Eve."

Eve's eyes widened. Ryan just had to be kidding! But he looked completely sincere as he brushed a lock of wet hair from her forehead. That was when Eve realized the source of the bright white light. An enterprising reporter from Channel Seven had climbed over the fence at the back of the property. A cameraman was with him, and they were taping the whole scene for the evening news!

Eve couldn't help it. She started to laugh. For the first time in her life, she didn't care at all about her appearance. She was alive, and Ryan thought she looked beautiful. And wasn't that all that really counted?

EPILOGUE

It was Christmas Eve, and they were giving their first Christmas party. Eve had been serious about moving out of the sorority house, and she'd convinced Beth to pool their resources so they could move into a rental house just off campus. Of course they had pets, five of them to be exact. Eve had the puppy Beth had told her about, Beth had brought her own dog, and they were bottle-feeding three abandoned kittens until they were old enough to be adopted.

Eve was in the kitchen, making appetizers. The holiday season was a time to be with friends, and Eve felt a little melancholy. Five of her friends were dead, victims of the tragedy at the Sutler Mansion. She thought about Cheryl and Tracie, and she smiled a sad smile. They would have loved this party. Scott would have come. And Marc. And even Jeremy, although Eve was sure he wouldn't have missed the opportunity to play another practical joke. Jeremy would have hung an ornament that exploded with worms or something equally gross on their Christmas tree.

"Do you need some help, Eve?" Ryan came into the kitchen just as Eve was taking a tray of baked appetizers out of the oven.

"I think I've got it under control." Eve arranged the appetizers on a tray. "You can start passing these around if you want to."

"Okay. But first, a kiss for the cook." Ryan bent over and kissed Eve lightly on the lips. It was a sweet kiss, a social kiss, but it promised much more when the party was over.

"I talked to Professor Hellman today." Eve smiled. "He's got some good news about your book. They're going to publish it, Ryan. And you're going to get an advance!"

Ryan grinned from ear to ear. "That's great! How about yours?"

"Not yet." Eve shook her head. "We're still working on the rewrite, but Professor Hellman thinks it shows promise."

"Anything about Dean's rock-opera?"

"Yes, and no." Eve smiled. "He's gotten a couple of nibbles, but there's real interest in the songs he wrote with Beth. They've already sold three."

"And Beth's poems?"

"One should be out next month." Eve looked very happy for her friend. "She doesn't get any money. It's a literary magazine, and they pay her in extra copies. But Beth's really thrilled."

"Good for her! I probably shouldn't bring this up, but what did you find out about . . . well . . . you know."

"Angela?"

"How is she doing?"

"Not very well. I talked to her psychiatrist at Shadybrook Sanitarium, and he explained the whole thing to me. Angela really wanted to write fiction, Ryan, but her parents didn't approve. She used to write anyway, locked in her room, hiding what she wrote from them. By the time she graduated from high school, she'd finished a whole book. And that book was *Ten Little Writers*."

Ryan looked surprised. "You mean she wrote it *before* she came to the workshop?"

"That's right. It's the reason why Angela could work so fast. Didn't you ever wonder how she had time to write her chapters when she was so busy helping everyone else? And didn't you think it was strange that her chapters were so professional?"

"I didn't think about it at the time, but you're right. No wonder they were so good! She'd had all that time to perfect them. But Angela didn't even know us before she got to the workshop. How did she put us in her book?"

"She didn't. Angela just substituted our names for the characters she'd already written. Her book was set in a mansion so she didn't have to change that. It was a simple revision, Ryan. It probably didn't take her more than five minutes. And then she just printed it out."

Ryan sighed. "It really was a good book. Did her parents ever read it?"

"Yes. Angela finally got the courage to show it to them. They read it, but they didn't like it. They told her she'd wasted her time and she should be working on something more serious than fiction. That's when Angela began the split."

"Split personality?"

"Exactly." Eve did her best to explain. "Angela was an only child, and her parents were away a lot. She already had an imaginary playmate. A lot of only children do."

Ryan looked surprised. "I was an only child, and I used to pretend I had a friend. His name was Tom, and he did all the things I wished I could do. Is that an imaginary playmate?"

"It sounds like it." Eve smiled at him. "Mine was Margo, and she was really horrible. I blamed her for every nasty thing I did. I outgrew it, but Angela didn't. Her imaginary playmate turned into Wicked."

"Wicked?"

"Wicked is Angela's alter ego. It's the dark side of her personality. Angela really wanted to please her parents, but she also wanted to write fiction. She felt guilty about what she was writing, and that's when Wicked came out. Wicked tried to protect Angela from her parents' displeasure."

"By turning her fiction into fact?"

"That's right. Before the workshop started, Wicked talked to the technician who installed our computer network. He told her the printer had a huge memory, and he showed her how to duplicate the pages we'd already printed out. That's how Wicked knew who Angela's victims would be."

"You mean Wicked didn't know what Angela was writing? Even though Wicked and Angela are the same person?"

"That's right. And they're not the same person,

Ryan. They just share the same body. Angela didn't know what Wicked was doing. She was just as horrified as we all were when the victims in her book started to die in real life."

Ryan looked confused. "But . . . how is that possible?"

"The psychiatrist said it's like a coin, placed flat on a tabletop. When one side faces up, you can't see the other. Angela had no awareness of Wicked. She didn't even know that Wicked existed. Angela's bright side, the real Angela, has a conscience. Wicked doesn't, and that's why that side of Angela's personality was capable of murder."

"That's pretty sick, isn't it?"

"I'm afraid so." Eve sighed. "Her psychiatrist told me he's trying to get in touch with Angela's bright side again, to bring her out so she's the dominant personality. But so far, he hasn't had any luck."

"Is there any hope that she'll get better?"

"Her psychiatrist thinks so. He's trying drug therapy and hypnosis, but Angela's bright side is still dormant. Wicked has control of Angela's body. And as long as Wicked is dominant, Angela will have to stay behind locked doors."

Ryan hugged Eve. "That's too bad, but I'm relieved. I'll never forget how Angela tried to kill you."

"It wasn't Angela. It was Wicked," Eve corrected him. "Angela was a really nice person with a lot of problems."

"Hey . . . let's change the subject. I didn't want to put your Christmas present under the tree. There's just too many people here. I wanted to give it to you when we were alone."

"Thank you, Ryan." Eve took the small, gift-wrapped box he handed to her. She unwrapped it, and a delighted smile spread over her face. It was a diamond engagement ring! She handed it back to Ryan and held out her hand. "You'd better do the honors."

"Does that mean you'll marry me?" Ryan looked very anxious as he slipped it on her finger.

"That's exactly what it means." Eve threw her arms around Ryan and hugged him. "I love you, Ryan. Any guy who thinks I'm beautiful when I look like a drowned rat is definitely the man for me!"

It was ten o'clock on Christmas Eve when Wicked typed the words, *The End*, on her laptop computer. She printed out her last chapter and added the pages to the three-ring binder that was titled *Ten Little Writers*. She'd finished her book, and now she had things she had to do.

Wicked put everything she needed in a backpack. She considered herself lucky that the regular staff never worked on the holidays. They called in replacements who didn't really know the cases, and Wicked had managed to fool them all.

"Good-bye, Nurse Thompson." Wicked stepped over the nurse she'd stabbed with a letter opener. She unlocked her door with the nurse's keys and stepped out into the hallway with a smile on her face. The staff was all in the day room, watching a movie on television, and the other patients had been sedated and put to bed. When Miss Thompson had come in to give Wicked her tranquilizer, Wicked had stabbed her.

The long hallway was deserted as Wicked unlocked the main door and slipped out into the cold, dark night. It didn't take long to find Miss Thompson's car. There were only a half dozen parked in the lot. Wicked started it and drove out through the wrought-iron gates.

As she traveled along the deserted highway, Wicked sang Christmas carols along with the radio. They were playing all her favorites—"Silent Night," "It Came Upon the Midnight Clear," and "Joy to the World." Of course there wouldn't be much joy at Shadybrook Sanitarium tonight, not when they discovered that Miss Thompson was dead and Wicked had escaped.

Wicked drove carefully, observing the speed limit and signaling whenever she changed lanes. She didn't want to be stopped by the police for a traffic violation. Wicked gave a sigh of relief as she parked the nurse's car at the bus terminal. She'd made it, and now she was on her way.

Her final destination was over two hundred miles away, and Wicked had thought about flying. But they were bound to ask for identification at the airport, and she couldn't take that chance. Anyone with money could buy a bus ticket, no questions asked.

The bus was late, but Wicked didn't mind. She used the time to perfect her plan. And then Wicked was on the bus, smiling happily as she rode through the snowy countryside.

Wicked was sitting next to a talkative woman who was coming home from a Christmas Eve dinner.

Wicked pretended to be Angela and she listened as
the woman told her all about the wonderful dinner
her daughter-in-law had served. But Wicked's mind
wasn't on the goose with cranberry sauce, or the
stuffing that had been made with roasted chestnuts.
Wicked was thinking about how wonderful it would
be when she got to the college and turned the rest of
Angela's book into reality.

**DISCOVER THE DELICIOUS MYSTERY
THAT STARTED IT ALL!**

No one cooks up a delectable, suspense-filled
mystery quite like Hannah Swensen,
Joanne Fluke's dessert-baking, red-haired heroine
whose gingersnaps are as tart as her comebacks,
and whose penchant for solving crimes—one
delicious clue at a time—has made her a
bestselling favorite. And it all began on these
pages, with a bakery, a murder, and some suddenly
scandalous chocolate-chip crunchies. Featuring a
bonus short story and brand new, mouthwatering
recipes, this very first Hannah Swensen mystery is
sure to have readers coming back for seconds . . .

**Please turn the page for an exciting sneak peek of
Joanne Fluke's first Hannah Swensen mystery**

CHOCOLATE CHIP COOKIE MURDER

**now on sale
wherever print and e-books are sold!**

CHAPTER ONE

Hannah Swensen slipped into the old leather bomber jacket that she'd rescued from the Helping Hands thrift store and reached down to pick up the huge orange tomcat that was rubbing against her ankles. "Okay, Moishe. You can have one refill, but that's it until tonight."

As she carried Moishe into the kitchen and set him down by his food bowl, Hannah remembered the day he'd set up camp outside her condo door. He'd looked positively disreputable, covered with matted fur and grime, and she'd immediately taken him in. Who else would adopt a twenty-five-pound, half-blind cat with a torn ear? Hannah had named him Moishe, and though he certainly wouldn't have won any prizes at the Lake Eden Cat Fanciers' Club, there had been an instant bond between them. They were both battle-worn—Hannah from weekly confrontations with her mother, and Moishe from his life on the streets.

Moishe rumbled in contentment as Hannah filled his bowl. He seemed properly grateful that he no longer had to scrounge for food and shelter and he showed his appreciation in countless ways. Just this morning, Hannah had found the hindquarters of a mouse in the center of the kitchen table, right next to the drooping African violet that she kept forgetting to water. While most of her female contemporaries would have screamed for their husbands to remove the disgusting sight, Hannah had picked up the carcass by the tail and praised Moishe lavishly for keeping her condo rodent-free.

"See you tonight, Moishe." Hannah gave him an affectionate pat and snatched up her car keys. She was just pulling on her leather gloves, preparing to leave, when the phone rang.

Hannah glanced at the apple-shaped wall clock, which she'd found at a garage sale. It was only six A.M. Her mother wouldn't call this early, would she?

Moishe looked up from his bowl with an expression that Hannah interpreted as sympathy. He didn't like Delores Swensen and he had done nothing to hide his feelings when she'd dropped in for surprise visits at her daughter's condo. After suffering through several pairs of shredded pantyhose, Delores had decided that she would limit her socializing to their Tuesday-night mother-daughter dinners.

Hannah picked up the phone, cutting off the answering machine in midmessage, and sighed as she heard her mother's voice. "Hello, Mother. I'm ready to walk out the door, so we'll have to keep this short. I'm already late for work."

Moishe raised his tail and shook it, pointing his posterior at the phone. Hannah stifled a giggle at his antics and gave him a conspiratorial wink. "No,

Mother, I didn't give Norman my phone number. If he wants to contact me, he'll have to look it up."

Hannah frowned as her mother went into her familiar litany on the proper way to attract a man. Their dinner last night had been a disaster. When she'd arrived at her mother's house, Hannah had encountered two additional guests: her mother's newly widowed neighbor, Mrs. Carrie Rhodes, and her son, Norman. Hannah had been obligated to make conversation with Norman over sickeningly sweet Hawaiian pot roast and a chocolate-covered nut cake from the Red Owl Grocery as their respective mothers beamed happily and remarked on what a charming couple they made.

"Look, Mother, I really have to . . ." Hannah stopped and rolled her eyes at the ceiling. Once Delores got started on a subject, it was impossible to get a word in edgewise. Her mother believed that a woman approaching thirty ought to be married, and even though Hannah had argued that she liked her life the way it was, it hadn't prevented Delores from introducing her to every single, widowed, or divorced man who'd set foot in Lake Eden.

"Yes, Mother. Norman seems very nice, but . . ." Hannah winced as her mother continued to wax eloquent over Norman's good qualities. What on earth had convinced Delores that her eldest daughter would be interested in a balding dentist, several years her senior, whose favorite topic of conversation was gum disease? "Excuse me, Mother, but I'm running late and . . ."

Moishe seemed to sense that his mistress was frustrated because he reached out with one orange paw and flipped over his food bowl. Hannah stared at him in surprise for a moment, and then she began to grin.

"Gotta run, Mother. Moishe just knocked over his food bowl and I've got Meow Mix all over the floor." Hannah cut off her mother's comments about Norman's earning capabilities in midbreath and hung up the phone. Then she swept up the cat food, dumped it in the trash, and poured in fresh food for Moishe. She added a couple of kitty treats, Moishe's reward for being so clever, and left him munching contentedly as she rushed out the door.

Hannah hurried down the steps to the underground garage, unlocked the door to her truck, and climbed in behind the wheel. When she'd opened her business, she'd bought a used Chevy Suburban from Cyril Murphy's car lot. She'd painted it candy-apple red, a color that was sure to attract notice wherever it was parked, and arranged for the name of her business—The Cookie Jar—to be painted in gold letters on the front doors. She'd even ordered a vanity license plate that read: "COOKIES."

As Hannah drove up the ramp that led to ground level, she met her next-door neighbor coming home. Phil Plotnik worked nights at DelRay Manufacturing, and Hannah rolled down the window to pass on the warning that their water would be shut off between ten and noon. Then she used her gate card to exit the complex and turned North onto Old Lake Road.

The interstate ran past Lake Eden, but most of the locals used Old Lake Road to get to town. It was the scenic route, winding around Eden Lake. When the tourists arrived in the summer, some of them were confused by the names. Hannah always explained it with a smile when they asked. The lake was named "Eden Lake," and the town that nestled next to its shore was called "Lake Eden."

There was a real nip in the air this morning, not unusual for the third week in October. Autumn was brief in Minnesota, a few weeks of turning leaves that caused everyone to snap photographs of the deep reds, gaudy oranges, and bright yellows. After the last leaf had fallen, leaving the branches stark and bare against the leaden skies, the cold north winds would start to blow. Then the first snowfall would arrive to the delight of the children and the stoic sighs of the adults. While sledding, ice-skating and snowball fights might be fun for the kids, winter also meant mounds of snow that had to be shoveled, virtual isolation when the roads were bad, and temperatures that frequently dropped down to thirty or even forty below zero.

The summer people had left Eden Lake right after the Labor Day weekend to return to their snug winter homes in the cities. Their cabins on the lakeshore stood vacant, their pipes wrapped with insulation to keep them from freezing in the subzero winter temperatures, and their windows boarded up against the icy winds that swept across the frozen surface of the lake. Now only the locals were in residence and the population of Lake Eden, which nearly quadrupled over the summer months, was down to less than three thousand.

As she idled at the stoplight on Old Lake Road and Dairy Avenue, Hannah saw a familiar sight. Ron

LaSalle was standing by the dock of the Cozy Cow Dairy, loading his truck for his commercial route. By this time of the morning, Ron had finished delivering dairy products to his residential customers, placing their milk, cream, and eggs in the insulated boxes the dairy provided. The boxes were a necessity in Minnesota. They kept the contents cool in the summer and protected them from freezing in the winter.

Ron was cupping his jaw with one hand and his pose was pensive, as if he were contemplating things more serious than the orders he had yet to deliver. Hannah would be seeing him later, when he delivered her supplies, and she made a mental note to ask him what he'd been thinking about. Ron prided himself on his punctuality and the Cozy Cow truck would pull up at her back door at precisely seven thirty-five. After Ron had delivered her daily order, he'd come into the coffee shop for a quick cup of coffee and a warm cookie. Hannah would see him again at three in the afternoon, right after he'd finished his routes. That was when he picked up his standing order, a dozen cookies to go. Ron kept them in his truck overnight so that he could have cookies for breakfast the next morning.

Ron looked up, spotted her at the stoplight, and raised one hand in a wave. Hannah gave him a toot of her horn as the light turned green and she drove on by. With his dark wavy hair and well-muscled body, Ron was certainly easy on the eyes. Hannah's youngest sister, Michelle, swore that Ron was every bit as handsome as Tom Cruise and she'd been dying to date him when she was in high school. Even now, when Michelle came home from Macalester College, she never failed to ask about Ron.

Three years ago, everyone had expected the star quarterback of the Lake Eden Gulls to be drafted by the pros, but Ron had torn a ligament in the final game of his high school career, ending his hopes for a spot with the Minnesota Vikings. There were times when Hannah felt sorry for Ron. She was sure that driving a Cozy Cow delivery truck wasn't the glorious future he'd envisioned for himself. But Ron was still a local hero. Everyone in Lake Eden remembered his remarkable game-winning touchdown at the state championships. The trophy he'd won was on display in a glass case at the high school and he volunteered his time as an unpaid assistant coach for the Lake Eden Gulls. Perhaps it was better to be a big fish in a little pond than a third-string quarterback who warmed the Vikings' bench.

No one else was on the streets this early, but Hannah made sure that her speedometer read well below the twenty-five-mile limit. Herb Beeseman, their local law enforcement officer, was known to lie in wait for unwary residents who were tempted to tread too heavily on the accelerator. Though Hannah had never been the recipient of one of Herb's speeding tickets, her mother was still livid about the fine that Marge Beeseman's youngest son had levied against her.

Hannah turned at the corner of Main and Fourth and drove into the alley behind her shop. The square white building sported two parking spots, and Hannah pulled her truck into one of them. She didn't bother to unwind the cord that was wrapped around her front bumper and plug it into the strip of power outlets on the rear wall of the building. The sun was shining and the announcer on the radio had promised that the temperatures would reach the high forties today. There was no need to use her head bolt heater for another few weeks, but when winter arrived and the mercury dropped below freezing, she'd need it to ensure that her engine would start.

Once she'd opened the door and slid out of her Suburban, Hannah locked it carefully behind her. There wasn't much crime in Lake Eden, but Herb Beeseman also left tickets on any vehicle that he found parked and unlocked. Before she could cover the distance to the rear door of the bakery, Claire Rodgers pulled up in her little blue Toyota and parked in back of the tan building next to Hannah's shop.

Hannah stopped and waited for Claire to get out of her car. She liked Claire and she didn't believe the rumors that floated around town about her affair with the mayor. "Hi, Claire. You're here early today."

"I just got in a new shipment of party dresses and they have to be priced." Claire's classically beautiful face lit up in a smile. "The holidays are coming, you know."

Hannah nodded. She wasn't looking forward to Thanksgiving and Christmas with her mother and sisters, but it was an ordeal that had to be endured for the sake of family peace.

"You should stop by, Hannah." Claire gave her an appraising look, taking in the bomber jacket that had seen better days and the old wool watch cap that Hannah had pulled over her frizzy red curls. "I have a stunning little black cocktail dress that would do wonders for you."

Hannah smiled and nodded, but she had all she could do to keep from laughing as Claire unlocked the rear door to Beau Monde Fashions and stepped inside. Where could she wear a cocktail dress in Lake Eden? No one hosted any cocktail parties and the only upscale restaurant in town had closed down right after the tourists had left. Hannah couldn't remember the last time she'd gone out to a fancy dinner. For that matter, she couldn't remember the last time that anyone had asked her out on a date.

Hannah unlocked her back door and pushed it open. The sweet smell of cinnamon and molasses greeted her, and she began to smile. She'd mixed up several batches of cookie dough last night and the scent still lingered. She flipped on the lights, hung her jacket on the hook by the door, and fired up the two industrial gas ovens that sat against the back wall. Her assistant, Lisa Herman, would be here at seven-thirty to start the baking.

The next half hour passed quickly as Hannah chopped, melted, measured, and mixed ingredients. By trial and error, she'd found that her cookies tasted better if she limited herself to batches that she could mix by hand. Her recipes were originals, developed in her mother's kitchen when she was a teenager. Delores thought baking was a chore and she'd been happy to delegate that task to her eldest daughter so that she could devote all of her energies to collecting antiques.

At ten past seven, Hannah carried the last bowl of cookie dough to the cooler and stacked the utensils she'd used in her industrial-sized dishwasher. She hung up her work apron, removed the paper cap she'd used to cover her curls, and headed off to the coffee shop to start the coffee.

A swinging restaurant-style door separated the bakery from the coffee shop. Hannah pushed it open and stepped inside, flipping on the old-fashioned globe fixtures she'd salvaged from a defunct ice-cream parlor in a neighboring town. She walked to the front windows, pulled aside the chintz curtains, and surveyed the length of Main Street. Nothing was moving; it was still too early, but Hannah knew that within the hour, the chairs that surrounded the small round tables in her shop would be filled with customers. The Cookie Jar was a meeting place for the locals, a choice spot to exchange gossip and plan out the day over heavy white mugs of strong coffee and freshly baked cookies from her ovens.

The stainless-steel coffee urn gleamed brightly and Hannah smiled as she filled it with water and measured out the coffee. Lisa had scoured it yesterday, restoring it to its former splendor. Lisa was a pure godsend when it came to running the bakery and the coffee shop. She saw what needed to be done, did it without being asked, and had even come up with a few cookie recipes of her own to add to Hannah's files. It was a real pity that Lisa hadn't used her academic scholarship to go on to college, but her father, Jack Herman, was suffering from Alzheimer's and Lisa had decided to stay home to take care of him.

Hannah removed three eggs from the refrigerator behind the counter and dropped them, shells and all, into the bowl with the coffee grounds. Then she broke them open with a heavy spoon and added a dash of salt. Once she'd mixed up the eggs and shells with the coffee grounds, Hannah scraped the contents of the bowl into the basket and flipped on the switch to start the coffee.

A few minutes later, the coffee began to perk and Hannah sniffed the air appreciatively. Nothing smelled better than freshly brewed coffee, and everyone in Lake Eden said that her coffee was the best. Hannah tied on the pretty chintz apron she wore for serving her customers and ducked back through the swinging door to give Lisa her instructions.

"Bake the Chocolate Chip Crunches first, Lisa." Hannah gave Lisa a welcoming smile.

"They're already in the ovens, Hannah." Lisa looked up from the stainless-steel work surface, where she was scooping out dough with a melonballer and placing the perfectly round spheres into a small bowl filled with sugar. She was only nineteen, ten years younger than Hannah was, and her petite form was completely swaddled in the huge white baker's apron she wore. "I'm working on the Molasses Crackles for the Boy Scout Awards Banquet now."

Hannah had originally hired Lisa as a waitress, but it hadn't taken her long to see that Lisa was capable of much more than pouring coffee and serving cookies. At the end of the first week, Hannah had increased Lisa's hours from part-time to full-time and taught her to bake. Now they handled the business together, as a team.

"How's your father today?" Hannah's voice held a sympathetic note.

"Today's a good day." Lisa placed the unbaked tray of Molasses Crackles on the baker's rack. "Mr. Drevlow is taking him to the Seniors' Group at Holy Redeemer Lutheran."

"But I thought your family was Catholic."

"We are, but Dad doesn't remember that. Besides, I don't see how having lunch with the Lutherans could possibly hurt."

"Neither do I. And it's good for him to get out and socialize with his friends."

"That's exactly what I told Father Coultas. If God gave Dad Alzheimer's, He's got to understand when Dad forgets what church he belongs to." Lisa walked to the oven, switched off the timer, and pulled out a tray of Chocolate Chip Crunches. "I'll bring these in as soon as they're cool."

"Thanks." Hannah went back through the swinging door again and unlocked the street door to the coffee shop. She flipped the "Closed" sign in the window to "Open," and checked the cash register to make sure there was plenty of change. She'd just finished setting out small baskets of sugar packets and artificial sweeteners when a late-model dark green Volvo pulled up in the spot by the front door.

Hannah frowned as the driver's door opened and her middle sister, Andrea, slid out of the driver's seat. Andrea looked perfectly gorgeous in a green tweed jacket with politically correct fake fur around the collar. Her blond hair was swept up in a shining knot on the top of her head and she could have stepped from the pages of a glamour magazine. Even though

Hannah's friends insisted that she was pretty enough, just being in the same town with Andrea always made Hannah feel hopelessly frumpy and unsophisticated.

Andrea had married Bill Todd, a Winnetka County deputy sheriff, right after she'd graduated from high school. They had one daughter, Tracey, who had turned four last month. Bill was a good father on his hours away from the sheriff's station, but Andrea had never been cut out to be a stay-at-home mom. When Tracey was only six months old, Andrea had decided that they'd needed two incomes and she'd gone to work as an agent at Lake Eden Realty.

The bell on the door tinkled and Andrea blew in with a chill blast of autumn wind, hauling Tracey behind her by the hand. "Thank God you're here, Hannah! I've got a property to show and I'm late for my appointment at the Cut 'n Curl."

"It's only eight, Andrea." Hannah boosted Tracey up onto a stool at the counter and went to the refrigerator to get her a glass of milk. "Bertie doesn't open until nine."

"I know, but she said she'd come in early for me. I'm showing the old Peterson farm this morning. If I sell it, I can order new carpeting for the master bedroom."

"The Peterson farm?" Hannah turned to stare at her sister in shock. "Who'd want to buy that old wreck?"

"It's not a wreck, Hannah. It's a fixer-upper. And my buyer, Mr. Harris, has the funds to make it into a real showplace."

"But why?" Hannah was honestly puzzled. The

Peterson place had been vacant for twenty years. She'd ridden her bicycle out there as a child and it was just an old two-story farmhouse on several acres of overgrown farmland that adjoined the Cozy Cow Dairy. "Your buyer must be crazy if he wants it. The land's practically worthless. Old man Peterson tried to farm it for years and the only things he could grow were rocks."

Andrea straightened the collar of her jacket. "The client knows that, Hannah, and he doesn't care. He's only interested in the farmhouse. It's still structurally sound and it has a nice view of the lake."

"It's sitting smack-dab in the middle of a hollow, Andrea. You can only see the lake from the top of the roof. What does your buyer plan to do, climb up on a ladder every time he wants to enjoy the view?"

"Not exactly, but it amounts to the same thing. He told me that he's going to put on a third story and convert the property to a hobby farm."

"A hobby farm?"

"That's a second home in the country for city people who want to be farmers without doing any of the work. He'll hire a local farmer to take care of his animals and keep up the land."

"I see," Hannah said, holding back a grin. By her own definition, Andrea was a hobby wife and a hobby mother. Her sister hired a local woman to come in to clean and cook the meals, and she paid baby-sitters and day-care workers to take care of Tracey.

"You'll watch Tracey for me, won't you, Hannah?" Andrea looked anxious. "I know she's a bother, but it's only for an hour. Kiddie Korner opens at nine."

Hannah thought about giving her sister a piece of her mind. She was running a business and her shop wasn't a day-care center. But one glance at Tracey's hopeful face changed her mind. "Go ahead, Andrea. Tracey can work for me until it's time for her to go to preschool."

"Thanks, Hannah." Andrea turned and started toward the door. "I knew I could count on you."

"Can I really work, Aunt Hannah?" Tracey asked in her soft little voice, and Hannah gave her a reassuring smile.

"Yes, you can. I need someone to be my official taster. Lisa just baked a batch of Chocolate Chip Crunches and I need to know if they're good enough to serve to my customers."

"Did you say *chocolate*?" Andrea turned back at the door to frown at Hannah. "Tracey can't have chocolate. It makes her hyperactive."

Hannah nodded, but she gave Tracey a conspiratorial wink. "I'll remember that, Andrea."

"I'll see you later, Tracey," Andrea said and blew her daughter a kiss. "Don't be any trouble for your aunt Hannah, okay?"

Tracey waited until the door had closed behind her mother and then she turned to Hannah. "What's hyperactive, Aunt Hannah?"

"It's another word for what kids do when they're having fun." Hannah came out from behind the counter and lifted Tracey off the stool. "Come on, honey. Let's go in the back and see if those Chocolate Chip Crunches are cool enough for you to sample."

Lisa was just slipping another tray of cookies into

the oven when Hannah and Tracey came in. She gave Tracey a hug, handed her a cookie from the tray that was cooling on the rack, and turned to Hannah with a frown. "Ron hasn't come in yet. Do you suppose he's out sick?"

"Not unless it came on suddenly." Hannah glanced at the clock on the wall. It was eight-fifteen and Ron was almost forty-five minutes late. "I saw him two hours ago when I drove past the dairy, and he looked just fine to me."

"I saw him, too, Aunt Hannah." Tracey tugged on Hannah's arm.

"You did? When was that, Tracey?"

"The cow truck went by when I was waiting outside the realty office. Mr. LaSalle waved at me and he gave me a funny smile. And then Andrea came out with her papers and we came to see you."

"Andrea?" Hannah looked down at her niece in surprise.

"She doesn't like me to call her Mommy anymore because it's a label and she hates labels," Tracey did her best to explain. "I'm supposed to call her Andrea, just like everyone else."

Hannah sighed. Perhaps it was time to have a talk with her sister about the responsibilities of motherhood. "Are you sure you saw the Cozy Cow truck, Tracey?"

"Yes, Aunt Hannah." Tracey's blond head bobbed up and down confidently. "It turned at your corner and went into the alley. And then I heard it make a loud bang, just like Daddy's car. I knew it came from the cow truck because there weren't any other cars."

Hannah knew exactly what Tracey meant. Bill's

old Ford was on its last legs and it backfired every time he eased up on the gas. "Ron's probably out there tinkering with his truck. I'll go and see."

"Can I come with Aunt Hannah?"

"Stay with me, Tracey," Lisa spoke up before Hannah could answer. "You can help me listen for the bell and wait on any customers that come into the coffee shop."

Tracey looked pleased. "Can I bring them their cookies, Lisa? Just like a real waitress?"

"Absolutely, but it's got to be our secret. We wouldn't want your dad to bust us for violating the child-labor laws."

"What does 'bust' mean, Lisa? And why would my daddy do it?"

Hannah grinned as she slipped into her jacket and listened to Lisa's explanation. Tracey questioned everything and it drove Andrea to distraction. Hannah had attempted to tell her sister that an inquiring mind was a sign of intelligence, but Andrea just didn't have the necessary patience to deal with her bright four-year-old.

As Hannah pulled open the door and stepped out, she was greeted by a strong gust of wind that nearly threw her off balance. She pushed the door shut behind her, shielded her eyes from the blowing wind, and walked forward to peer down the alley. Ron's delivery truck was parked sideways near the mouth of the alley, blocking the access in both directions. The driver's door was partially open and Ron's legs were dangling out.

Hannah moved forward, assuming that Ron was stretched out on the seat to work on the wiring that

ran under the dash. She didn't want to startle him
and cause him to bump his head, so she stopped
several feet from the truck and called out. "Hi, Ron.
Do you want me to phone for a tow truck?"

Ron didn't answer. The wind was whistling down
the alley, rattling the lids on the metal Dumpsters,
and perhaps he hadn't heard her. Hannah walked
closer, called out again, and moved around the door
to glance inside the truck.

The sight that greeted Hannah made her jump
back and swallow hard. Ron LaSalle, Lake Eden's
local football hero, was lying faceup on the seat of
his delivery truck. His white hat was on the floorboards, the orders on his clipboard were rattling in
the wind, and one of Hannah's cookie bags was open
on the seat. Chocolate Chip Crunches were scattered
everywhere and Hannah's eyes widened as she
realized that he was still holding one of her cookies
in his hand.

Then Hannah's eyes moved up and she saw it: the
ugly hole ringed with powder burns in the very center
of Ron's Cozy Cow delivery shirt. Ron LaSalle had
been shot dead.

Everyone in Lake Eden, Minnesota, may have had their doubts, but at long last, Hannah Swensen is getting married!

Hannah is thrilled to be marrying Ross Barton, her college crush. And her excitement only grows when she learns he'll be able to join her on her trip to New York City for the Food Channel's dessert chef contest. They get a taste of the Big Apple before Hannah wins the Hometown Challenge and the producers bring all the contestants to Lake Eden to tape the remainder of the show. It's nerve-wracking enough being judged by Alain Duquesne, a celebrity chef with a nasty reputation. But it's even more chilling to find him stabbed to death in the Lake Eden Inn's walk-in cooler—before he's even had a chance to taste Hannah's Butterscotch Sugar Cookies! Now Hannah has not only lost her advantage, she'll have to solve a mystery with more layers than a five-tiered wedding cake . . .

Please turn the page for an exciting sneak peek of Joanne Fluke's newest Hannah Swensen mystery

WEDDING CAKE MURDER

now on sale wherever print and e-books are sold!

CHAPTER ONE

"No, it's not the wedding I dreamed of, but it *is* the wedding I want!" Hannah Swensen's hands shook slightly as she replaced her cup of coffee in the bone china saucer. She'd been so startled by Grandma Knudson's question that a few drops had sloshed out of her cup and landed in its matching saucer. The matriarch of Holy Redeemer Lutheran Church was known for being outspoken, but Hannah hadn't expected to be grilled about her upcoming nuptials when Grandma Knudson had called her at The Cookie Jar, Hannah's coffee shop and bakery, and invited her to the parsonage for coffee.

"Everyone's talking, you know," Grandma Knudson confided, leaning forward in her chair. "No one can understand why they haven't been invited to the wedding. I told them you preferred a small, intimate family affair, but they feel left out. And almost everyone from my Bible study group asked me if there was something wrong."

"Wrong?" Hannah repeated, not certain what Grandma Knudson meant.

"Yes. People always think that there's something wrong when a wedding takes place behind closed doors. Weddings aren't supposed to be private. They're supposed to be joyous celebrations."

"I *am* joyous! I mean, *joyful.* And so is Ross. I just thought it might be easier for everyone if we didn't have a big public display."

"Because of Norman and Mike?"

"Well . . . yes. That's part of the reason. This is rather sudden, and they haven't had time to get used to the idea that Ross and I are getting married. I thought it would be . . ." Hannah paused, trying to think of another word, but only one came to mind. "I thought it would be *easier* for them this way," she finished.

Grandma Knudson was silent as she stared at Hannah, and that made Hannah want to explain. "You know . . ." she continued. "If I'd invited everyone to a huge wedding and reception, it would be almost like . . . like . . ."

The older woman let her struggle for a moment, and then she gave a nod. "Like rubbing their noses in it?"

"Yes! I mean, not exactly. But some people might think that that's what I was doing."

"Perhaps," Grandma Knudson conceded. "Tell me about Ross. Did he think that a small, private wedding was a good idea?"

"I . . . actually . . ." Hannah paused and took a deep breath. "Ross and I didn't really talk about that. He just told me that anything I wanted to do about the wedding would be fine with him."

"I see. Did you at least meet with Mike and Norman and talk to them about what you'd decided?"

"No. I wanted to spare their feelings. I thought it might be too painful for them to discuss it."

"You mean you thought it might be too painful for *you* to discuss it, don't you?" Grandma Knudson corrected her bluntly.

Hannah sighed heavily. She had to be truthful. "Perhaps you're right," she admitted, and made a move to pick up her cup and saucer rather than meet the older woman's eyes. "I guess I really wasn't thinking clearly, and I certainly didn't think that a small wedding would cause all this fuss. I just wanted to get married before I had to leave for the Food Channel *Dessert Chef Competition*. I thought that Ross could go with me and it would be our honeymoon."

"I see. And the competition is in three weeks?"

"That's right." Hannah managed to take a sip of her coffee and then she put it back down on the table again. Why was Grandma Knudson asking all these questions? There must be a reason. As Hannah sat there, trying to think of why Grandma Knudson was giving her the third degree, the light dawned. "Mother!" Hannah said with a sigh.

"What did you say?"

"I said *Mother*. She put you up to this, didn't she? She wanted me to have a big wedding and I refused. So Mother came running to you to see if you could convince me to change my mind! Isn't Mother the reason you invited me here for coffee?"

"She's part of the reason. But the other part is that I wanted you to taste my lemon pie. It's the easiest pie I've ever made. All you need is a lemon, sugar, butter, and eggs. You put everything in a blender, pour it into one of those fancy frozen piecrusts Florence carries down at the Red Owl, and bake it. But you haven't even sampled it yet."

Hannah looked down at the dessert plate resting next to her cup and saucer. Grandma Knudson's pie did look delicious. "Is that crème fraiche on the top?"

"Yes. It's your crème fraiche, the one you use on your strawberry shortcake. And if you don't want to go to the bother of making that, you can use vanilla ice cream or sweetened whipped cream. Taste it, Hannah. I want your opinion."

Hannah picked up her fork and took a bite. And then she took another bite. "It's delicious," she said. "It has exactly the right amount of tartness to balance the sweetness."

"I'm glad you like it, but let's get back to Mike and Norman. You're not getting off the hot seat so easily. Your mother's very upset, you know. People have been stopping her on the street and asking when your wedding invitations will arrive."

"Did she tell them that it was a small, private wedding?"

Grandma Knudson shook her head. "No. She was too embarrassed. You know as well as I do what people think when you get married so fast in a small, private ceremony."

"They think I'm . . . ?" There was no way Hannah could finish her question. She was too shocked.

"Of course they think that. It's usually the case, especially with a first marriage like yours. There's even a betting pool that Hal McDermott set up down at the café for the date the baby will be born."

Hannah's mouth dropped open and she shut it quickly. And then she gave a rueful laugh. "What happens to the betting pool if there's no baby? Because there isn't!"

"Good question. My guess is that Hal gets to keep the proceeds, and that's not right. I think I'll have Bob and Claire go down there and convince him to give all that money to the local charities. That would serve people right for betting on something like that!"

"Do you think Hal will agree to give the money to charity?"

"He'll have to. Betting pools are illegal in Winnetka County, and Hal knows it. So is playing poker for money behind that curtain of his in the back room of the café. He'll knuckle under. You don't have to worry about that. And if he doesn't, Bob will give a rousing sermon about gambling the next time Rose drags Hal to church."

Hannah couldn't help it. She laughed. Grandma Knudson always got what she wanted, and this would be no exception.

"That's better," Grandma Knudson commented. "It's good to hear you laugh. Now what are you going to do about Mike and Norman?"

"What do *you* think I should do? Invite them to be Ross's groomsmen at a huge church wedding?"

"I think that's *exactly* what you should do! Give Mike and Norman a chance to step up to the plate. As it stands right now, everyone's buzzing about the fact that their hearts are broken. If both of them are in the wedding party, it'll put all those wagging tongues to rest. Believe you me, they'll jump at the chance to do that!"

"Are you sure?"

"I'm positive." Grandma Knudson locked eyes with Hannah. "Neither one of those men enjoys being the butt of gossip, and both of them like Ross. Of course they're disappointed that you didn't choose one of them, but they'll do the right thing if you ask them."

Hannah thought about that for a moment. Norman and Mike *did* like Ross. The three men were friends. And she knew that Ross liked Mike and Norman. If she'd said she wanted a big wedding and asked Ross to choose two men to be groomsmen, he would probably have chosen Mike and Norman.

"Well?"

Grandma Knudson was waiting for an answer, and Hannah hedged a little. "You may be right, but I'll have to ask Ross what he thinks of the idea."

"I did that this morning. I called Ross at work and he said it was fine with him if that was what you wanted. And Mike and Norman are definitely on board. I double-checked with them right afterwards. And both of them told me that they'll accept if you ask them."

"You called Mike and Norman, too?"

"Of course I did. I wanted to make sure this would work."

Hannah gave a little groan. Railroaded. She'd been railroaded, but Grandma Knudson had a point she couldn't ignore. If everyone in town was gossiping about her and Hal had even set up a betting pool, she had to do something to turn things around. And then she remembered what Grandma Knudson had said. "You said you double-checked with Mike and Norman this morning?"

"Yes."

"If you *double*-checked, that means you or someone else had checked with them *before* this morning. Was that someone you?"

Grandma Knudson looked slightly flustered. "Actually . . . no."

With a burst of lightning clarity, Hannah saw the whole picture. Her eyes narrowed and she faced the matriarch of the church squarely. "*Mother* checked with them before you did. Is that right?"

Grandma Knudson sighed. "Yes, but she didn't want you to know that it was her idea."

"That figures," Hannah said with a sigh.

"Your mother is an expert when it comes to gossip," Grandma Knudson attempted to explain, "but she was afraid you'd reject her plan out of hand if she was the one to suggest it. That's why she asked me to talk to you about it. And I did. Your mother, Andrea, and Michelle are already working out the details of your wedding."

"They're planning my wedding without me?"

"Yes, but you know how long wedding plans take. Delores and the girls have everything organized, but nothing's been firmed up yet. All they need is for you to give them the go-ahead."

Hannah was silent. She wasn't quite ready to cave in yet.

"Your mother said to tell you that she knows you're busy at The Cookie Jar and you have to be in

New York for the dessert competition very soon. She's absolutely certain that everything will be ready so that you can get married, have a reception at the Lake Eden Inn, and leave for New York the next morning."

"Mother can pull off a big wedding in less than three weeks?"

"Yes. And you don't have to do any wedding planning. Your sisters and Delores are completely prepared to arrange everything."

Again, Hannah was silent. She didn't like the idea of turning everything over to her mother and sisters, but it seemed like the only reasonable option since she'd made such a mess of it on her own.

"Delores said to tell you that there are only two things you have to do," Grandma Knudson spoke again. "The first thing is to choose your wedding dress. Your mother has already consulted with Claire at Beau Monde, and Claire has ordered more than a half-dozen gowns for your approval. When they come in, Claire will let you know so that you can run next door to try them on. All you have to do is choose the one you want to wear and Claire will do any alterations you might need."

Hannah gave a slight smile. At least they were letting her choose her own wedding gown! And it was true that she didn't have time to organize a big wedding. The nightmare of trying to arrange Delores's wedding was still fresh in her mind. There was no way she wanted to get involved in a morass like that again, but she was the bride and it was a bit disconcerting not to be involved in any of the planning.

"What's the second thing they want me to do?" she asked.

"Show up at the church on time."

Hannah's sarcastic nature kicked in, and the question popped out of her mouth before she could exercise restraint. "Do they want me to show up with or without Ross?"

Grandma Knudson burst into laughter. "With Ross. Not even your mother could accomplish a wedding without a groom." The older woman reached out to take Hannah's hand. "Are you all right with this plan, Hannah? If you're not, we can try to come up with something else that'll work."

Grandma Knudson was waiting for an answer and Hannah took a deep breath. "Yes, I'm all right with it as long as Ross and I can get married before the Food Channel competition. Do you think that's possible?"

"Your mother assured me that it was."

Hannah gave a reluctant nod. "All right then. I'll do it, if you'll do something for me."

"What's that?"

"I'd like a second piece of your lemon pie, and I'd also like to have the recipe. It's the best non-meringue lemon pie I've ever tasted!"

EASY LEMON PIE

Preheat oven to 350 degrees F., rack in the middle position.

Note from Grandma Knudson: I got this recipe from my friend, Lois Brown, who lives in Phoenix, AZ. She has a lemon tree in her backyard so she always has lemons to make this pie.

Hannah's 1st Note: You can make this recipe in a food processor or a blender. We use a food processor down at The Cookie Jar.

 1 frozen 9-inch piecrust *(or one you've made yourself)*
 1 whole medium-size lemon
 ½ cup butter *(1 stick, 4 ounces, ¼ pound)*
 1 cup white *(granulated)* sugar
 4 large eggs

_____

 Sweetened whipped cream to put on top of your pie before serving

If you used a frozen pie crust, take it out of the package and set it on a cookie sheet with sides while you make the filling for the pie.

If you made your own piecrust, roll it out, put it in a 9-inch pie pan, cut it to fit the pie pan, and crimp the edges so it looks nice. Then set it on a cookie sheet with sides to wait for its filling.

Cut the tough ends off your lemon. Cut it in half and then cut each half into 4 slices. *(The slices should be round, like wagon wheels.)*

Cut the other half-lemon into 4 similar slices to make 8 slices in all.

Examine the slices and pick out any seeds. Throw the seeds away.

Place all 8 seedless slices in a blender *(or a food processor)*.

Turn on the blender or food processor and process the lemon slices until they are mush. *(This is not a regular cooking term, but I bet you know what I mean!)*

Melt the half-cup of butter in the microwave or on the stovetop. *(If you'd rather do it in the microwave, this should take about 50 seconds on HIGH.)*

Pour the melted butter over the lemon mush in the blender.

Add the cup of white sugar.

Crack open the 4 eggs and add them one by one.

Turn on the blender or food processor and blend everything until it is a homogenous mush. *(Another nonregulation cooking term.)*

Pour the lemon mixture into the crust.

Bake your Easy Lemon Pie at 350 degrees F. for 40 minutes or until the mixture turns solid and the top is brown.

Take your pie out of the oven and cool it on a cold stove burner or a wire rack. Once it is cool, cover it with foil or plastic wrap and refrigerate it until you're ready to serve.

Hannah's 2nd Note: I like to use my Crème Fraiche on this pie. Here's the recipe just in case you don't have it handy:

HANNAH'S WHIPPED CRÈME FRAICHE

(This will hold for several hours. Make it ahead of time and refrigerate it.)

   2 cups heavy whipping cream
   ½ cup white *(granulated)* sugar
   ½ cup sour cream *(you can substitute*
      unflavored yogurt, but it won't hold as well
      and you'll have to do it at the last minute)
   ½ cup brown sugar *(to sprinkle on top after*
      you cut your pie into pieces)

Whip the cream with the white sugar until it holds a firm peak. Test for this by shutting off the mixer, and "dotting" the surface with your spatula. Once you have firm peaks, gently fold in the sour cream. You can do this by hand or by using the slowest speed on the mixer.

Transfer the mixture to a covered bowl and store it in the refrigerator until you are ready to serve your Easy Lemon Pie.

To serve your pie, cut it into 6 generous pieces or 8 smaller slices and put each slice on a pretty dessert plate.

Top each slice with a generous dollop or two of Hannah's Whipped Crème Fraiche.

Sprinkle the top of the Whipped Crème Fraiche with brown sugar.

Hannah's 3rd Note: If you want to get really fancy, cut a paper-thin slice of lemon, dip it in granulated sugar, and put it on top of each slice of pie.

CHAPTER TWO

Hannah breathed a deep sigh of relief as she hurried in the back door of The Cookie Jar and sat down on a stool at the stainless steel work island. She'd been manipulated by two master manipulators, but she couldn't be angry with either one of them. If everything Grandma Knudson had told her was correct, she had to change her small, intimate wedding plans and endure a huge church wedding and a reception with all the bells and whistles. Delores, Andrea, and Michelle would plan an elaborate affair, but there was no other recourse. And thankfully, there was nothing for her to do except choose her wedding gown and show up for the ceremony.

One quick cup of coffee later and Hannah was on her feet, mixing up sugar cookie dough. She was just getting ready to mix in a cup of chopped pecans when Lisa Herman Beeseman, Hannah's young partner, rushed through the swinging restaurant-style door that separated the coffee shop from the kitchen.

"There's a phone call for you, Hannah," Lisa

announced breathlessly. "It's somebody named Eric, and he said he was from the Food Channel. I think it's about the *Dessert Chef Competition.*"

Hannah handed the wooden spoon to Lisa and gestured toward the bowl. "Will you stir in those pecans while I take the call? I'm making a variation of sugar cookies with maple flavoring and pecans."

"Sure. No problem. Aunt Nancy and Michelle have got everything covered out in the coffee shop."

Lisa began to stir, and Hannah headed for the phone on the kitchen wall. She flipped to a blank page in the shorthand notebook she kept on the counter, picked up a pen, and grabbed the receiver. "This is Hannah."

"Hi, Hannah. It's Eric Connelly from the Food Channel. We're in a little time crunch here and we had to move the *Dessert Chef Competition* up a week and a half. Can you clear the decks back there and be here on October tenth instead of October twentieth?"

"Oh!" Hannah was so flustered, it took her a moment to think of something intelligent to say. "Yes. Of course I can."

"Good. And I'm telling all four contestants that we've added a new wrinkle to the contest."

He seemed to be waiting for her to respond, and Hannah gave a little nod she knew he couldn't see. "What's the new wrinkle? Or is that something we'll find out when we get there?"

Eric laughed, a nice deep laugh that ended in a chuckle. "It's no secret. We just thought it would be more interesting if we went off-location for most of the episodes. We'll start here in our home studio, but the winner that night will have the hometown advantage from then on."

"Hometown advantage?"

"Yes. If you win, the remainder of the contest moves to your hometown in Lake Eden, Minnesota."

Hannah glanced at the one industrial oven she owned and began to frown. "But . . . my place is rather small. I don't have room for four other chefs."

"I know that. Your sister sent in a photo of your kitchen when she entered you in the competition. I took care of that, Hannah. I checked with your friend Sally Laughlin at the Lake Eden Inn, and she has enough room in her kitchen for four baking stations. That's only if you win the hometown challenge, of course. The other four contestants all have large restaurants in their home cities, so it's not a problem for them."

The frown remained on Hannah's face. "Doesn't that put me at a disadvantage?"

"Not at all. The Lake Eden Inn can hold as many people as the other four restaurants. If you win, it won't be a problem at all."

"Oh . . . good."

"We're all set then? I can send you the travel arrangements and you'll be here on the tenth?"

Hannah blinked twice, trying to dear her thoughts. "Yes. That'll be fine with . . . oh, no!"

"What was the *oh, no!* for?"

"My wedding! It's scheduled for Sunday, the eighteenth!"

"That's not a problem. The contest will be over by then. And . . ." Eric paused for a moment. "This is just off the top of my head, but maybe we can find a way to incorporate part of your wedding into the *Dessert Chef Competition*."

Hannah was genuinely puzzled. "How could you do that?"

"If you win the hometown challenge, we'll be in Lake Eden. And we might just stick around to film it. You're having a reception at a local place, aren't you?"

"Yes. At the Lake Eden Inn."

"Perfect! Let us think about that for a couple of days and see what we can come up with. This could really bump up the ratings. Everyone loves a wedding. And everyone will love you as a bride-to-be. You'll definitely have the viewer vote. That much is for sure."

"There's a popular vote in addition to the judges' decisions?"

"No, but that's what keeps people watching. And that's what we want . . . viewers."

"Oh, yes. Of course you do. Ratings are everything . . . right?"

"Right." Eric chuckled again. "All right, Hannah. It was nice talking to you. My secretary will get back to you in the next couple of days with the travel arrangements. I've got her working on it right now. You do know that you can bring an assistant chef with you for the competition, don't you?"

"Yes. It was in the letter I received that told me I was a contestant. There was also a copy of the rules."

"Do you know who your assistant will be?"

"Yes, I do. My assistant is Michelle Swensen. She's my youngest sister."

"Good. The audience enjoys getting to know our

chefs' family members. Your sister isn't under eighteen, is she?"

"No, she turned twenty-one this past year."

"Good. The reason I asked is because we have to make special provisions for anyone under the age of eighteen on the set."

"I see," Hannah said, even though she didn't.

"Now that I think about it, your wedding will make a perfect ending to our competition. We were afraid we'd run short after one of the contestants dropped out for personal reasons. Is your sister one of the bridesmaids?"

"Yes, she is. And so is my other sister, Andrea."

"Wonderful! It was too late to add another new contestant so the more bodies we can film, the better."

Hannah winced slightly. *Bodies* obviously meant something different to Eric than it meant to her!

"Have you decided which desserts you'll be baking for the competition?"

"No, not yet."

"That's all right. You have some time. As long as you give us a list of the ingredients you'll need when you get to New York, it'll be fine."

Hannah came close to groaning out loud. She hadn't done any preparation for the competition. "When do you need my list?"

"When you get off the plane in New York."

"All right. I'll have my list ready for you."

"Good. That's all then, Hannah. We'll send your itinerary and your plane reservations in the next few days. We're going to put you up at the Westin in the Theater District."

"That sounds wonderful," Hannah said, and she meant it. Michelle would be thrilled to be in New York's Theater District.

"We're all set then. Good luck in the competition, Hannah. I'm looking forward to meeting you and your sister."

"I'm looking forward to meeting you, too. Thank you, Eric."

Hannah said good-bye and hung up the phone. When she turned to face Lisa, there was a frown on her face. If she won the hometown challenge, they might show her wedding on television! Could Delores and her sisters get everything ready in time? And would the fact that the wedding might be televised throw Delores into a tizzy?

Lisa looked up from her stirring. When she saw Hannah's expression, she looked concerned. "What's the matter, Hannah?"

"It's the Food Channel competition. They moved up the date. I have to be in New York by the tenth!"

"But how about the wedding?"

"They said the competition would be over by then and my wedding can go on as planned. And they're thinking about televising it!"

"Oh boy! You'd better tell your mother right away! It may make a difference in what she plans."

"You're right." Hannah took a moment to think about that. "Actually . . . this might not be a bad thing. I'm sure Mother and Andrea will do a great job. And they can consult with me by phone if there's a problem when I'm in New York."

"How about Michelle?"

"She's going with me as my assistant, so she's off

the wedding team. I wonder if Mother and Andrea can handle it alone. They may have bitten off more than they can chew."

"I doubt that. Your mother's a force. She knows how to get things done."

"That's true." Hannah thought of something else that Eric had told her and she sighed heavily. "Will you call your dad and Marge and ask them if they can handle the coffee shop for us while we have a meeting to plan what I'll bake for the contest?"

"I'll ask them right now. They're here at a table in the back. Dad will be really pleased. He loves to help out up front and so does Marge."

"Is your Aunt Nancy here today? I know she's been helping you out in front."

"She's here. She says it's a wonderful way to meet the people in Lake Eden, now that she's moved here."

"Good. I'll need you, Michelle, and Aunt Nancy to come back here for the meeting. And I'll text Mother and Andrea to come here right away. I have to decide which desserts to bake so that I can give the producer a list of the ingredients I'll need."

"Okay. I just filled the display cookie jars and made a fresh pot of coffee. That should hold them out front for at least an hour."

"Thanks, Lisa."

"You're welcome. Do you want me to make some white chocolate cocoa for us? I've got a new recipe that uses cinnamon and white chocolate chips."

"That sounds great. I have to talk to all of you, and we'll meet right here around the work island."

"Okay. But if this is about the baking contest, why do you need your mother and Andrea? Andrea doesn't bake anything except whippersnapper cookies, and your mother doesn't bake at all."

"I know, but both of them have tasted everything we've ever baked in here. And if I don't invite them, I'll just have to explain everything all over again."

"That makes sense. And you need Aunt Nancy because she's such a good baker?"

"Exactly. Aunt Nancy has more recipes than anyone I know, and she may be able to suggest some desserts that haven't even occurred to me. I have to come up with some real winning recipes before I leave for the competition, and there's not that much time."

"How many desserts do you need?"

"I need one super dessert for the hometown challenge. That's on the first night. It has to be the best thing I've ever baked."

"What's the hometown challenge?"

"It's the only part of the competition that'll be held in New York. The winner of the challenge gets to move the rest of the competition to his or her restaurant."

"If you win, they'll move the contest *here*?" Lisa glanced around their kitchen in dismay. "But that's impossible, Hannah! We only have one oven!"

"That's exactly what I told the producer, but he was one step ahead of me. He called Sally at the Lake Eden Inn, and she agreed to hold the competition in her kitchen if I win the challenge."

"Well, that's a relief! I was wondering how we could fit all those contestants in here."

"It's not just the contestants. There'll be a New

York film crew here, too. The Food Channel is going to be airing the whole competition live."

"How many will be in the film crew?"

Hannah shrugged. "I'm not sure, but it's bound to be a lot of people."

"Thank goodness for Sally's big kitchen! If we had to crowd everyone in here at The Cookie Jar, we'd have to knock out a wall and expand to include the whole block!"

CHAPTER THREE

Hannah gave a relieved sigh as she glanced down at her shorthand notebook. "All right. I've got seven desserts to try. Which one do you think I should bake for the hometown challenge?"

"None of them."

Hannah, Lisa, and Michelle turned to stare at Aunt Nancy in confusion. "*None* of them?" Hannah repeated.

"That's right. The first night is really important. You'll need something that'll knock their socks off."

"You're absolutely right," Delores said, smiling at Aunt Nancy. "Hannah simply *has* to win the hometown challenge." She turned to Hannah. "Just think about the business it'll bring to Lake Eden if you win, dear. They'll be shopping in the stores. Claire's Beau Monde is every bit as classy as a New York boutique. And Claire is a real person, not at all snooty the way most of those pseudo-French salesladies are."

"That's true," Hannah conceded the point, "but

they'll probably be staying at the Lake Eden Inn for the entire time they're here. They may not even come into town."

"They'll come into town," Andrea said, taking up the argument. "There's not much to do out at the Lake Eden Inn. It's way out on the other side of Eden Lake. You can't swim this time of year and winter hasn't really hit yet. There's not enough ice to go ice fishing or skating, and it's not the season for regular fishing. The lake's beautiful, but you can only take so many walks around the lake. And that means they'll be bored silly, especially since you said most of them are from big cities."

"That's right." Hannah looked down at her notes again. "They're from Chicago, New York, Los Angeles, and Atlanta. I'm the only one from a small town."

"Big cities have entertainment. The Lake Eden Inn is nice, don't get me wrong. You can sleep in a beautiful room, eat great food, and drink fine wine, but that's about it. You can't cross-country ski, or go on the snowmobile trails if there's no snow yet. And there's no snow right now."

"Andrea's right," Michelle said. "They're going to get bored out there by the lake. If we can figure out some way to provide transportation, they'll come into town at least a couple of times. I'm sure of it."

Delores put her cell phone down. There was a smug expression on her face as she turned to Hannah. "Ross agrees," she said. "I just texted him, and he said it was bound to bring business to Lake Eden. He said the film crew from the Food Channel works hard and they play hard, too. They'll come into town to go bowling, hang out at the Red Velvet Lounge at the Albion Hotel, and do some background shots of your hometown. They'll probably even interview some locals."

Hannah stared at her mother in shock. "You sent a text message to Ross before I even had time to tell him about it?"

"Well . . ." Delores equivocated for a moment and then she nodded. "Yes, I did. I had no idea you hadn't told Ross. He's your fiancé. Why didn't you tell him before you told us?"

There was no way that Hannah wanted to say that she hadn't even thought of it, so she simply sighed. "I didn't want to bother him at work. I was going to tell him tonight when I saw him for dinner. Really, Mother! It's not like we're joined at the hip."

"I see," Delores said, and everyone around the table, including Hannah, realized that the mother of the bride thought that her daughter was in the wrong.

Hannah turned to Andrea. "When you were engaged to Bill, would you have sent him a message telling him that the competition had been moved up before you told anyone else?"

Andrea looked down at the table. It was clear she didn't want to meet Hannah's eyes. "I don't know," she said.

"It's a moot point," Michelle pointed out. "They didn't have text messaging then."

"But they had phones," Hannah argued, zeroing in on Andrea again. "Would you have called Bill, even at work, if something like this had happened to you?"

"Uh . . . well . . ." Andrea paused and the expression on her face resembled that of a rabbit trapped by a much larger predator. "I'm really not sure, but . . . maybe?"

"Was that a question?" Hannah asked.

Andrea sighed again. And then she took a deep breath. "Yes, I would have called Bill right away. But . . . it's different for you, Hannah."

"What do you mean?"

"I mean . . . you're older. You're established. You're more . . . secure with yourself. You don't need the constant approval from Ross that I needed from Bill."

Hannah wasn't sure she liked what Andrea was implying, but she did understand. "You think I'm more capable of making my own decisions and I don't need a husband the way you needed Bill."

This time, it was definitely a statement and no one said a word. Except Andrea, who gave a nod and said, "Yes. That's it, Hannah. You're much more self-reliant than I was at nineteen."

"Okay," Hannah said, and reached out to pat her sister's hand. "I ought to be more self-sufficient. I'm more than ten years older than you were when you got married."

"And she wasn't even preg—" Michelle stopped short and shot a guilty glance at Delores. "Sorry."

"And I'm not either," Hannah said, glaring at her, and then the humor of the situation got to her and she smiled. "Sorry. Grandma Knudson hit me with the same thing this morning. I really didn't realize that people would think I was . . . you know." There was an uncomfortable silence, and then Hannah went on, "Grandma Knudson is going to make sure that all the money people bet on the birthdate of the nonexistent baby is given to charity."

"Good! It serves those people right!" Delores looked outraged. "I, for one, never thought for a minute that . . ."

"Of course we didn't!" Andrea jumped in. "It was just that it was so sudden and nobody expected it, and . . ."

"And you shocked the pants off everybody in Lake Eden," Michelle finished.

"Michelle!" Delores turned to give her the glance that all three of her daughters called *Mother's icy glare of death.*

"Well, she did," Michelle defended herself. "Nobody in Lake Eden ever thought she'd make up her mind. You know that, Mother."

Delores didn't bother to reply, but the flush on her cheeks, coming through under her makeup, was answer enough for Hannah.

"Back to the recipes," Lisa said, rescuing all of them from a difficult discussion. "What do you think Hannah should bake first, Aunt Nancy?"

"Patience, Lisa. I need more information from Hannah before I can answer that. Who are the judges, Hannah?"

"There are five of them." Hannah looked down at her notebook. "Jeremy Zales is the first one. He won some kind of prestigious award."

"The Golden Knife," Aunt Nancy said. "It's almost as important as the James Beard Award."

"Another judge is LaVonna Brach."

"She writes cookbooks," Aunt Nancy informed her. "They're the kind of little paperbacks you can find at grocery store checkout counters, and they're extremely popular. She's written over a hundred. It says so on the front cover."

"Are they any good?" Andrea asked her.

"Surprisingly, yes. Sometimes those little books are worthless, but I've followed some of her recipes and they work perfectly. I've been collecting her cookbooks for at least five years and I have two shelves of them in the bedroom. Heiti says I'd better stop collecting before I run out of wall space."

Lisa frowned slightly. "Haiti? Like the country?"

"That's how it's pronounced, but it's spelled differently. Heiti is an Estonian name. That's where his ancestors come from."

"But who is this Heiti?"

"He's a friend I met at church and he's building my bookshelves. Heiti's a fine carpenter. You'll have to come over to see them. He also restores classic cars and he's promised to fix the old Thunderbird in my garage."

"He lives around here?" Lisa looked a bit nervous about her aunt's *friend*.

"He does now. He moved here from Connecticut." Aunt Nancy addressed Hannah, and it was obvious that she wanted to change the subject. "Who's the third judge, Hannah?"

"The third judge is Helene Stone."

"I've never heard of her," Aunt Nancy said,

turning to Michelle. "Can you find out more about her on that phone of yours?"

"I'm already Googling her." There was a brief pause, and then Michelle read the information on her screen. "Helene Stone is a well-known purveyor of gourmet ingredients. She has a small store in New York that carries exotic spices and imported vegetables and fruits."

"Who's the fourth judge?" Delores asked.

Hannah referred to her notebook again. "Christian Parker."

"I know who he is!" Andrea said with a smile. "He has his own show on the Food Channel. He seems very nice, Hannah."

"You watch the Food Channel?" Hannah tried not to look as shocked as she felt. To put it nicely, Andrea was culinarily challenged. The closest she came to preparing a gourmet meal was when she made peanut butter and jelly sandwiches.

"Yes, I *do* watch the Food Channel. It's Tracey's favorite channel, and she loves Christian Parker's show. We watch every weekday when she gets home from school. It's our private mother-daughter alone time."

Hannah knew she shouldn't ask, but she had to know. "Have you learned anything about cooking?"

"Yes!" Andrea pointed to the foil-covered platter in the center of the counter. "That's where I got the idea for my newest whippersnapper cookies."

"Christian Parker made whippersnappers?" Delores asked.

"No, but what he said about chips made me want to try some whippersnappers that way."

"He's an excellent chef," Aunt Nancy said. "What did he say about chips?"

"He said to mix and match them in cookies. His example was peanut butter cookies with peanut butter chips, milk chocolate chips, and dark chocolate chips. Would you like to taste my Chips Galore Whippersnapper Cookies? I brought some with me."

"We would!" Delores answered for all of them, and Hannah was glad. So far, Andrea had only made one type of cookie, but everyone, including her husband, hoped that her experimentation with baking would spread out to include additional successful culinary efforts.

Lisa jumped up to fill their cups and fetch fresh napkins. Even though they'd already had two of Hannah's Molasses Crackles, there was always room to taste one more cookie.

"These are just great, Andrea," Hannah said after her first bite. "You chopped the chips up in little pieces."

"That was Christian Parker's idea. He said that if the chips are in smaller pieces, you get different flavors of chips in each bite."

"I really like these," Hannah said, reaching out to take another cookie from the platter to prove it. "They're good, Andrea. You'll give me the recipe, won't you?"

"Of course. And you'll use it here in The Cookie Jar?"

"We will. I think our customers will love these, especially the peanut butter and chocolate fanatics."

Andrea looked very happy. "So everybody likes them?"

Delores laughed. "I've eaten two already, and I'm about to go for my third. They're wonderful, dear."

"Yes, they are." Aunt Nancy took another cookie, and then she turned to Hannah. "Didn't you say there were five judges?"

"Yes. The fifth judge is Alain Duquesne. I don't know anything about him."

"I do," Andrea said. "He was a guest chef on Chef Christian's show and he was really picky. He didn't like the way Chef Christian sautéed all the vegetables together. He said that each vegetable should be sautéed separately to get the full flavors."

"He said that on someone else's show?" Aunt Nancy began to frown when Andrea nodded. "He's known for being very critical, but it wasn't even his show!"

"That's what Tracey said. She said the only reason he was there was because Chef Christian had invited him and it was wrong to criticize your host."

"That's very adult of her," Delores commented.

"It certainly is," Aunt Nancy agreed, and then she turned to Hannah again. "You've named all five judges. Which one is the head judge?"

"Alain Duquesne."

"That's a stroke of bad luck," Aunt Nancy said, wearing the same expression she would have worn if she'd tasted something unpleasant. "He's a nasty know-it-all. And his recipes aren't worth the powder to blow them up!"

Hannah burst into laughter. She couldn't help it.

Aunt Nancy looked terribly irate. "Sorry. I've just never heard you be so disapproving of anyone before. And what you said about his recipes was really funny."

"Well, it's true. They're unnecessarily compli- cated, incredibly time-consuming, and the results don't warrant that amount of work. The man doesn't know what *shortcut* means! Of course he's got as many assistants as he wants to do all the prep work and clean up his mess."

"Do you know him personally?" Lisa asked, gazing at her aunt in something very close to awe.

"You could, say that. He was born less than five miles from my parents' farm, and I went to school with him. Of course his name wasn't Alain Duquesne then. He changed it when he became an important celebrity chef."

"What was his name back then?" Michelle asked.

"Allen Duke. He was the youngest of three children and his mother babied him. He grew up thinking that he was better than anyone else."

Hannah was silent for a moment, and then she asked, "Did he have any favorite foods?"

"I see where you're headed, and it won't do you a parcel of good." Aunt Nancy shook her head. "Allen doesn't really like food. When he was in third grade, he brought a peanut butter sandwich and a thermos of milk to school every day for lunch. And he never tried to trade with any of the other kids whose mothers packed different sandwiches and home-baked cookies."

"He didn't have dessert?" Lisa looked shocked.

"Yes, he did. Allen always had a little bowl of Jell-O or butterscotch pudding, the kind you can buy ready-made in the grocery store. He was crazy about Jell-O and butterscotch pudding."

"He ate them every day?" Andrea asked, and Hannah could tell she was surprised.

"Almost every school day, or at least every day that I was in the lunchroom with him. And I'm willing to bet that he had Jell-O or butterscotch pudding for dessert on the weekends, too. My mother always said that Allen's mother wasn't much of a cook."

Hannah jotted that down. She wasn't sure if it would come in handy, but it was a piece of personal information about the head judge. "Is there anything else you remember about him?" she asked Aunt Nancy. "I really need an edge for the hometown challenge."

"I have that covered," Aunt Nancy declared, looking very proud of herself. "I think you should bake something that Chef Alain Duquesne loves, but something he never could bake successfully."

"What's that?"

"A white chocolate soufflé. He adores soufflés, and he's crazy about white chocolate. I saw him interviewed on television and he mentioned that it was the one dessert he had trouble baking."

"Aren't soufflés difficult to bake?" Lisa asked.

"Normally, yes. I tried to perfect a chocolate soufflé for years," Aunt Nancy admitted. "But then my friend Anne Elizabeth gave me a never-fail recipe." She turned to Hannah. "That's what you can bake for the hometown challenge."

"A chocolate soufflé?"

"Yes, but not just any chocolate. You should make yours white chocolate. Allen loves soufflés, and he's crazy about white chocolate. I'm convinced that'll bring you right back here to Lake Eden for the next Food Channel challenge."

"Perfect!" Delores told her. And then she turned to Hannah. "What's the next challenge, dear?"

Hannah glanced down at her notebook. "The cake challenge."

"Wonderful!" Aunt Nancy clapped her hands. "I've got that one covered, too. The Allen I knew in high school was a dyed-in-the-wool romantic. As a matter of fact, when we were older, he took me to the senior prom."

"So he was your high school boyfriend?" Delores asked.

"Oh, no. Not at all. Allen wasn't anyone's boyfriend. He had someone he spent time with, but that wasn't exactly a boyfriend-girlfriend relationship. Allen was too in love with himself to love anyone else."

"If you felt that way about him, why did you go to the prom with him?" Hannah asked.

"I wanted to go and I didn't have a date. And Allen wanted to go so that he could show off in a white tuxedo. No one had ever worn a white tuxedo to a prom before. And he wanted his date to wear the black dress and long black gloves that Audrey Hepburn wore in *Breakfast at Tiffany's* because it would complement his white tuxedo so well. Allen fancied himself as a trendsetter."

"Do you think he's still that way?" Lisa asked.

"Oh, yes. You can tell that by the food he creates. I wouldn't want to eat some of his meals, but they're very successful and trendy. That man can put together the most unusual ingredients and make people eat them and rave about it."

Delores began to frown. "I'd like to know more about that prom. Did Allen go shopping with you to help you choose your prom dress?"

"Yes, and no. He handed me a photo of Audrey Hepburn wearing the dress and he asked me if I could sew a dress just like it if he paid for the material. And since I'd always loved to sew and I was good at it, I said, 'Yes, of course I can. What size do you need?' And I still remember how he leaned back and looked at me critically. I got the feeling he could see right through my clothes, and it made me terribly uncomfortable. I was about to tell him to forget it, that I couldn't make a dress like that after all, when he said, 'You'll do if you wear your hair up like it is in the picture. And I'll buy the gloves. Make the dress in your size.' And then he asked me to be his date for the prom."

"That's not exactly romantic!" Lisa looked dismayed.

"I knew that then. And I also knew that he thought of himself as a sophisticated and debonair man of the world. He didn't care who he took to the prom as long as she looked the way he wanted her to look. His date was just a prop to make him appear even more suave and urbane. But I wanted to go to the prom, and he was the class president, the most

desirable date I could possibly have, so . . ." Aunt
Nancy gave a little shrug. "I made the dress, put it
on, and went to the prom with Allen Duke."

"Did you have a good time?" Andrea asked her.

"I had a great time! All the girls admired my
dress, and their dates couldn't take their eyes off me.
We were the most stunning couple there. Allen was
a superb dancer, and we spent the whole night on the
dance floor. When the prom was over, Allen took
me home and then he went out on a late date with
another girl he said wouldn't have looked good in the
Audrey Hepburn dress."

Delores just stared at Aunt Nancy. It was the first
time that Hannah had ever seen her mother speech-
less. It took Delores several seconds to recover and
then she said, "How awful for you!"

"Not really. I knew that Allen was all show, and I
wasn't interested in him anyway. And I knew from
the start that he wasn't interested in me. On the
whole, he was a perfect prom date."

"But prom dates are supposed to be romantic,"
Lisa objected. "How could he be a perfect date?"

"Allen *looked* romantic. I'm talking about movie-
star romantic. I looked the part of the ingénue, and
Allen looked the part of the handsome lover. And
that's the reason I told you this story. Chef Alain
Duquesne appreciates someone who looks the part."
Aunt Nancy turned to Hannah. "Everyone at the
Food Channel knows you're getting married right
after the competition. And by the time you arrive in
New York, the judges will know it, too. That's why I
think you should bake a wedding cake for the cake

challenge. And you should present it to the judges wearing your wedding veil. Allen will really appreciate that, and I can almost guarantee that he'll give you a perfect score so that you can win that challenge, too!"

CHIPS GALORE
WHIPPERSNAPPER COOKIES

DO NOT preheat your oven quite yet—this cookie dough needs to chill before baking.

  1 box *(approximately 18 ounces)* yellow cake mix, the kind that makes a 9-inch by 3-inch cake *(I used Duncan Hines—18.5 ounces net weight)*
  1 large egg, beaten *(just whip it up in a glass with a fork)*
  2 cups of Original Cool Whip, thawed *(measure this—a tub of Cool Whip contains a little over 3 cups and that's too much!)*
  1 teaspoon vanilla extract
  1 cup assorted chips, chopped into little pieces *(regular chocolate, white chocolate, milk chocolate, butterscotch, peanut butter, or whatever you have left over from other cookies you've baked)*

  ―――――

  ½ cup powdered *(confectioner's)* sugar *(you don't have to sift it unless it's got big lumps)*

Pour HALF of the dry cake mix into a large bowl.

Use a smaller bowl to mix the two cups of Cool Whip with the beaten egg and the vanilla extract. Stir gently with a rubber spatula until everything is combined.

Add the Cool Whip mixture to the cake mix in the large bowl. STIR VERY CAREFULLY with a wooden spoon or a rubber spatula. Stir only until everything is combined. You don't want to stir all the air from the Cool Whip.

Sprinkle the rest of the cake mix on top and gently fold it in with the rubber spatula. Again, keep as much air in the batter as possible. Air is what will make your cookies soft and have that melt-in-your-mouth quality.

Sprinkle the cup of chopped, mixed-flavor chips on top and gently fold the chips into the airy cookie mixture. *(You can easily chop the chips in a food processor by using the steel blade and processing them in an on-and-off motion.)*

Cover the bowl and chill this mixture for at least one hour in the refrigerator. It's a little too sticky to form into balls without chilling it first.

Hannah's 1st Note: Andrea sometimes mixes whippersnapper dough up before she goes to bed on Friday night and bakes her cookies with Tracey in the morning.

Hannah's 2nd Note: If you see our mother, please don't mention that I told you Andrea always gives Bethie a warm whippersnapper cookie for breakfast on Saturday mornings.

When your cookie dough has chilled and you're ready to bake, preheat your oven to 350 degrees F., and make sure the rack is in the middle position. DO NOT take your chilled cookie dough out of the refrigerator until after your oven has reached the proper temperature.

While your oven is preheating, prepare your cookie sheets by spraying them with Pam or another non-stick baking spray, or lining them with parchment paper.

Place the confectioner's sugar in a small, shallow bowl. You will be dropping cookie dough into this bowl to form dough balls and coating them with the powdered sugar.

When your oven is ready, take your dough out of the refrigerator. Using a teaspoon from your silverware drawer, drop the dough by rounded teaspoonful into the bowl with the powdered sugar. Roll the dough around with your fingers to form powdered-sugar-coated cookie dough balls.

Andrea's 1st Note: This is easiest if you coat your fingers with powdered sugar first and then try to form the cookie dough into balls.

Place the coated cookie dough balls on your prepared cookie sheets, no more than 12 cookies on a standard-size sheet.

Hannah's 3rd Note: I've said this before, but it bears repeating. Work with only one cookie dough ball at a time. If you drop more than one in the bowl of powdered sugar, they'll stick together.

Connect with

Us

Visit us online at
KensingtonBooks.com
to read more from your favorite authors, see books
by series, view reading group guides, and more.

Join us on social media

for sneak peeks, chances to win books and prize packs,
and to share your thoughts with other readers.

facebook.com/kensingtonpublishing
twitter.com/kensingtonbooks

Tell us what you think!

To share your thoughts, submit a review,
or sign up for our eNewsletters, please visit:
KensingtonBooks.com/TellUs.